The Viscount Tastes Like Trouble

THORNS & TEMPTATIONS

ARABELLA KENT

The Viscount Tastes Like Trouble
Thorns & Temptations, Book 1
ISBN: 979-8-9930526-4-9

Published by Arabella Kent
For permissions, inquiries, or licensing requests:
authorarabellakent@gmail.com

For every woman who built a life with shaking hands.
For the ones who left in the dark and found the light anyway.
For the women who ran — and for the ones still deciding to.
For everyone who survived someone else's hands and chose to live soft again.

Author's Note

The Viscount Tastes Like Trouble is a steamy Regency romance with a guaranteed happily ever after. It also contains themes and scenes that may be difficult for some readers, including:

•Domestic abuse (past, depicted in flashback)

•Stalking and blackmail

•Children in peril

•On-page gun violence

•Death of an abuser (on page)

•Emotional manipulation by a secondary character

•Explicit sexual content

Your comfort matters to me. If any of these topics are sensitive for you, please read at your own pace — or reach out before diving in.

authorarabellakent@gmail.com

xo, Arabella

Chapter One

Eleanor Ashford—Nell to those who love her—stood behind the counter of The Mill Street Bakery, arranging cranberry tarts in neat rows while dawn crept through the misted windows. Flour dusted her dark sleeve. The scent of butter and sugar hung warm in the cold air, and the brick oven at her back radiated heat that seeped through her wool dress.

The shop bell could ring at any moment. Every time it jangled, her heart seized, a quick, animal spasm she'd never learned to control. She pressed her thumb into the edge of the counter until the wood bit her skin, and the sharpness brought her back. This was her bakery. Her counter. Her morning.

Her body was built of full breasts, generous hips, and a soft belly that had carried twins and showed every evidence of it. She'd been taught to be ashamed of it.

But before the twins, before her body had changed, there had been a different kind of shame.

The women on their street in Cheapside had been less kind. Barren, they'd whispered over their washing, their gazes sliding toward Nell's flat stomach while their own had swelled year after year. Eight years married and not a single quickening to show for it—there had to have been something wrong with her. Something broken inside.

They were wrong, of course. There had been two babes. The first bled out of her in the fifth month, alone on the kitchen floor while her husband, Gabriel, played cards in Southwark. The second came and went so quickly she might have imagined it—a fortnight of hope crushed to nothing in a single night of cramping and grief. After that, a midwife had pressed a pouch of dried pennyroyal into Nell's palm. She had used it for five years without faltering, hiding the bitter tea behind the flour bin, drinking it before Gabriel stirred. Let them call her barren. Barren was a word she could survive. The alternative—bringing a child into that house, into those hands—she could not.

Then Gabriel found the herbs. He upended the flour bin in a rage, scattering white powder across the kitchen like snow, and when the pouch tumbled free he held it up between two fingers with a look she would never forget. He burned it in the grate. Called her a scheming, ungrateful wretch. Took her that night with the ash still warm in the hearth.

She quickened within the month. And Gabriel, who had raged about a barren wife for years, turned his fury on the cost of what was coming instead. Built like a brood mare, he'd said, his eyes scraping over her thickening waist. Good for nothing else. She had fled before the twins drew breath—eight months gone and nothing to her name but her mother's green silk, a small pouch of jewelry she'd hidden beneath a loose floorboard after Gabriel had found her mother's garnet brooch and sold it to cover his gambling debts, and the desperate certainty that her children would never know his hands.

Gabriel was dead. She had watched them pull the body from the rubble herself, stood dry-eyed while the constable told her she was a widow. Dead and buried and gone. But the dead had long memories, and Gabriel Hyde had left his ugly fingerprints on every corner of her life.

Five years she'd owned this place. The business barely broke even most months, and the lodgings upstairs were cramped—two rooms for her and the children, a third rented to Martha, a seamstress friend. But it was hers. Every creaking floorboard, every temperamental oven brick, every smudge on the windows. She had bled for it in ways she did not intend to discuss with anyone, and it belonged to her, and no one would take it from her again.

A thud from upstairs; then a shriek, followed by the unmistakable sound of a pillow striking a wall.

"Oliver, give it back!" Lily's voice cut through the floorboards.

"It's mine! You borrowed it three weeks ago and never returned it!" Oliver's reply came muffled, like he was speaking from beneath a blanket or possibly a sister.

A smile pulled at the corner of her mouth despite herself. She crossed to the foot of the stairs. "If I come up there and find feathers on the floor," she called, resting one hand on the banister, "you are both sweeping the shop after lessons. With the small broom."

Silence. The small broom was a punishment of legendary cruelty in the Ashford household, its bristles so sparse it took an hour to clean what should take ten minutes.

"We're getting dressed!" Lily announced, her tone shifting

to angelic cooperation so quickly it could give a person whiplash.

Nell shook her head and returned to the counter, and they were nine years old and growing far too fast. Lily had her spectacles and her sharp tongue and her mother's stubbornness. Oliver watched everything in silence. He had a gentleness that made her chest ache. She knew where he learned it. He did not learn it from kindness. He learned it in a house where silence meant safety.

She didn't think about that. Not this morning.

The back door swung open, letting in a gust of cold air and the sound of cheerful humming. Her assistant, Daphne, was twenty-seven and built like Nell—soft, round, and utterly unapologetic about it. Her cheeks were ruddy and her fingers were perpetually stained with berry juice or flour.

"Morning, Nell!" Daphne shook the rain from her cloak before hanging it on the peg by the door, water pooling beneath the hem onto the stone floor. She scraped her boots on the mat, leaving streaks of mud. "It's coming down something terrible out there, and the lane's turned to soup. But I brought my appetite."

Nell felt the tension in her shoulders ease the way it always did when Daphne arrived. "You always bring your appetite," Nell said, wiping a stray smudge of flour from the counter. "I am starting to think that's why you took this position."

"Starting to think?" Daphne pressed a hand to her chest in mock offense and leaned against the workstation. "Nell, I told you plain as day when you hired me. I said, 'I will work hard, but I expect to eat well.' And you shook my hand and said, 'Fair enough.'"

Daphne plucked a broken piece of cranberry tart from the

tray, one of the pieces too misshapen to sell, and popped it into her mouth. “Best decision you ever made,” she added around a mouthful of pastry, grinning as she reached for her apron.

“Modest as ever.” Nell arched an eyebrow, her hands still working the dough with rhythmic, grounding pressure.

“Modesty is for people who haven’t earned the right to brag.” Daphne moved to the seed cakes, arranging them with practiced, nimble hands. “It’s a shame Dr. Hartley is still in London. He would have bought half of these by now.” She cut a glance at Nell, the corner of her mouth twitching in a silent tease. “That man finds a great many excuses to visit your shop, Nell.”

Nell kept her eyes on the tarts, refusing to look up. “He is a physician, Daphne. He buys cakes because he likes cakes.”

“He buys cakes because he likes you.” Daphne’s tone remained light, but her stare sharpened as she leaned over the tray. “Don’t think I have failed to notice the way he looks at you. It’s like you are the only tart worth having.”

“That’s enough.” Nell’s cheeks burned despite the cold air whistling through the window frame. She busied herself by straightening her apron with a sharp tug.

“Is it, though?” Daphne’s grin widened, her teeth catching her bottom lip as she waited for a reaction.

Heat crept up Nell's neck, for Edmund Hartley was kind and steady. He had come to the village just six months ago. He possessed dark brown hair going silver at the temples, gentle hands, and a laugh that came easily. His fiancée had deserted him last winter, after four years of engagement. She was a baron's daughter who ran off with a French count, if Mrs. Pemberton's breathless retellings were to be believed. The scandal had apparently been the talk of London for months.

"The children will be wanting breakfast," Nell said, changing the subject with a forced briskness as she reached for a clean towel. "Lily's chest was rattling last night."

Daphne's teasing expression softened instantly. "Poor lamb. This damp weather does her no favors."

The bell above the door jangled.

Nell looked up, her shopkeeper's smile already forming, only to feel it freeze on her face. A man filled her doorway. He was impossibly tall, towering more than a foot above her, with shoulders broad enough to block out the grey morning light. Dark hair fell in damp waves across his forehead, rain dripping from the ends onto her clean floor. He had sharp cheekbones and a jaw cut as clean as glass, and his full lips might have been pretty on a softer face. He was the kind of handsome that belonged in oil paintings or grand ballrooms, far away from her shop.

Except for the scar.

It ran from his temple to his jaw, a thick rope of raised tissue that pulled the corner of his mouth into a permanent near-sneer. Rain tracked down the ruined flesh like tears on marble, but a war wound, she realized. It was too clean for an accident.

He could not be more than eight and twenty. She saw it in the soft curl at his temples and the smooth skin the scar had spared. His look belonged to a much older man. Storm-grey and set deep beneath dark brows, heavy-lidded, fixed on her with bored arrogance that made her back teeth clench.

"I'll fetch the next batch from the oven." Daphne squeezed Nell's arm and slipped through the curtain to the back room, though her glance lingered on the stranger a moment too long before she disappeared.

His attention moved over her shop. It dragged across the display cases and the modest counter. It paused at her apron and judged the lot of it lacking.

"Quaint." He let the word hang as he tapped a gloved finger against the doorframe. He took the room in again. One brow rose in quiet dismissal.

He spoke the word like a verdict, a judge passing sentence on something beneath his notice. His accent was cultured and aristocratic, dripping with the particular disdain of men who had never wanted for anything. Nell's spine stiffened, and her smile turned to glass. The accent was different, the clothes finer, but she knew that tone — that cold certainty that the world existed to serve him. Gabriel had worn it too, in cheaper cloth.

He stepped inside properly, shaking rain from his shoulders. He hadn't intended to come in, she realized. He simply wanted shelter from the downpour, and her shop was a convenient, dry place to stand until the weather passed. He approached the counter with boots that struck the floor. He moved like a predator, accustomed to rooms parting around him.

He scanned her display, then let his attention slide to her. It paused at her bodice long enough to make the point. Then it moved back to her face, taking its time.

"The rain should pass shortly, sir." Nell let the words drip with false sweetness while she wiped a spot on the counter that was already clean. "Though you are welcome to purchase something while you wait."

His eyebrow rose a fraction. "The tarts. Are they fresh?" he asked, flicking his attention to her hands.

"Baked this morning." She gestured to the display, keeping

her movements controlled. "Cranberry. Seed cake. Lemon curd, if your tastes run sweeter."

He reached past her, coming close enough that she caught the scent of rain, horse, and sandalwood. He picked up a cranberry tart, turning it in his long fingers, inspecting it the way one might a disappointing artifact. He set it down without care, leaving it slightly askew from its fellows.

"I will take six," he commanded, pulling a leather purse from his coat.

There was no warmth in the order; he placed a gold sovereign on the counter. The coin gleamed against the worn wood. It was far too much for six tarts, a deliberate display of wealth or perhaps a test to see how quickly she would grovel for it.

Nell slid the sovereign back toward him with the tip of her finger. "I don't keep change for gold, sir. Sixpence will do."

His eyes narrowed as he looked from the coin to her face. "You are refusing my coin?"

"I am requesting appropriate payment." She held his stare without flinching, the way she'd learned to hold Gabriel's eyes in the early days, before she understood that meeting them only made him angrier.

"This is a bakery. It's not a counting house." Nell kept her hand extended, her palm unyielding.

A muscle twitched along his face. For a moment, she thought he might argue, or worse, simply leave the sovereign and walk out, forcing her to either keep it or chase after him. Instead, he reached into his waistcoat and produced a handful of smaller coins. He counted out sixpence, then dropped them into her palm.

Their fingers brushed. The contact was brief and accidental, yet it felt electric.

Nell pulled her hand back and busied herself wrapping the tarts in brown paper—her pulse quickened, though she refused to examine the reason. She tied the package with string and slid it across the counter.

He took the parcel without a word of thanks and turned toward the door. The rain still hammered against the windows, grey sheets of it turning the street beyond into a blurred watercolour.

Daphne came out from the back room with fresh loaves stacked in her arms. She stopped short when she saw the stranger leaving. "Was there something else you needed, sir?" she asked as she shifted the warm bread against her hip. "We have meat pies fresh from the oven if you're hungry."

The man paused at the door. He looked over his shoulder. That cold stare found Nell across the shop.

"I have what I came for," he said, his attention lingering on Nell for a breath too long before he pulled his hat lower and stepped into the rain.

Then he was gone. The bell jangled behind him like a mocking laugh. Daphne exhaled a long, low breath. "Who was that?" she asked, setting the loaves down on the counter and crossing her arms over her chest.

Nell stared at the door, watching the water pool on the floor where he'd stood. "I have no idea. Some lord who wandered in from the rain."

"Some lord," Daphne repeated. "With a face like that and manners like a wet cat." She tilted her head, studying Nell. "You've gone pale."

"I'm fine." Nell kept her eyes on the floor and reached for the mop.

"You're not fine. You look like you've seen a ghost." Daphne shook her head, her expression uncharacteristically serious. "What did he say to you?"

Nell didn't answer because her heart was still racing, and it was not the old, familiar fear that Gabriel had trained into her bones. This was something else, something she didn't have a name for and didn't want to examine too closely. Gabriel's cruelty had been hidden, sweetness masking poison. He gave pretty words and charming smiles until the door closed and the mask came off. But this man, with storm-grey eyes and a tongue sharp enough to cut, wore his disdain openly. There was no mask.

There was something almost honest about it.

Nell shook herself and bent to mop up the water he'd tracked in, for if he returned, she would be ready. She wouldn't let a stranger unsettle her again.

Chapter Two

Dominic Westmore rode through the gates of Bramwell Park as the rain finally began to ease. He tried to convince himself that the tarts were the only reason his thoughts kept returning to the baker.

The estate looked smaller than he remembered. The grand oak trees lining the drive had grown wild in his absence, their branches reaching toward each other like old friends embracing. The gravel was patchy, and weeds pushed through in stubborn clumps. The house itself—grey stone with tall windows—seemed to sag under the years of standing empty.

He dismounted in the stable yard, handing the reins to a groom. The staff here were new, most of the old ones having found positions elsewhere when the family decamped to London. They looked at him the way everyone looked at him now: quick glances at his face, then away, a careful neutrality that couldn't quite hide the flinch.

Bramwell Park had sat empty for four years, maintained by a skeleton staff who aired the rooms and waited for a family that never came. His mother preferred London. His younger sister had married well and produced two children already, heirs to someone else's estate. No one needed Bramwell Park anymore. No one except him.

London had become unbearable. The ballrooms, the dinner parties, and the endless social rounds had curdled into a particular kind of torture. The stares followed him everywhere. "Poor Lord Westmore", they murmured behind their fans. Such a tragedy. And always, the unspoken addition: And Lady Vivienne, for well, one could hardly blame her, could one?

He'd written ahead to have the house opened, telling his mother he needed country air. He didn't tell her he needed to stop seeing pity in every face he passed.

The study was cold when he entered. The fire was not yet lit. He rang for Graves, the one servant who had been his family since he was a boy and one of the few who had agreed to return, then sank into his father's chair.

It was his chair now. It still did not feel that way. His father had died eight years ago in a hunting accident. It had seemed almost mundane at the time. Now Dominic understood that death rarely announced itself. It simply arrived.

The scar pulled when he moved his jaw, though two years healed and still angry-looking, still tight in cold weather. Before the war, before Waterloo, he'd been considered handsome. Dark hair, storm-grey eyes, a smile that had made debutantes blush and their mothers calculate his income. Now he avoided mirrors entirely.

Waterloo. The word sat in his mind like a stone.

He remembered the chaos of battle: smoke so thick it turned noon to dusk, screaming that came from everywhere and nowhere, the earth bucking beneath cannon fire until his teeth rattled and his bones felt loose in his skin. He remembered Alistair Thorne at his side, the friend who had been closer than a brother since their Eton days. He remembered the French cavalry officer who had broken through their line, saber raised, heading straight for Alistair with murder in his swing.

Dominic hadn't thought. Hadn't calculated or weighed the consequences. He simply moved. The blade meant for Alistair's throat caught Dominic across the face instead, opening him from temple to jaw in one clean, terrible stroke. He went down in a spray of his own blood while the world turned red and then black.

He woke in a field hospital with his face stitched shut and Alistair gone.

Missing. Three days, no word, yet the regiment assumed him dead, though Dominic had refused to believe it. He'd pulled the bandages from his own face, still seeping, and gone back into the wreckage alone. Against orders. Against reason. Against every instinct except the one that mattered—Alistair was alive, and Dominic would find him.

He found him.

What happened after that belonged to a locked room in Dominic's mind, a door he had sealed shut and would not open. Not for the army chaplain who had asked careful questions. Not for the regimental surgeon who had noted injuries in Alistair's file that did not match any known weapon of war. Not for himself, in the small hours when sleep refused to come and his hands remembered things his mouth would never speak.

The official report said Alistair Thorne had been separated from his regiment and recovered by Viscount Westmore. That was the truth the army needed. The rest of it—the real and ruinous rest of it—Dominic had buried so deep that some days he almost believed it had happened to someone else.

Almost.

Alistair wrote letters now. They arrived every fortnight, full of concern and invitations and gentle prods to rejoin the living. Dominic read each one, and he could not bring himself to answer a single one. Every time he saw that handwriting, his hands went cold and the locked door rattled on its hinges, and he had to sit very still until the shaking stopped.

It was not that he didn't care. It was that he cared so much it had curdled into something he could not name, something that tasted of smoke and iron and a darkness he would carry to his grave.

And Vivienne.

He'd loved her since childhood. She was golden-haired and blue-eyed, with a laugh like bells and a smile that had haunted his dreams through every bloody mile of the campaign. He'd carried her portrait into battle, pressed against his heart. He'd written her letters full of longing and promises, fueled by the desperate hope that he would survive to keep them.

She'd been waiting when he returned. She stood in the drawing room of her father's house, wearing pale blue and looking like an angel descended to welcome him home. He'd reached for her, but she stepped backward—one step, then two, while her eyes fixed on his face with an expression he'd never seen before.

Horror.

"I cannot marry a monster." She pressed her lace handkerchief to her mouth, her shoulders trembling as she backed away.

Five months later, she married a baronet with an unmarked

face and a comfortable estate in Surrey. Dominic had heard she was expecting their first child.

He shoved the memory away and reached for the package of tarts. The brown paper crinkled as he unwrapped it, and the scent of cranberry and butter rose to meet him. He bit into one —and the pastry crumbled perfectly, rich and flaky, yet the cranberry filling was tart-sweet, bright against his tongue. It was exceptional.

The baker had made these—yet he pictured the woman with raven hair escaping its pins in dark wisps. She had brown eyes too large for her face, set above round cheeks dusted pink from the heat of her ovens. She had a rosebud mouth that had pursed at him in disapproval. She'd barely reached his chest. The top of her head might graze his collarbone if she stood close, yet she'd looked up at him the way she could bring him to his knees with a single word.

She hadn't flinched when she saw his face.

He turned the thought over in his mind, examining it from every angle. Everyone flinched. Even the servants who had known him since childhood always showed that first moment, that quick flash of shock before training took over and they smoothed their expressions into careful neutrality. But the baker had simply looked at him as if he were an inconvenience. The rain had blown something unpleasant into her shop and she was waiting for it to leave.

It was the most refreshing thing anyone had done in two years.

He'd been rude to her. He knew this. He'd called her shop "quaint" and dropped the sovereign on her counter like a challenge. He'd given her a once-over, noticing the generous swell of her hips beneath that apron and the soft fullness of her figure. He'd seen curves upon curves that his palms itched to learn, and he'd been daring her to react. It was an old habit, part of the armor he put on without thinking. If people were going to stare at him like a monster, he might as well act like one.

But she hadn't backed down. She'd refused his gold. She looked at him the way she'd look at any other customer who'd tracked rain onto her floor. She spoke to him like he was ordinary. To her, his scar was only a scar. It was not a mark that demanded pity or fear.

He didn't know her name. He hadn't thought to ask. He hadn't thought he would care. He shouldn't return. She was a shopkeeper. She was a widow, judging by the black ribbon at her collar. She was beneath his notice and far beneath his station. He had no reason to go back.

But he reached for another tart. He knew, despite himself, that he would find a reason.

Chapter Three

Dominic Westmore stood at the window of the study at Bramwell Park, watching groundskeepers hack at hedges that had grown wild in his absence. He couldn't stop thinking about the baker.

Three days had passed. The crumpled tart wrappers littered his desk, six of them, empty—he'd meant to ration them, perhaps one per day. Instead, he'd eaten two that first night, standing at this very window while rain streaked the glass. The remaining four had vanished by the second morning, devoured over coffee he barely tasted.

The house pressed around him. He'd paced the halls yesterday like a caged animal, opening doors to rooms shrouded in dust sheets, finding nothing but memories and silence. He saw the library where his father had taught him to play chess. He passed the music room where his mother had practiced scales that once echoed through the corridors. The nursery remained untouched since he'd outgrown it, still holding the wooden soldiers he'd lined up for imaginary battles.

He turned from the window. His reflection caught in the glass, the scar a dark slash against pale skin, and he looked away.

The door opened behind him. Graves entered with the particular silence of a man who had spent thirty years learning not to startle his employers. "Will you be taking luncheon in the dining room today, my lord?" Graves kept his eyes level, his tone neutral.

"I will be riding to the village." Dominic reached for his coat where it hung by the door, his movements stiff. "Don't hold supper for me."

"Very good, my lord." Graves moved to the side table, retrieving gloves that Dominic hadn't asked for. "The grey mare has been saddled."

Dominic paused, his coat half-shrugged onto his shoulders. "I hadn't told you I was going out," he noted, his brow furrowing as he met the servant's eye.

"No, my lord." Graves held out the gloves, his expression unchanged. "You hadn't."

Something loosened in Dominic's chest. Graves had seen the crumpled tart wrappers littering the study desk, the restless trips down corridors that led nowhere, and drawn whatever quiet conclusion he was entitled to draw.

"Thank you, Graves," Dominic said, taking the leather gloves and pulling them tight over his knuckles.

"My lord." Graves inclined his head and stepped back, his hands folded behind him in a posture of perfect patience.

~

The roads were dry and the air was crisp with the promise of autumn. Dominic kept the mare to an easy canter, though his blood thrummed with an urgency he refused to examine too closely. People stopped to stare as he passed: a farmer mending a fence, a woman hanging washing, and two children who gaped until their mother pulled them inside. He kept his eyes forward, for he was used to being a spectacle.

The village of Cresswell emerged from the trees like something from a painting. It was a collection of thatched roofs and cobblestone streets, with a church spire reaching toward clouds that threatened rain but hadn't yet delivered.

"Quaint," he'd called her shop three days ago. He'd meant it as an insult. Now he wished he could pull it back.

He tied the mare outside the haberdashery and walked the rest of the way to The Mill Street Bakery. His heart was beating faster than it should, and his palms were damp inside his gloves. It was ridiculous. She was a shopkeeper and a widow, while this was nothing but a craving for decent pastry.

He pushed open the door.

Nell had been braced for Mrs. Pemberton since half past nine, when she'd spotted the woman's distinctive purple bonnet bobbing past the haberdashery window. Mrs. Pemberton never simply walked anywhere. She processed like a ship under full sail, and her course this morning had clearly been set for The Mill Street Bakery.

The bell jangled at half past ten. Mrs. Pemberton swept through the door with Felicity trailing behind like a pale ghost.

"Mrs. Ashford!" Mrs. Pemberton's smile showed too many

teeth as she tapped her parasol against the floorboards. "How well you look today. Does she not look well, Felicity?"

Felicity murmured something that might have been an agreement as she adjusted her shawl.

"You are too kind, Mrs. Pemberton." Nell kept her hands busy arranging seed cakes, though they needed no arranging. That particular brightness in Mrs. Pemberton's eyes meant gossip or scheming, and usually both. "The usual order?"

"Cranberry tarts, yes. A dozen today, I think. We are expecting company this afternoon." Mrs. Pemberton settled herself against the counter like she owned it, arranging her skirts with practiced grace. "Felicity, dear, go look at those lovely biscuits in the window. Take your time."

Felicity drifted away without protest, her slippered feet barely making a sound on the wooden floor. Nell watched her go and felt a familiar pang of sympathy. The girl was pretty enough, with fair hair and blue eyes, but there was something extinguished about her. She was like a candle that had been snuffed too many times and had forgotten how to hold a flame.

"Now then." Mrs. Pemberton leaned close enough that Nell could smell her perfume, something cloying with too much rose. "You must tell me everything."

Nell reached for the brown paper, keeping her movements steady despite the woman's prying stare. "Everything about what, Mrs. Pemberton?"

"Oh, don't play coy with me." The fan snapped open, fluttering against Mrs. Pemberton's considerable bosom. "You've heard, of course, that Bramwell Park is occupied? Lord Westmore has returned. The viscount himself has come back after two years of hiding away like some wounded animal." She paused for effect. “And he was seen leaving this very shop three days ago.”

Nell’s stomach dropped. The rude man. The one who had called her shop quaint and dripped rainwater on her clean floor. The one she’d refused the sovereign from and told that the street was behind him. She'd insulted a viscount—she'd told a viscount to leave her shop.

She kept her face neutral through sheer force of will, her hands continuing to fold the brown paper into crisp edges. “He came in from the rain, bought some tarts, and left. I did not know who he was. That was the whole of it.”

Mrs. Pemberton pressed a hand to her chest in theatrical delight, her silk skirts rustling. “You didn’t know who he was? Oh, how marvelous! How perfectly marvelous! Tell me, what was he like? Is the scar very dreadful? They say he was beautiful before the war, absolutely beautiful. One of the most eligible bachelors in England, if you can believe it. And now,” she made a sharp tsking sound with her tongue, “such a tragedy.”

“It’s a scar, Mrs. Pemberton.” Nell wrapped the tarts with more force than necessary, the twine biting into her thumb. “I didn’t study it closely. I was occupied with him dripping on my floors.”

“But you spoke with him? What did he say? Was he pleasant? Rude?” Mrs. Pemberton’s fan beat faster. “They say his temperament has soured since the injury. That he barely speaks to anyone, even his own family. His poor mother has been beside herself.”

“He bought tarts.” Nell tied the package with string, pulling the knot tight until the paper groaned. “He paid. He left. I am afraid there’s nothing more interesting to report.”

Mrs. Pemberton's brows lifted slightly, but her smile didn't falter. "Such a shame he has become a recluse. A viscount in his prime, unmarried, with a fortune and an estate." She glanced toward Felicity, who remained motionless by the biscuit display. "Of course, a man in his condition cannot afford to be particular. Twenty-eight, a fortune, and an estate—and yet the London mamas will not be lining up the way they once did. Not with a face like that. He will need a wife who does not flinch." Her expression sharpened with calculation as she smoothed her gloves. "Felicity would suit him perfectly, don't you think? So gentle. So accommodating. A man with his challenges would benefit from a wife who knows when to be quiet."

Nell bit back the response that wanted to escape, her jaw tightening as she looked at the young girl. "I am sure Miss Pemberton has many fine qualities."

"You must tell me if he returns." Mrs. Pemberton reached for the package, her gloved fingers brushing Nell's with a lingering pressure. "Anything he says, anything he seems to want, any indication of his preferences. A mother must be prepared, you understand. One doesn't simply wait for opportunity to knock, one must be standing at the door with refreshments ready."

"I doubt he will return." Nell slid the tarts across the counter, meeting Mrs. Pemberton's eyes with a pleasant smile that didn't reach her own. "I was not particularly welcoming."

Mrs. Pemberton's laugh was sharp and knowing as she adjusted her shawl. "All the more reason he might. Difficult men don't want simpering, Mrs. Ashford. They want someone who treats them like they are normal." She collected her package, tucking it under her arm like a prize. "Come along, Felicity. We've taken enough of Mrs. Ashford's time."

They left in a rustle of silk and a lingering cloud of rose perfume. Nell stood behind her counter, blood drumming against her ribs, replaying every word she'd said to a viscount three days ago.

She'd mocked him. She'd refused his coin. She'd looked him in the eye and told him this was a bakery, not a counting house. Men like that could destroy women like her with a single word to the right people. A complaint about her rudeness, a suggestion that her establishment was not fit for decent custom, and she would be ruined. Everything she'd built, the shop, the lodgings, the fragile safety she'd carved out for herself and the children, all of it could crumble because she'd let her temper get the better of her.

She forced herself to breathe. No. He'd been rude first. Arrogant and dismissive, looking at her shop like it offended him, looking at her like she was merchandise to be assessed and found wanting. A title didn't excuse behavior, and a fortune didn't buy the right to treat people like dirt beneath expensive boots.

But still. She should have curtsied, should have recognized quality when it walked through her door. She should have swallowed her pride and been properly deferential, the way women like her were supposed to be deferential to men like him.

The back door swung open. Daphne emerged with flour on her apron, wiping her hands on a rag. "Was that Mrs. Pemberton sniffing about again? I could smell her perfume from the kitchen. What is she scheming now?"

Nell turned away from the counter. "The man from three days ago. The rude one who dripped everywhere."

"The one with the scar?" Daphne moved to the bread shelf, straightening loaves that were already straight. "What about him?"

"He is Lord Westmore." Nell's voice sounded strange in her own ears, thin and hollow. "The viscount. Owner of Bramwell Park."

Daphne's face went pale beneath her freckles, her hands freezing mid-reach. "The one I offered meat pies to?" She pressed a hand to her chest, her eyes wide. "Lord above. I spoke to a viscount like he was any common tradesman."

"We both did." Nell picked up her cleaning cloth and attacked the counter with vicious, circular strokes. "I practically threw him out."

Daphne was quiet for a moment, her teeth worrying at her lower lip. "Well, he deserved it." She paused, her tone wavering. "Did he not?"

"He did." Nell's hands were still shaking, and she couldn't quite convince herself that being right would matter when a viscount decided to take offense.

The bell above the door jangled.

Nell looked up, her shopkeeper's smile already forming, and felt it die on her face.

He filled the doorway. No rain this time. Just clean boots and a coat that hadn't been slept in. His hair was neatly combed back from his forehead, and the scar stood out starkly in the bright light, a raised ridge of tissue that pulled at the corner of his mouth.

Daphne sucked in a breath beside her.

He stepped inside, the floorboards creaking under his

weight. He closed the door behind him with a soft click and stood there for a moment, hands clasped behind his back, looking at Nell with those iron eyes that gave nothing away.

"Baker," he spoke the word through clenched teeth, his focus fixed on a point just above her head.

Nell blinked, her hand pausing mid-motion over the counter. "I beg your pardon?"

He cleared his throat, his fingers flexing where they were clasped behind his back. "I don't know your name. I realized, riding here, that I never asked." His mouth set in a harder line. "Baker seemed, at best, insufficient."

Daphne gave Nell a look that said, plain as day, *a viscount is in your shop and you have flour on your elbow.* She turned back to the counter and busied herself shaping the next batch of loaves, though her hands moved slower than usual and her ears were plainly working harder than her fingers.

Nell felt every bit of it. The smudge on her sleeve. The stray strand of hair escaping her pins. The oldest work dress she owned, the grey one with the patched elbow.

"Mrs. Ashford." The greeting landed flat, stripped of warmth. She set down her cleaning cloth and folded her hands primly in front of her. "Eleanor Ashford."

"Mrs. Ashford." He repeated the name slowly, his attention dropping to the black ribbon at her collar the way it had three days ago. He'd already drawn his conclusion then, she realized. He'd known the moment he first saw it.

"Widowed." She held his stare despite the frantic hammering of her heart against her ribs. "My lord."

The title landed between them like a stone dropped into a still pond. His eyes narrowed, and his shoulders stiffened beneath the fine wool of his coat.

"Ah." His mouth twisted in a gesture that was not quite a smile and not quite a grimace. "Someone has been talking."

"The village talks, my lord." Nell lifted her chin, refusing to shrink from his scrutiny. "It's what villages do."

"And now we are to have 'my lords'." He shifted his weight. Disappointment crossed his face before he flattened it to nothing. "How tedious. I had rather enjoyed being treated like a common nuisance."

"Would you prefer I continue not knowing who you are?" The words escaped before she could catch them, her chin lifting higher in defiance. "I could arrange to forget, if it would make you more comfortable."

Daphne made a small, strangled sound, her hand flying to cover her mouth. Nell didn't dare look away from the man before her.

Lord Westmore didn't stiffen with offense. Instead, the hard line of his mouth softened by a fraction. The storm behind his eyes quieted, and something softer surfaced.

"I would prefer," he said slowly, taking a measured step closer to the counter, "that you stop looking at me the way I am about to have you arrested."

Nell let out a long breath, her shoulders dropping from their defensive hunch. "I did tell you to leave. Rather forcefully. And I refused your coin. I believe I also implied you were incapable of conducting a simple transaction."

"You did." He approached the counter, his boots striking the floor without the predatory weight of their first meeting. "And I deserved it. I was," he paused, his brow furrowing as he searched for the proper word, "insufferable."

She hadn't expected an apology, or anything resembling one, from a man of his station. Her eyebrows rose before she could check the impulse. "You were," she agreed, allowing herself a small, sharp nod. "Somewhat."

"Somewhat." The corner of his mouth twitched, fighting a budding smile. "You are very generous, Mrs. Ashford."

"I am very practical." She gestured toward the display case with one flour-dusted hand. "Insulting customers is bad for business. Even customers who deserve it."

He moved closer to the counter, close enough that she could catch the scent of leather, rain-washed horse, and the warm, woody depth of sandalwood. She could see the faint lines at the corners of his eyes.

"Your tarts, however," he said, nodding toward the glass display, "were not insufferable. They were exceptional." He spoke simply, without flattery, his ashen eyes meeting hers directly. "The cranberry especially."

Warmth crept up Nell's neck despite her efforts to remain cool. She busied her hands with straightening a sheet of paper she'd already adjusted twice. "Thank you, my lord."

"I found them even tastier the second morning." He turned his eyes to the tarts, and something in his posture eased as his hands unclenched at his sides. "Richer, somehow. I thought perhaps I was imagining it."

"You were not." She reached for a fresh sheet of brown paper, grateful for the task. "The flavor develops overnight. The tartness mellows and allows the butter to come through. Most people eat them too quickly to notice."

"I ate most of them too quickly as well." He glanced at her, a rueful twist to his mouth.

She smiled. It was a real smile, and she was surprised by the way it tugged pleasantly at her cheeks. "Then you've a discerning palate, my lord."

"I have a weakness for good food." He straightened, reaching into his waistcoat with a soft rustle of silk. "Four cranberry tarts. If you've them."

"I do." She turned to the case and selected four of the best ones, their golden crusts glistening under the afternoon sun.

He produced the coins, the correct amount this time, and placed them on the counter with a soft clink. Nell swept them into her palm and turned to wrap the pastry, hyperaware of him watching her back. She folded the paper and tied the string in a neat, firm bow.

She turned back and held the package out to him. He took it. Their hands hovered over the brown paper for a beat. His fingers brushed the edge where hers had been. He did not touch her, yet he stood close enough that she felt his warmth.

"I will return, Mrs. Ashford." He tucked the package under his arm and kept his focus on her. "Your establishment may be quaint, but the proprietor is..." He paused and tilted his head as if weighing a grave question. "Tolerable."

She snorted. The sound slipped out before she could stop it. Her hand flew to her mouth. "High praise indeed, my lord."

"I am not known for my effusiveness." Warmth touched his face. The hard line of his mouth curved into a real smile. "Good day, Mrs. Ashford."

He walked toward the door at an easy pace. He stopped at the threshold with his hand on the latch and glanced back. The afternoon light struck his scar and cast it in sharp relief. Nell realized she no longer saw the damage. She saw only the force in him and a mouth that could soften toward kindness.

"Dominic," he said, the words dropping to a low, quiet register. "My name is Dominic."

She didn't use it. The name sat on her tongue and she tucked it away in her mind for safety.

"Good day, Lord Westmore." She inclined her head, her hands folded before her.

He inclined his head in return, opened the door with a jangle of the bell, and stepped out. The door swung shut—yet Nell pressed her hand to her chest, feeling her heart racing.

"Did a viscount just flirt with you?" Daphne's voice came from beside her, sounding both strangled and incredulous.

Nell didn't answer. She moved to the window and watched as Dominic untied his horse and swung into the saddle with easy grace. She watched him turn the mare toward Bramwell Park until he disappeared around the corner.

This is dangerous, she thought, her reflection watching her from the glass. A viscount and a baker. A man with a fortune and a woman with a past that could swallow her whole if anyone looked too closely. There was no sense in it, only trouble.

But she was smiling anyway, and she couldn't seem to stop.

Chapter Four

The green silk had been in Nell's wardrobe for seventeen years, wrapped in muslin to protect it from dust, moths, and time. She stood before the open wardrobe now, running her fingers over the fabric through its protective covering. French silk, her mother had told her once. It had been purchased before the war with France made such luxuries impossible to find. Her mother had worn it the night she met Nell's father at a country dance in Derbyshire, an evening not unlike the one planned for the village green tonight.

Something beautiful should go with you, her mother had whispered, pressing the dress into Nell's hands the night she'd run away with Gabriel. *Even if everything else about this is wrong.*

Nell hadn't worn it since. She hadn't dared. Beautiful things invited attention, and attention invited pain. She'd learned that lesson well in the years that followed.

A knock sounded at her bedroom door. Martha entered without waiting for an invitation, her sewing basket tucked under one arm. "You are still staring at it." She crossed the small room and pulled the muslin away with brisk movements. "Staring won't make it fit. Let us see what we are working with."

The silk spilled free, catching the candlelight like water. It was a deep green, the colour of spring leaves and new growth, of things that hadn't yet learned to be afraid.

"French silk, pre-war." Martha lifted the bodice, examining the seams with a seamstress's critical eye. "You've been hiding quality in that wardrobe, Mrs. Ashford."

"It was my mother's." Nell touched the fabric, half-expecting it to crumble under her fingers, but the weave held firm.

"Strip down, then." Martha began threading a needle with efficient movements. "Let us see what needs adjusting."

Ten minutes later, Nell stood before the small mirror above her dresser while Martha worked the buttons up her spine. The glass was old and slightly warped, giving back a reflection that seemed to belong to someone else entirely.

"Another inch in the bust." Martha murmured the words around a mouthful of pins, her breath warm against Nell's neck. "Half at the waist. It sits properly now." She tugged at the bodice, checking her work and smoothing the fabric over Nell's ribs. "You fill it the way it was meant to be filled."

The dress curved over her fuller breasts. It draped instead of pulling tight. Below the high waist, the silk followed the soft roundness of her belly and the flare of her hips. The colour warmed her skin and made her dark hair shine.

Gabriel's voice slid through her memory.

You think a silk dress changes what you are? Mutton dressed as lamb.

She shut her eyes and forced air into her lungs. She pushed him back into the place where she kept everything she refused to let break her. When she looked again, the woman in the mirror remained. She still wore green silk. She still looked like someone worth seeing.

She remembered him in the rain-streaked doorway. She remembered how Lord Westmore had regarded her across the counter. Not with pity. Not with disgust. With something that made her pulse quicken. She had spent years making herself fade into grey dresses with her head lowered.

Tonight she wanted something different. Just for one evening, she wanted to feel like the woman her mother had been. She wanted to be the woman who had worn this dress to a dance and believed that beautiful things were meant to be enjoyed. Not for anyone, but for herself.

"It's good to see you like this." Martha stepped back as she admired her handiwork. "Like a woman who remembers she is allowed to be beautiful."

Nell reached for a ribbon on her dresser, her fingers trembling slightly against the wood. "I am only going to sell baked goods."

"That's not all." Martha took the ribbon from her and began to thread it through Nell's hair with deft, soothing movements. "You deserve one night where you are not just the baker, the mother, or the widow. You deserve to be Nell."

Nell's throat tightened, making it difficult to swallow. She watched in the mirror as Martha tied off the ribbon, the green silk catching the light with every shallow breath. "What if I have forgotten how?"

Her fingers drifted to the small black ribbon still pinned at her collar. For nine years she'd worn it; nine years of being the untouchable widow. It was a scrap of fabric that told the world she belonged to a dead man so she wouldn't have to explain why she belonged to no one at all.

She unpinned it. The silk felt soft between her fingers, worn thin from years of washing—it was such a small thing to carry so much weight.

"Nell?" Martha's voice was careful and low as she watched her friend's reflection.

Nell crossed to the window and pushed it open. The cool evening air rushed in, smelling of woodsmoke and autumn leaves. She looked at the ribbon one last time, this lie she'd wrapped around her throat like a collar, and threw it into the darkness. It fluttered once, caught the dying light, and vanished into the shadows of the alleyway.

"I am done." The words came out rough, scraped from somewhere deep inside her. "I am done being his widow. I am done wearing his death like a shield." She turned back to Martha, and something in her chest cracked open. It was not a break, but a release. "I want to be Nell tonight. Just Nell."

Martha's eyes glistened in the candlelight. She pressed her palm to Nell's cheek. "Then go be her. She has been waiting a long time."

The walk to the village green took ten minutes on a good day. Tonight, with Lily bouncing ahead and doubling back every few steps, it took nearly twenty.

"Mama, do you think there will be fire-eaters?" Lily tugged at Nell's hand, her spectacles sliding down the bridge of her nose. "Sarah Martin said there were fire-eaters last year, but I don't believe her because Sarah Martin is a liar."

"Lily." Nell reached down and adjusted her daughter's spectacles with gentle fingers. "We don't call people liars."

"But she is one." Lily kicked at a stray stone in the path, her small face set in a scowl. "She said her father caught a fish as big as a horse, and that's not even possible."

"Perhaps it was a very small horse." Oliver spoke from Nell's other side, his hand tucked firmly in hers. He was trying to look dignified, the way he always did when they went somewhere public, but his eyes kept darting toward the distant glow of torchlight.

Martha walked behind them, shifting the burden of the basket of goods they hadn't been able to fit on Daphne's cart. "Fire-eaters, puppet shows, and enough roasted meat to feed an army. You will have plenty to see."

The village green opened before them like a scene from a fairy story. Lanterns were strung between ancient oak trees, their light dancing in the autumn breeze. Long tables groaned with food, including roasted chickens, meat pies, wheels of cheese, and baskets of crusty bread. Musicians stood on a wooden platform, already playing a lively tune that made Nell's feet itch with a forgotten rhythm.

Everyone was here. Farmers in their best coats stood near merchants and their wives, while gentry nodded politely to servants they would ignore come morning. The Harvest Festival was one of two nights a year when hierarchies softened, when ale and torchlight made everyone equal, or close enough to it.

Nell spotted her stall near the edge of the green. It was a simple wooden table covered with a clean cloth, already laden with seed cakes and ginger biscuits. Daphne stood behind it, waving her arms frantically.

"There's Daphne." Nell quickened her pace, suddenly self-conscious of the green silk and the way it swished against her legs with every step. "Martha, can you," she trailed off, gesturing vaguely toward the children.

"I will keep them fed and out of trouble." Martha was already reaching for Lily's hand, her dark eyes glinting with a knowing look. "You work. And maybe," she paused, a sly smile touching her lips, "don't work too hard."

"Mama!" Lily broke free long enough to throw her arms around Nell's waist, nearly upsetting her balance. "You look like a princess!"

Nell hugged her back, breathing in the clean soap and sugar smell of her daughter's hair. "Go on, then. Stay with Martha. Don't eat so many sweets that you make yourself sick."

"I make no promises." Lily was already pulling Martha toward the puppet show, chattering loudly about fire-eaters and the dishonesty of Sarah Martin.

Oliver lingered. He didn't say anything about the dress, for he rarely spoke of things that mattered, but he squeezed her hand once, his small fingers tight around hers. His eyes met hers, looking far too old for a boy of nine, carrying questions he didn't know how to ask.

"I am fine." Nell spoke quietly, stroking his hair away from his forehead. "Go have fun. That's an order."

The ghost of a smile crossed his face. Then he was gone, following his sister into the crowd. His dark head bobbed between the bodies of the villagers until she lost sight of him.

Daphne's eyes went wide when Nell reached the stall, her

mouth dropping open. "Nell!" She pressed both hands to her cheeks, her face lighting up. "You look, you look like a painting. A proper painting, the kind that hangs in rich people's houses."

Nell busied herself straightening the seed cakes, though they were already perfectly aligned. "It's just a dress, Daphne."

"It's not just a dress." Daphne's grin stretched from ear to ear as she began to rearrange a stack of biscuits. "Half the village is going to trip over their own feet when they see you."

"Then half the village should watch where they are walking." Nell smoothed the tablecloth, trying to ignore the heat rising in her cheeks.

The evening fell into a familiar rhythm. Customers approached, coins changed hands, and tarts disappeared into eager mouths. Mrs. Pemberton swept by in a cloud of rose perfume, Felicity trailing behind like a silent shadow. She bought half a dozen ginger biscuits without mentioning viscounts or anything more inflammatory than the cool evening air.

As the evening deepened and the torches burned brighter, Nell noticed other things. Eyes lingered a moment too long, and heads turned as she moved. The green silk caught the light, drawing attention she was not used to drawing, for she felt exposed, but beneath the nerves, she felt something else. It was a sensation that felt remarkably like being alive.

"Go." Daphne nudged her elbow, breaking her reverie as she took a coin from a customer. "Walk around. I can manage the biscuits here."

"I should stay and help." Nell reached for the tongs, but Daphne swatted her hand away.

"You didn't wear that dress to stand behind a table."

Daphne's grin turned mischievous as she jerked her chin toward the music. "Go. Be seen. You've earned one night of not hiding."

Nell hesitated, her hands finding the familiar, rough wood of the stall. But Daphne was right. She hadn't worn her mother's dress to sell seed cakes—she had worn it because she was tired of being invisible. She wanted to remember what it felt like to be something other than careful.

She stepped away from the stall, out into the crowd and the flickering torchlight. She walked toward a feeling that was dangerously like hope.

The music swelled as she made her way past the food stalls and the ale tent, toward the clearing where couples spun in country reels. She stopped at the edge of the circle, her hands clasped in front of her as she watched. Farmers and their wives moved together with the ease of long practice. Young people laughed and stumbled through steps they hadn't quite mastered, and children darted between legs, chased by harried parents.

"Mrs. Ashford?" She started slightly, turning to see who had spoken.

Mr. Willoughby stood beside her, his weathered face creased in a gentle smile. He was sixty if he was a day, with kind eyes and hands that still bore the thick calluses of a lifetime working his own land. He'd lost his wife three winters past to consumption, the village whispered, and everyone in Cresswell respected the quiet dignity with which he bore his grief.

"Would you do me the honor?" He gestured toward the dancers, his smile turning almost shy as he dipped his head.

Nell hesitated, her fingers twisting a fold of her silk skirt. "I am not much of a dancer, Mr. Willoughby."

"Neither am I." He offered his hand, holding it patiently. "But the music is fine, and my old bones could use the exercise. Will you humor an old man?"

She looked at his outstretched hand. It was a broad palm with gentle fingers, possessing nothing demanding or dangerous. Something loosened in her chest, a tightly wound spring that had been coiled there for years.

She took his hand.

The dance was a simple country reel, far removed from the elaborate figures she'd learned as a girl. Mr. Willoughby was true to his word, while he was not much of a dancer. He stepped on her foot within the first minute and his face crumpled with immediate apology.

"Forgive me, Mrs. Ashford." He stumbled slightly, regaining his footing with a grimace. "I am afraid these old legs don't bend the way they used to."

Nell laughed. It was a clear, genuine sound that surprised her as it escaped. "No harm done, Mr. Willoughby. I have survived worse than a stepped-on toe."

They fumbled through the rest of the dance together, neither of them graceful, yet both of them smiling. The music was bright, the torchlight felt warm on her face, and for one perfect, fleeting moment, she forgot to be afraid. She forgot to be careful. She forgot that she was a woman with secrets and a past that could swallow her whole if anyone looked too closely. She smiled a real smile, the kind she used to give freely before Gabriel taught her that smiling invited attention, and attention invited pain.

The music ended with a final flourish of the fiddle. Mr.

Willoughby bowed, his old knees creaking audibly, and Nell found herself curtsying in return. It was a muscle memory from another life, performed with an elegance she'd thought long dead.

"Thank you, Mrs. Ashford." He straightened, his eyes crinkling at the corners. "You've made an old man's evening."

"Thank you." She squeezed his hand briefly, meaning the words more than he could know. "For asking."

He melted back into the crowd. Nell stood there for a moment, flushed and breathless, the green silk swirling against her legs. Her throat was dry from laughing and her cheeks were warm from the exertion, yet she felt lighter than she'd felt in years.

She made her way to the cider stall, suddenly parched. She accepted a cup from the ruddy-faced woman manning the barrel, offering a small nod of thanks. She stood at the edge of the crowd to catch her breath, allowing herself to believe she might deserve this simple happiness.

Chapter Five

Dominic stood at the far edge of the green, tankard in hand, wondering what in God's name had possessed him to come. He hated festivals. He loathed the noise, the press of bodies, and the way people's eyes slid to his scar and then quickly away, like he couldn't see them doing it. He'd avoided every village gathering for the four years he'd been away.

But Graves had mentioned, far too casually while laying out Dominic's evening coat, that Mrs. Ashford always kept a stall at the Harvest Festival. He'd noted that her cranberry tarts sold out within the hour and suggested it might be worth attending if one were in the mood for decent pastry.

Dominic had told himself he was in the mood for pastry.

So here he was. He lurked in the shadows like a fool, nursing ale he didn't want and watching villagers enjoy themselves in ways he'd forgotten. The music grated on his nerves, and the laughter felt like mockery, but every sidelong glance at his face reminded him why he'd stopped attending social functions.

Then he saw her.

The green silk caught the torchlight, shimmering with every movement. Her raven hair gleamed, the distinctive streak of white showing bright at her temple. Every curve was on display without apology, like she'd every right to take up space in a world that told women like her to shrink. She was laughing with an old man. She was dancing badly, stumbling through steps, and looking more alive than anything he'd seen in two years.

His breath stopped in his chest. She was not beautiful the way London debutantes were beautiful, porcelain and practiced, each smile calculated for effect. She was beautiful like a storm. She was like something wild and dangerous that could break a man who got too close.

He wanted to get closer.

He watched the dance end. He watched her curtsy to the old man and make her way to the cider stall. He watched her stand alone at the edge of the crowd with a cup in her hands and a flush on her cheeks. He set down his tankard on a nearby bench and moved before he could think better of it.

The crowd parted as he approached. It always did, whether from deference or discomfort, he had long since stopped trying to determine. She hadn't seen him yet. She was looking at the dancers, that almost-smile still playing on her lips. The green silk hugged her waist and draped over her hips, making his hands itch with a sudden, sharp urge to touch.

He stopped a few feet away, merely looking at her and taking her in.

She turned and saw him. The smile faded from her face, and her shoulders stiffened beneath the fine green silk. She didn't run, however. She lifted her chin instead, her brown eyes meeting his grey ones without flinching as she waited for him to speak.

"Mrs. Ashford." He inclined his head, a sudden, unintended grit catching in the back of his throat. "You are looking… festive."

"Lord Westmore." She held her cider cup like a shield between them, her knuckles white against the wood. "I didn't expect to see you here."

"I came for the tarts." He shifted his weight, the lie obvious. Her stall was across the green, and he hadn't so much as glanced in its direction.

Her mouth curved, not quite a smile but close. "Of course you did. Should I fetch you some?"

"Later, perhaps." He moved closer, drawn by a pull he couldn't name. "That dress is new."

"Old, actually." She didn't step back, though her fingers tightened further on the cup. "It belonged to my mother."

"It suits you." The words scraped out of him, sounding more like a confession than a compliment.

She looked away first, her lashes sweeping down to hide her eyes. "Thank you, my lord."

The noise of the festival pressed around them with its music, laughter, and the crackle of torches. It all felt distant and muted, the way they existed in a bubble separate from the village.

"Walk with me." He gestured toward the quieter edge of the green, away from the dancers and the notice already turning toward them.

She hesitated and looked around the crowd. She took in the faces that might be watching and the mouths already shaping gossip. "Five minutes." She lifted her chin in challenge. "Then I return to my stall."

They walked side by side, away from the torchlight and into the cooler dark at the edge of the green. Their steps brushed through grass still damp with evening dew. "Why did you really come?" She asked without turning to him. Her focus stayed on the dark ahead.

"I heard you would be here." He could lie. He should lie. The truth carried risk. The words came anyway. "I wanted to see you."

She stopped and faced him. Her expression gave nothing away in the dim light. "That is a dangerous thing to say, my lord."

"I am aware." He held his place. His hands stayed clasped behind his back.

"People will talk." She motioned toward the festival. Toward the torchlight and the press of bodies. "They are likely talking already."

"Let them." He lifted one shoulder. He did not look away from her.

"Easy for you." Her expression sharpened. "You are a viscount. Gossip does not touch you. I am a widow with a shop and two children. Gossip decides whether I earn or starve."

He had not thought of that. He had thought only of his need to be near her. It was selfish. It was reckless. "I did not mean," he began.

"You did not think." Her tone stayed calm. "Men like you rarely do."

He accepted the blow, for he knew he deserved it. "You are right. I saw you across the green in that dress and I," he stopped, raking a hand through his hair and feeling the familiar pull of the scar along his jaw. "I will go. If that's what you want."

She should want that. He could see the war playing out on her face. The sensible part of her was screaming to end this, to send him away, and to protect the fragile life she'd built. But she didn't move, and neither did he.

"I have bought your tarts. I have learned your name." He leaned in until the space between them shrank to almost nothing, his words dropping low. "But I know nothing else about you."

Her brow furrowed as she looked up at him. "And yet here you are."

"Here I am." He tilted his head, studying the planes of her face.

"Tell me something true, Mrs. Ashford. One thing that's not about tarts or shops or proper distances between viscounts and bakers."

Wariness flickered in her eyes as she took a small, cautious sip of her cider. "Why?"

"Because you intrigue me." He offered the truth simply, though it was possibly the most foolish thing he'd ever said. A long moment passed. The festival swirled in the distance, but she seemed to notice none of it — yet she watched him, searching for something he couldn't name.

"I used to play the pianoforte." She said it quietly, almost reluctantly, as if the words were being pulled from deep within. "Before. I was quite good, actually. I haven't touched one in years."

He filed this away, treasuring the small piece of herself she'd offered. "Why did you stop?"

A subtle tension pulled at her face. "I stopped having access to pianofortes."

There was a story there of pain carefully buried. He didn't push.

"Your turn." She lifted her chin, her eyes meeting his, with a renewed sense of challenge. "Tell me something true."

He considered her request. A dozen lies rose to his lips, easy deflections and charming evasions of the kind he'd used in London ballrooms. But she'd given him something real, and he felt she deserved the same.

"I came back to Hampshire because I couldn't stand the way people looked at me in London." The words felt like gravel in Dominic's throat as he stared into the trees. "Here, at least, some of them remember what I looked like before. They remember the boy who raced his horse through the village. In London, I am only the scarred viscount. A cautionary tale mothers whisper to their daughters."

Nell held his stare. The wariness in her expression shifted, softening into something that might have been understanding. They stood as two people who had lost pieces of themselves, two people hiding from what they had been.

Then she stiffened and glanced toward the distant torchlight of the festival she'd left behind. "I should return to my stall. Daphne will be wondering where I have gone." She was pulling away. Dominic could feel the walls going back up, the moment of openness closing like a heavy door.

"Mrs. Ashford." He reached for her arm without thinking, his fingers brushing the air.

She stepped back, moving quickly out of reach. Her face shuttered, the brief warmth gone like it had never existed.

"Goodnight, Lord Westmore." She turned and walked away, back toward the festival.

Dominic stood alone at the edge of the green, watching her disappear into the crowd. The music seemed louder now, more grating. The laughter felt like it was directed at him.

Something on the ground caught his eye. It was a shawl of cream-coloured wool, simple but well made. It must have slipped from her shoulders while they talked, while she'd told him about the pianoforte and he'd confessed why he'd fled London. He bent and picked it up; the fabric was soft beneath his fingers, still holding the warmth of her body.

He brought it to his face without thinking and breathed in. He smelled vanilla, sugar, and something underneath that was simply her, warm and alive. He felt lost. He was standing in the dark like a besotted fool, holding a shopkeeper's shawl to his face like it was the most precious thing he'd ever touched.

"Westmore!" His breath hitched, trapped in a lungful of vanilla, as he stood paralysed with the shawl still pressed to his cheek.

Someone called out from beyond the trees. Dominic let the shawl fall behind him, the cream-coloured wool pooling in the grass at his heels as he turned to find Sir Richard Hale emerging from the shadows. Sir Richard's tankard was sloshing, his grin too wide and his eyes bright with the particular gleam of a man who had spotted gossip. Mrs. Pemberton materialized at Sir Richard's elbow, her purple bonnet bobbing and her fan already fluttering.

They approached him from the direction of the festival and stopped a few feet away. Their backs were to the torchlight and to the path anyone returning from the green would take.

"Saw you walking with the baker." Sir Richard studied

Dominic with barely concealed curiosity as he took a long draught of his ale. "Taking quite an interest in village life, are we?"

"What is this about a baker?" Mrs. Pemberton's voice dripped with false innocence.

"Westmore and the baker." Sir Richard chuckled, swirling the remaining ale in his cup. "I caught them taking a cozy stroll in the dark. Very cozy indeed."

Dominic's mouth set in a grim line. They were both watching him now, cataloguing every twitch of his expression and every shift of his weight. Tomorrow the whole village would know—by the week's end, the rumor would reach the whole county.

Her words echoed in his mind: *Gossip decides whether I earn or starve.*

He had to kill this now, before it destroyed everything she'd built. He arranged his face into the cold mask he'd worn in London ballrooms, bored, dismissive, and utterly uninterested. It was the mask that had earned him a reputation for arrogance and driven away everyone who might have cared.

"The baker?" He let boredom drip from every syllable, his lip curling with practiced disdain as he looked past them. "She is nothing of consequence."

Sir Richard laughed, delighted by the cruelty. Mrs. Pemberton giggled behind her fan.

There was a movement behind them, a flash of green in the darkness. Dominic's eyes lifted over Mrs. Pemberton's shoulder, over her ridiculous purple bonnet, and his blood turned to ice.

Nell stood ten feet away. She was frozen in the path, her shawl-less shoulders pale in the dim light. Their eyes met.

She'd heard. Every word. He could see it in her face, in the way her expression shuttered and the light died in her eyes. Her whole body went rigid as though she were bracing for a blow.

I am a fool. The thought was cold and clear, cutting through the fog of his own stupidity.

He watched her stand there like a statue. Mrs. Pemberton was still talking, her fan beating the air between them, and Dominic could not move, could not follow, could not undo a single word without proving every one of them true.

"Can't blame you for looking, though." Sir Richard's voice crashed through the moment, oblivious and jovial as he clapped a hand on Dominic's shoulder. "That dress does do remarkable things. For a shopkeeper."

Mrs. Pemberton tittered, her fan beating faster against her chest. "One can hardly fault a man for appreciating the scenery."

Nell didn't run. That was the worst part. She didn't gasp or cry or cause a scene. She simply looked at him, looked through him. Then she backed away. One step. Two. Controlled and dignified, the green silk swaying gently as she retreated. She turned and walked into the crowd without looking back.

Sir Richard was still talking, something about viscounts and village diversions, but Dominic heard none of it. He stood rooted to the spot, staring at the space where she'd been, feeling something crack open in his chest.

The shawl lay in the grass behind him, still warm and still carrying her scent. He'd told her she intrigued him and asked her for something true—then he'd repaid her trust by calling her nothing.

Mrs. Pemberton's fan snapped shut with a sharp click. "My lord? Are you quite well?"

"Fine." He replied coldly. Dominic cleared his throat and forced his expression back into the cold mask of the aristocracy. "The night air has a chill. If you will excuse me."

He didn't wait for their response. He didn't look back at the shawl lying abandoned in the grass. He walked in the opposite direction from where Nell had gone, toward the stables and his horse, toward Bramwell Park and the empty rooms that were all he deserved.

Chapter Six

Nell found Daphne at the stall, busy counting coins into a small leather pouch. Her hands were not shaking, yet she was distantly proud of that.

"Nell!" Daphne looked up with a grin that faded the moment she saw Nell's face, her hands going still over the coins. "What is wrong? What has happened?"

"A headache." The lie came easily. "I need to collect the children and go home."

Daphne's eyes narrowed, but she didn't push. She swept the remaining coins into the bag with a quick motion. "I can close up here. You go on."

"Thank you." Nell offered a stiff nod, already turning away. She walked through the festival like a ghost, her feet carrying her toward the puppet show where Martha had taken the children.

She is nothing of consequence.

The words kept replaying over and over, like a wound she couldn't stop touching.

She'd seen his face when their eyes met — the flicker of

regret or surprise before his expression had shuttered completely. He'd known she was there—and he'd known she'd heard. And he'd said nothing.

She found Martha near the sweet stall. Lily was half asleep against her shoulder, while Oliver stood guard with a stick of honeyed almonds clutched in one hand.

"Mama!" Lily stirred enough to protest. She rubbed her face with a sticky fist. "We have not seen the fire eater yet!"

"Another time, love." Nell kept her voice steady as she took Lily's small hand. "Mama is tired."

Oliver studied her face. He said nothing. He slipped his free hand into hers and held on tight.

The boy had never asked about his father. He knew Gabriel was dead. He knew, in the way children know things they are never told, that the man had hurt her. He had seen it in the way she flinched when a door slammed too hard, the way she checked the locks three times every night, the way she went rigid when a man stood too close. He had pieced together the shape of the monster without ever being shown its face. And he had decided, somewhere in the quiet of his own small heart, that no man would ever hurt her again.

They walked home together through the quiet streets. Martha carried Lily, whose protests had faded into soft, rhythmic snores. Oliver matched his pace to Nell's, shooting worried glances at her profile that she pretended not to notice.

At home, she sent the children to bed with kisses and murmured promises. Martha squeezed her shoulder in the hall-way, a silent question in her dark eyes, but Nell merely shook her head. She couldn't talk about it. Not yet. Perhaps not ever.

Alone in her bedroom, she stood before the mirror and looked at the woman in green silk.

That dress does remarkable things. For a shopkeeper.

She'd been a fool. She had danced with Mr. Willoughby, and laughed as if she had nothing to fear. She'd walked into the darkness with a viscount who had asked her for something true, as though truth were something safe to give.

She is nothing of consequence.

The green silk came off. Button by button, she undid Martha's careful work, her fingers remaining steady even as something inside her crumbled. The fabric pooled at her feet. She picked it up, folded it, and wrapped it in muslin before returning it to the dark corners of the wardrobe. It was hidden away where it belonged — where she belonged.

She climbed into bed in her shift and pulled the covers up to her chin. The sheets were cold, the room was dark. And somewhere across the village, a viscount had looked her in the eyes and called her nothing. She didn't cry. She'd learned not to cry during her years with Gabriel. But she lay awake for a long time, staring at the ceiling, feeling the last fragile pieces of hope crumble to dust in her chest.

Dominic sat alone in the study of Bramwell Park, a single candle guttering on the desk before him. He hadn't gone back for the shawl—he couldn't bear to. He would just let it rot in the grass or let some villager find it. It didn't matter. Nothing mattered except the look on her face when their eyes had met.

He'd seen betrayal before. He'd seen it on Vivienne's face when she'd looked at his scar, seen it curdle into disgust and then pity. But that had been different. Vivienne had betrayed him. She'd looked at the man who had nearly died for his country and found him wanting. Tonight, he'd been the one doing the betraying.

She is nothing of consequence.

He'd said it to protect her. That was the lie he told himself. He'd said it to kill the gossip before it could spread, to make Sir Richard and Mrs. Pemberton lose interest, and to spare her the slow poison of village scandal.

But that was not the whole truth. He'd said it because it was easy. He'd chosen the mask because it was familiar and comfortable, the path of least resistance. For one craven moment, it had been simpler to play the cold aristocrat than to stand up and declare that the baker with flour on her sleeve and fire in her eyes mattered more to him than the opinion of every titled fool in Hampshire.

He'd taken her trust, the story of the pianoforte, and the softness that had crept into her expression, and he'd ground it under his heel. And she'd seen him do it.

Dominic reached for the decanter on his desk and poured whiskey into a glass. He didn't drink it. He simply watched the amber liquid catching the candlelight. He didn't know how to fix this, or if it could be fixed at all.

But he knew one thing with absolute certainty. Eleanor Ashford was not nothing. She was everything. And he'd just proven himself utterly unworthy of her.

The candle guttered and died, plunging the study into darkness. Dominic sat alone in the black and hated himself more than he'd hated anything in his ruined life.

Chapter Seven

Two weeks later.

Dominic stood at the window of the study at Bramwell Park, watching rain streak the glass in jagged lines. He tried to remember the last time he'd slept through the night, for the answer was the night before the festival. It was before he'd seen her in green silk. It was before he'd asked her for something true and she'd given it to him. He remembered the pianoforte, the softness in her eyes, and the brief, unguarded moment when she'd looked at him like he might be worth knowing.

He'd destroyed it all with three words.

The decanter on his desk was half empty. It had been half empty for days. He couldn't bring himself to finish it or pour it out, so it sat there. He hadn't returned to the shop. He couldn't face her. Couldn't face the memory of how she'd looked at him—the hope dying in her eyes, the shuttering of her expression, the careful dignity with which she'd backed away and disappeared into the crowd.

The door opened behind him with a soft groan of hinges.

"My lord." Graves stood in the doorway, his hands clasped in front of his waistcoat. "Lady Philippa's carriage has just come through the gates."

Dominic turned from the window, his brow furrowing as he checked the mantle clock. "I was not expecting her until Christmas."

"No, my lord." Graves permitted himself the smallest twitch of a smile as he stepped aside. "I believe that was her intention."

Commotion erupted in the entrance hall. A voice commanded servants with the authority of a general marshaling troops. Dominic barely had time to straighten his waistcoat before the study door swung wide and Lady Philippa Westmore swept into the room.

Travel dust clung to her deep blue pelisse. Her silver hair had escaped its pins, disheveled from hours in a rattling coach. But her eyes, sharp as ever and missing nothing, swept the study with the efficiency of a battlefield commander. She noted the untouched correspondence, the half empty decanter, and the curtains drawn against the light though it was barely past noon.

Her mouth pursed into a thin line. "Nephew."

"Aunt." Dominic crossed the room to kiss her cheek, breathing in the familiar scent of lavender and road dust. She'd always understood him in ways the rest of his family hadn't troubled themselves to try. "What has happened? Is something wrong?"

"Your mother wrote to me." Philippa settled into the chair across from his desk, waving away his offer of refreshment with an impatient flick of her wrist. "Three letters in as many weeks. She is worried about you."

Dominic snorted, dropping into his own chair and leaning back. "Mother hasn't worried about me since I was in leading strings."

"She worries in her own way." Philippa's voice softened, though her attention remained fixed on his tired features. "She says you've refused every invitation since returning from London. She says you don't leave the estate and that the servants whisper about you pacing the halls at night."

"The servants gossip too much." Dominic looked away, his jaw tightening.

"The servants see what is in front of them." She leaned forward, her weathered hands gripping the carved arms of the chair. "You are not well, Dominic. I can see it in your face. You look like you haven't slept in a fortnight."

He hadn't. But he wouldn't tell her why.

"I am fine." He offered the lie, though it sat bitter on his tongue.

"You are hiding." Philippa gestured at the stack of unopened invitations on the corner of his desk. "What are these? Lady Morton. Sir Russel." She picked them up, sorting through the cream-coloured cards with brisk efficiency. "Will you decline them all?"

"I don't like parties." He offered a casual shrug, his expression remaining entirely unreadable as he looked past her toward the exit.

"You used to." She retreated into a sudden, heavy stillness. "Before the war. Before Vivienne."

He flinched at the name. It still cut him, even now.

Philippa set the invitations down and picked up one that had been separated from the rest. She examined it, her lips curving into a slow smile. "Sir Huxley's autumn garden party.

This afternoon." She looked up, meeting his eyes with a challenge. "We are going."

"Aunt, please." He shook his head, a long, ragged breath escaping him.

"Don't argue with me." She rose, brushing the travel dust from her silk skirts. "I have just spent hours in a rattling coach because your mother was afraid you'd drink yourself to death. The least you can do is escort me to one garden party."

"It will be tedious." He felt his resistance weakening. It always did when she was involved.

"Then we shall be tedious together." She paused at the door, turning back to rake her eyes over him one final time. "One hour. A clean coat. And shave, for God's sake. You look like a highwayman."

Nell stood in her kitchen, kneading bread she didn't need to knead. She tried not to think about the harvest festival.

The shop was closed for the Sabbath. Upstairs, she could hear the muffled sounds of her children. There was Lily's occasional cough and the soft, repetitive scrape of Oliver's whittling knife against wood. It was quiet domesticity, this was the life she'd built, as it was the life that should have been enough.

She punched the dough harder than necessary, her knuckles dusting with flour.

The green silk was still in her wardrobe. She couldn't look at it, yet she couldn't give it away. She couldn't decide which would hurt more: keeping it as a ghost or letting it go forever.

She is nothing of consequence.

She'd heard those words in her dreams for fourteen nights now. She heard them in the creak of floorboards, in the jangle of the shop bell, and in the heavy silence between heartbeats. He'd looked at her, or rather, he'd looked through her while Mrs. Pemberton giggled and the whole fragile fantasy she'd allowed herself to believe came crashing down.

The bell at the front of the shop rang. Nell's hands stilled in the dough. Her shoulders tensed and every muscle went rigid before she forced herself to draw a breath. It wouldn't be him. He hadn't come in two weeks and he was not going to come now. Nell wiped her hands on her apron and made her way to the front of the shop. Her heart hammered despite her best efforts to still it.

Dr. Hartley stood in the doorway with his medical bag in hand, his quiet smile already forming. "Mrs. Ashford. I hope I am not intruding."

Relief flooded through her immediately. She pressed a hand to her chest and felt foolish for her earlier panic. "Dr. Hartley. You are back from London."

"I arrived last evening." He stepped inside, removing his hat and setting it on the counter with a gentle thud. "I wanted to check on Lily before anything else. How has she been?"

"The cough comes and goes." Nell smoothed her apron, grateful for something to do with her hands. "It's worse at night. The apothecary's tonics don't seem to help as much as yours."

"Then let me examine her." He gestured toward the stairs.

Upstairs, Lily was propped against pillows with one of her beloved novels open in her lap. Her spectacles had slid down her nose, but she pushed them up with one finger as Hartley entered, her face brightening.

"Dr. Hartley! Have you read *The Mysteries of Udolpho*?" Lily gripped the edges of the book, her eyes wide. "It's ever so thrilling. There's a castle and a wicked Italian, and Emily is trapped, and—"

"I confess I haven't." Hartley's eyes crinkled as he set down his bag and pulled up a chair beside her bed. "But if you recommend it, I shall have to remedy that. Now, let me listen to your breathing."

He was gentle and patient. He asked questions in a voice that never condescended. Lily, usually shy with strangers, answered him easily as she chattered about castles and villains.

Oliver appeared in the doorway, a half carved bird clutched in one hand and his dark eyes watchful. He said nothing, but he leaned against the doorframe and observed the scene—and Hartley noticed the boy. He finished his examination, tucked his monaural back into his bag, and turned to Oliver with a respectful nod.

"Oliver." He gestured toward the carving. "That's fine work you are doing."

Oliver's chin lifted as he tightened his grip on the wood. "It's for Lily. She likes birds."

"She is lucky to have a brother who looks after her." Hartley rose from the chair and crossed to where Oliver stood, crouching slightly to meet him at eye level. "Your mother tells me you help in the shop. You carry flour sacks and mind the ovens."

"Someone has to do it." Oliver's voice was guarded, his stare probing the doctor's face.

"Indeed." Hartley held the boy's look without wavering. "A man's job, that. She is fortunate to have you."

Oliver's expression eased by a fraction. He nodded once, a

sharp jerk of his chin, and retreated to his corner by the window. Nell watched from the doorway, her throat tight. She knew in her bones that Gabriel would never have spoken to his son like this — not with patience, not with kindness. He would have used the boy the way he used everything, until there was nothing left worth using. Perhaps it was a mercy that he'd died before the children were born. Perhaps God had granted her that one small grace.

Downstairs, the back door burst open. Daphne tumbled through it, her cheeks pink from the autumn air and her eyes bright with excitement.

"Nell! Dr. Hartley!" She spotted them on the stairs and bounded up two at a time. "Have you heard? Sir Huxley's garden party is today. Everyone is going. The Mortons, the Whitfields, even old Mrs. Crenshaw, and she never goes anywhere."

"Actually." Hartley descended the last few steps, reaching into his coat pocket. "I was about to mention that. The Huxleys are old friends of my family, and Sir Huxley specifically asked me to attend." He paused, glancing at Nell with a shy light in his eyes. "I was hoping, that's, I wondered if you might accompany me. Both of you."

Nell hesitated, her hand finding the banister for support. "A garden party? I am not sure I would be welcome. I am just—"

"The Huxleys are good people." Hartley's voice was earnest as he took a step toward her. "Sir Huxley doesn't care about titles or trade. He cares about conversation and kindness. And I," he stopped and started again, "I would very much like your company."

Daphne bounced on her heels beside them. "Say yes, Nell.

When was the last time you did anything for yourself? Please?"

Nell looked at Hartley. She saw his kind eyes and the way he had spoken to her son as a person of worth. "All right." The word escaped almost instinctively. "But I have nothing suitable to wear."

Daphne's grin spread from ear to ear as she grabbed Nell's arm. "You could wear a flour sack and outshine every lady there. Come. I shall help you dress."

Chapter Eight

The Huxley gardens were everything Nell had imagined and nothing she belonged to. Old oaks threw shade across lawns clipped short enough to make her teeth hurt, and a string quartet played on the terrace, their music drifting across grounds dotted with ladies in fine muslins.

Nell felt every eye that flickered her way. Her dress was a modest, pale blue, and she was acutely aware of every silk gown and diamond pin. Daphne walked beside her in her Sunday best, her eyes wide with undisguised wonder. Hartley stayed close, his hand resting light on Nell's elbow.

Sir Huxley found them near the rose garden, his ready laugh booming across the lawn. "Hartley! Delighted you could come." He turned to Nell and Daphne with a genuine smile. "And you have brought guests. Wonderful, wonderful."

"Sir Huxley, may I present Mrs. Ashford." Hartley's voice carried a note of pride. "She owns The Mill Street Bakery, the bakery in the village. And Miss Daphne Wells, her assistant."

"Mrs. Ashford!" Sir Huxley beamed, clasping her hand

between both of his own. "I have heard nothing but praise for your baking. You must send some to the house. And Miss Wells, welcome, welcome."

Lady Huxley was equally gracious, her shrewd eyes missing nothing as she offered a polite tilt of her head. "Any friend of Dr. Hartley is a friend of ours. Please, enjoy yourselves."

Nell felt the knot in her chest begin to loosen. Perhaps this afternoon wouldn't be so terrible after all.

They found a spot near the rose garden, away from the thickest press of bodies. Daphne chattered about the dresses, the music, and the sheer scale of the estate while she spun in a slow circle. Hartley listened with patient amusement, his shoulder brushing Nell's as they stood together.

"You look happy," he said quietly, leaning in so the words were for her ears alone.

Nell considered the word. "I do feel lighter." She looked up at him and offered a small, tentative smile. "Thank you for bringing us, Doctor."

His smile deepened, warming his whole face. "Shall I fetch us some lemonade?" He gestured toward the terrace with a nod of his head. "I believe I saw a refreshment table near the stone steps."

"That would be lovely," Nell replied, smoothing the fabric of her skirt.

She watched him go. He was steady, reliable, and safe. She allowed herself, just for a moment, to imagine what it might be like to let someone like him into her life. She wondered if she could trust again, or believe that not all tenderness came with a price.

The moment Hartley was out of earshot, a shadow fell across the sunlight.

"Mrs. Ashford!" The voice dripped with saccharine sweetness. Mrs. Pemberton materialized before them. Felicity trailed behind her in pink muslin, her eyes fixed firmly on her slippers. "What a delightful surprise to see you here."

Nell's spine went rigid. "Mrs. Pemberton. How lovely to see you as well." She folded her hands tightly over her middle.

"Is it not just?" Mrs. Pemberton's smile widened, showing too many teeth as her fan snapped open. She began to flutter it vigorously against her bosom. "I was saying to Felicity only this morning how wonderful it's when people from all walks of life can mingle at these gatherings. It's so democratic. So modern."

Daphne stiffened beside her, clearly hearing the barb beneath the honey.

"Dr. Hartley was kind enough to invite us." Nell met the older woman's glittering eyes with an unblinking stare.

"Yes, the good doctor." Mrs. Pemberton pressed a hand to her chest and sighed theatrically. "Such a charitable soul. He is always taking an interest in those less fortunate. It's really quite touching."

Nell tightened her grip on her parasol and waited for the real blow, knowing it was coming.

"Though I must say, Mrs. Ashford." Mrs. Pemberton leaned closer, the scent of her heavy floral perfume turning cloying. She pitched her words loud enough for the nearby guests to catch every syllable. "You do seem to have a talent for attracting male attention. First an evening stroll with Lord Westmore at the harvest festival. And now the good doctor escorts you about like you are a lady of quality."

Beside her, Daphne went very still.

Nell felt it like a door slamming shut. She hadn't told Daphne about the walk. She hadn't told anyone. And now Mrs. Pemberton had laid it bare in the middle of a garden party.

"It was a brief conversation at a public event." Nell forced the words past the tightness in her throat, her fingers digging into her palms. "Nothing improper occurred."

"Oh, I am sure." Mrs. Pemberton's smile turned pitying as she tucked her fan beneath her chin. "But a widow of your position, with two children—one cannot afford to be seen as reaching above her station." She shook her head with a heavy, performative sigh. "People will talk, Mrs. Ashford. They already are."

"Then they should find better use of their tongues." Daphne's voice was low and sharp, her chin lifted and her jaw set tight.

Mrs. Pemberton blinked, her smile faltering for half a breath before she recovered. "I only mention it because I worry, dear."

"Mrs. Pemberton." Hartley stepped into the gap, two glasses of lemonade in hand and his expression pleasant. His eyes told a different story as they swept the group. "Miss Pemberton. If you will excuse us."

He didn't wait for a response. He handed the glasses to Nell and Daphne, offered Nell his arm, and steered them away. Mrs. Pemberton's expression curdled, but she held her tongue—one did not rebuke a doctor in a public setting. She retreated with Felicity in tow, already scanning the crowd for her next target.

They walked in silence until they reached a quieter corner of the garden, shielded by a towering yew hedge.

"Dr. Hartley!" A gentleman waved from a cluster of nearby guests. "A word, if you please?"

Hartley hesitated, glancing at Nell with concern as he placed a hand over hers on his arm. "Will you be all right for a moment? Mr. Patrick is a patient. I should acknowledge him."

"Go." Nell managed a smile she did not feel. "We are fine."

He squeezed her hand once and crossed the lawn. The moment he was out of earshot, Daphne turned on her.

"You walked with Lord Westmore at the festival." Her voice dropped low, barely above a breath, but the hurt in it carried like a shout. "And you didn't tell me."

Nell couldn't meet her eyes. She turned her head away, watching the colourful blur of the party. "I didn't want to talk about it."

"Nothing of consequence." Daphne spat the words like something poisonous she'd held too long on her tongue, her gaze fixed on a distant point across the lawn. "That arrogant, scarred—" She stopped herself and drew a sharp breath. "If I see him today, I swear I shall—"

"Daphne, please." Nell's voice cracked, her fingers nervously pleating the fabric of her skirt. "Not here. Not now."

"He hurt you." Daphne's voice softened, her anger gentling into something closer to grief as she reached out to touch Nell's shoulder. "I can see it. You have been different since that night. Quieter. Sadder. And now I know why."

Nell's throat closed, and she looked away, unable to deny the truth.

Daphne took her hand and squeezed tight. "I am sorry. I won't make a scene, but I shall not pretend to like him either."

"I know." Nell squeezed back, offering a small, grateful nod. "Thank you."

They stood together, watching the party swirl around them. The music, the laughter, and the glittering world that had never been theirs felt further away than ever.

Daphne's jaw worked for a moment as she sought a distraction. She nodded toward a woman passing in an elaborate gown. "That dress Lady Morton is wearing. Is that supposed to be fashionable?"

Nell felt a ghost of a smile tug at her lips, her tension easing just a fraction. "I believe it's meant to be."

"It looks like a curtain attacked her." Daphne sniffed, smoothing her own modest skirts. "Your blue is much prettier."

Hartley returned, his expression apologetic as he adjusted his waistcoat. "Forgive me. Mr. Patrick does go on about his ailments." He looked between them, sensing the shift but asking nothing. "Shall we find somewhere quieter?" He offered his arm to Nell, his eyes searching hers for comfort.

Chapter Nine

Dominic had expected tedium. He'd expected to stand at the edge of the party and count the minutes until he could escape, enduring the sidelong glances that followed him everywhere.

He hadn't expected her.

She wore a pale blue dress, modest but becoming, with curls escaping at her temples. She stood beside a man he didn't recognize, her hand resting on the stranger's arm with an ease that made a dangerous edge twist in Dominic's chest.

"Dominic." His aunt's words broke into his thoughts, her fan snapping shut with a rhythmic click. "You are staring."

He tore his attention away, but not quickly enough. Philippa followed his line of sight, studying the woman in blue with open curiosity.

"The woman in blue?" Philippa asked, tilting her head.

He didn't answer; his throat felt too tight, his jaw locked against the words he couldn't afford to say.

"She is lovely." Philippa's focus remained on the group,

her head tilting with a clinical interest. "Not in the fashionable way, perhaps, but there's something about her. Spirit."

"Aunt, don't—" Dominic started.

"Who is she?" Philippa was already in motion, her silk skirts hissing against the grass. "Come. Introduce me."

"No." The word snapped out like a whip, and Dominic stepped forward to intercept her. "She is no one. Just a… villager."

Philippa's eyebrow rose, her features sharpening into a look of pure, aristocratic skepticism. "A villager who has made you forget how to breathe?"

"Aunt, please." He caught her arm, his shoulders hunching as he leaned in close. "Don't."

She studied his face and read straight through him. Whatever she saw there softened her expression. "This is why you have not been sleeping."

He could not deny it. He stayed rooted to the spot and kept his focus on the distant treeline.

"Then I definitely need to meet her." Philippa patted his hand in a firm rhythm. "Come along, nephew."

"I cannot—" The words came out rough. He dropped his chin and looked at the dirt by his boots. "I said something at the festival. Something I should not have."

Philippa paused. Her hand went still on his arm. "What did you say?"

He kept looking at the grass. "I called her nothing of consequence. I thought it would protect her reputation, but she… I think she heard."

Philippa shut her eyes. A quiet sigh slipped out. "Oh, Dominic."

"I know," he whispered.

"You have your father's talent for cruelty when you are afraid." The words landed like a blow.

Dominic bowed his head. "I know."

"Then you will face it." Philippa linked her arm through his, her grip unyielding. "Come."

Nell saw them approaching before Daphne did. The silver-haired woman walked with purpose, her stride eating up the distance. Behind her, Westmore followed like a man being led to the gallows. Nell's spine went rigid, and she tucked her chin high. She wouldn't run. She wouldn't give him the satisfaction of seeing her flee. She just looked in the other direction.

Daphne's head turned, and recognition flashed across her face. She recognized the viscount. "Nell." Daphne whispered, her fingers digging into the fabric of her reticule. "He's here!"

"Yes." Nell kept her stare fixed ahead. "Let him come."

Daphne's jaw set. Hartley noticed the shift, his eyes moving between the women and the approaching pair, but he said nothing.

The silver-haired woman reached them first, her smile warm and her eyes missing nothing. "Forgive the intrusion. I am Lady Philippa Westmore." She adjusted her gloves with brisk tugs. "My nephew has been terribly remiss in introducing me to anyone."

Hartley stepped forward with a polite bow. "Lady Philippa. A pleasure. Dr. Hartley. I have a practice in the village."

"A physician!" Philippa tapped her chin with her folded fan. "How wonderful. We are in dire need of good doctors in Hampshire."

"And may I present Mrs. Ashford." Hartley gestured toward Nell. "She owns the bakery in the village. And Miss Daphne Wells, her dear friend and assistant."

Nell curtsied and kept her focus on Philippa. "Lady Philippa. An honour."

Philippa regarded her with open curiosity. "Mrs. Ashford. What a pleasure. And Miss Wells."

Daphne dipped into a stiff curtsy. Her lips pressed thin. "My lady."

"And this is my nephew." Philippa gestured behind her. "Lord Westmore."

Dominic stepped forward. His face held a careful mask. Tension touched his mouth. "Mrs. Ashford. Miss Wells."

Daphne did not curtsy. She watched him like a flint striking stone. Confusion crossed his brow before he turned to the doctor.

"Dr. Hartley." The words came tight. "How do you know Mrs. Ashford?"

"I am physician to Mrs. Ashford's daughter." Hartley's expression did not shift, yet his attention grew intent as he moved closer to Nell.

Philippa's attention swung to Nell, concern replacing pleasantry. "Your daughter is unwell?"

"My Lily has asthma, my lady." Nell smoothed the front of her skirt. "The damp weather troubles her lungs."

"Poor lamb." Philippa pressed a gloved hand to her collarbone. "Is she improving?"

"She is." Nell allowed herself a grateful glance toward Hartley. "Dr. Hartley has been very attentive."

Philippa regarded the two of them—the doctor standing close, his hand hovering at Nell's elbow—and something knowing flickered across her face. She tucked it away with practised ease.

Dominic stood rigid through the exchange, watching Nell with an intensity that bordered on indecent. Philippa glanced at him, one eyebrow arching in silent prompt.

He cleared his throat. "Her sweets are exceptional." The words came out rough, scraped raw. "The best in the county."

The praise landed heavy in the silence. He wouldn't meet Nell's eyes. Philippa's gaze darted between the two of them, her fan tapping once against her palm.

"High praise," she murmured. "My nephew rarely compliments anything."

"Mrs. Ashford." Dominic took a half-step forward, his voice strained. "I wondered if I might —"

"Dr. Hartley." Nell cut across him, turning to the doctor with a brightness sharp enough to draw blood. "I've heard there is a viewing platform by the lake. I should very much like to see it."

Hartley read the desperation in her shoulders. "Of course." He offered his arm. "The view is quite fine this time of year."

"Miss Wells." Hartley turned to Daphne. "Would you care to join us?"

Daphne looked at Dominic, then Philippa. "Actually, I think I shall stay. Lady Philippa, would you mind terribly if I walked with you?"

"I would be delighted, Miss Wells." Philippa offered her arm.

Nell squeezed Daphne's hand once—gratitude and warning compressed into a single press of fingers—then took Hartley's arm and did not look back.

Dominic watched her hand resting on another man's

sleeve. He watched her straight, proud back disappear down the gravel path. His gloves creaked where his fists tightened.

He should let her go. She'd made herself clear.

His feet moved anyway, drawn toward the lake at a distance he couldn't close and couldn't widen. Fools never knew when to stay away.

The path to the lake wound through manicured hedges and beneath ancient oaks with leaves just beginning to turn gold. Hartley walked beside her in comfortable silence, his presence steady and undemanding. "Thank you." Nell's voice came out shakier than she'd intended, and she reached up to tuck a stray curl behind her ear. "For getting me away."

"You seemed like you needed an exit." His smile was gentle, and he adjusted his pace to match her smaller steps. "I have found that garden parties often require strategic retreats."

The viewing platform jutted out over the lake, a wooden structure weathered by the elements. A few other guests stood at the far end, admiring the swans that drifted across the glassy surface. Nell stepped onto the platform, the boards creaking beneath her feet, though she moved to the railing, wrapping her fingers around the worn wood.

"It's beautiful." The tension in her shoulders began to unwind in the peaceful quiet.

Hartley joined her at the railing, standing close enough to offer warmth but not so close as to crowd her. "I come here sometimes when I need to think."

"What do you think about?" She turned to look at him, her curiosity piqued by his somber tone.

His smile turned wistful, and he looked out at the water. “The past, mostly. Paths not taken.”

“I think about those things too.” She looked down at her reflection in the shallows, understanding him better than he knew.

“Do you ever wonder what your life might have been?” He asked it quietly, his brown eyes raking over her face. “If you had made different choices?”

Every day, she thought. But she merely smoothed the lace at her wrist. “Sometimes. But I have my children and my shop. I wouldn’t trade those.”

“No.” His features softened, and his hand drifted a fraction closer to hers on the rail. “I don’t suppose you would.”

For a moment, Nell let herself believe this quiet companionship could be enough. Then, a sharp crack splintered the air. The boards beneath Hartley’s feet gave way without warning. He went down with a shout of surprise, plunging into the lake in a violent crash of churning water. Nell stumbled backward as the platform began to crumble, the boards beneath her own feet groaning as they tilted toward the dark gap.

Suddenly, strong arms caught her from behind. She was yanked back from the collapsing edge and pulled hard against a solid chest. She landed on safe ground, the gravel path solid beneath her shoes. His arms wrapped around her, holding her so tight she could feel his heart hammering against her spine. His rapid breath stirred the hair at her temple as he gasped for air.

Dominic had been approaching from the path when he saw the platform give way. He had sprinted the final yards, his boots thudding against the turf, to catch her just before she vanished. His arms tightened around her in an instinctive, protective clench, holding her like she might dissolve into the autumn mist.

For one breath—one single, treacherous breath—Nell let herself feel it. She leaned into the solid warmth of his coat and the staggering strength in his arms. Then she felt it.

Unmistakable and firm, the length of him pressed against the small of her back. Heat flooded through her, pooling low in her belly before a wave of pure horror crashed in behind it. She went rigid, every muscle locking with the force of a physical blow.

He felt the change. The moment she realized, his lungs froze mid-inhale and his entire body went still.

"Mrs. Ashford." The question emerged as a strangled rasp, rough as gravel as he peered down at her. "Are you hurt?"

She couldn't speak. Her mind refused to process the intimacy of the contact. In the water below, Hartley surfaced with a desperate gasp, sputtering as he treaded water.

"Mrs. Ashford! Are you—" The doctor's shout broke the silence, yet Dominic's arms didn't release her. Whether from shock or a stubborn inability to let go, she didn't know.

"Let go of me." The words hitched in her throat, barely carrying through the air as she struggled to find her footing. "Let go."

He released her instantly, stepping back so fast he nearly stumbled over a stray root. Nell spun to face him, her cheeks burning with a feverish heat and her eyes wide with outrage. He stood pale and stricken, his hands raised in front of him like a man proving he was unarmed.

She'd felt it. He knew she'd felt it, while there was no hiding the physical truth of what had occurred.

"I didn't—" His words broke, and his Adam's apple

bobbed in a frantic swallow. "The platform collapsed. I only meant to save you."

"Don't." She held up a shaking hand to silence him. "Don't say another word."

"Nell—" He started, reaching out a tentative finger.

"Don't touch me." She shoved him, her palms flat against his chest. She struck him hard enough to make him stagger back a step, his heels skidding on the grass.

She stumbled backward, away from him and toward the jagged edge. "Nell, wait!" Dominic lunged forward, his face showing terror.

She jerked away from his reaching hand, but her heel caught on a splintered piece of timber. She went over. Through the gap. Into the dark, waiting water.

"NELL!" Her name tore from his throat, stripped of all titles and propriety as he reached for the empty air.

The water hit her like a physical slap. It was October-cold, shocking the very breath from her lungs, yet she surfaced gasping, her heavy skirts tangling around her legs like leaden weights.

Hartley was already there. He waded toward her through the reeds. "Mrs. Ashford." He reached out, his steady hand an anchor in the chaos. "Take my hand. I have you."

She reached for Hartley. She reached for the man in the water, ignoring the man standing paralyzed on the bank. Dominic stood frozen on the shore, his coat half off and one arm free of its sleeve. He watched, motionless, as another man played the savior.

Hartley pulled her close, his arm solid around her waist as he supported the burden of her sodden skirts. "I have you. You are safe." He guided her toward the shallows where other guests had begun to gather, drawn by the commotion.

Someone wrapped a heavy wool coat around Nell's shoulders as she was helped onto the grass. It was not Dominic's, and he hadn't moved from his spot. Hartley climbed out beside her, his teeth chattering as he shivered, yet his first concern was for her.

"Are you hurt? Did you hit anything on the way down?" He brushed a wet strand of hair from her face, tenderly.

"N-no." The word was a mere wisp of air, barely holding together as a violent tremor took hold of her limbs. She wrapped her arms around herself, trying to anchor her frame. "I am f-fine."

She didn't look at Dominic. She wouldn't grant him even a glance. Daphne came running down the path, her skirts hiked shamelessly above her ankles, followed by a concerned Lady Philippa.

"Nell! What happened?" Daphne cried out, kneeling in the grass to take Nell's hand.

"The platform collapsed." Hartley's voice remained steady despite his pallor. "We both went in. She is unharmed but cold. We need to get her home immediately."

Daphne wrapped herself around Nell, shooting a glare at Dominic that could have curdled milk.

"My gig is nearby." Hartley accepted a dry coat from a bystander. "I will take them home."

"I can—" Dominic took a sharp step forward, his hand extending as if to catch her. The offer was stripped of its usual poise, jagged and exposed. "My carriage is at your disposal."

"No." The word left Nell's mouth before he'd finished speaking. It was the first time she'd looked at him since the fall, and her eyes were flat, cold, and entirely empty of warmth. "Thank you, Lord Westmore. Dr. Hartley will see us home."

The dismissal was absolute. It was public, humiliating, and entirely deserved, but Dominic stopped like she'd struck him across the face. Philippa reached his side, her expression unreadable as she placed a hand on his shoulder. He didn't move; he simply watched as Hartley guided Nell away, with Daphne flanking her other side, until the three of them disappeared toward the drive. "Come." Philippa took his arm, her grip firm. "We should leave as well." Dominic let his aunt lead him away, feeling numb and hollow.

At Bramwell Park, he went straight to his study and closed the door with a soft, final click. He stood at the window, staring at the darkening sky.

He replayed the moment again and again. The terror that had seized him when he saw her about to fall—and the way he'd moved without calculation, caring for nothing except her safety. She'd been in his arms. Pressed against him. Safe.

And then.

He closed his eyes and pressed his forehead against the cool glass. She'd felt him. The evidence of his desire had been impossible to hide, and there was no explaining it away to a woman he'd already insulted.

But that was not what haunted him. What kept circling in his mind was the single heartbeat before the horror had set in. She'd leaned into him. He was certain of it: for half a second, she'd relaxed against his chest.

She'd responded. Just for an instant, before memory and

fury had drowned the connection. It didn't matter that he was the man who had called her nothing. It didn't matter that he was an arrogant lord who had hurt her to save his own pride.

It mattered because if she could respond to him, then perhaps she didn't truly hate him. Perhaps there was still a chance to make this right. He opened his eyes and stared at his reflection. He would find a way, even if it destroyed him, he'd have to try.

Chapter Ten

Flour dust hung in the grey light of the kitchen like snow that refused to settle. Nell punched the dough down hard, folded it over, punched again. Her shoulders burned. Her fingers ached. Good. Pain kept the mind where it belonged—on the work, the shop, the next loaf.

Not on the lake.

She could survive the humiliation. Being fished out like a drowned cat while half the county gawked—fine. She'd fold that away into the locked box where she kept every other bruise life had handed her.

What she couldn't fold away was the moment before.

His chest against her back. His arms wrapped around her as though she were something worth saving. And then—the press of him. Hard and unmistakable against her hip. His body telling a story his mouth had spent weeks denying.

She slammed the dough against the worktable.

It meant nothing. Men were simple creatures. Warmth and softness, any woman's body pressed close enough—of course he'd responded. Biology. Instinct. Nothing more.

Nell.

Her name, torn from his throat when she'd fallen. Not Mrs. Ashford. Not the baker. *Nell.* Like it had cost him something to say it. Like he couldn't help himself.

The shop was empty, the morning rush long faded. Daphne was at the vicarage. The children were at Mr. Willoughby's farm. She was alone with the yeast and the sugar and the silence, and the silence was the worst of it.

The front door opened, the bell chiming overhead.

Her hands stilled in the dough.

Dr. Hartley stood in the doorway with his medical bag in hand. "Mrs. Ashford. I wanted to check on you," he said with a quiet, reassuring smile already forming as he closed the door behind him.

Relief flooded through her immediately. She wiped her floury hands on her apron, feeling foolish for her racing heart. "Dr. Hartley. You are back from your rounds early."

"I had a cancellation." He stepped inside, removing his hat and setting it carefully on the counter. "And I confess I have been worried. You took quite a chill at the lake. I wanted to see for myself that you are recovered."

"I am perfectly well." She gestured toward the kitchen with a slight wave of her hand. "Truly. Would you like some tea?"

"I would like that very much." He followed her into the kitchen, settling into a chair at the scarred worktable while she set the kettle over the flame. "The children are at the Willoughbys' today?" He asked, watching her move about the small space.

"Yes." Nell set out two cups of plain white china, noting the small chip on one rim as she placed them on the table. "They like Mr. Willoughby's farm."

"Good." His smile was genuine, crinkling the corners of his eyes as he rested his hands on the table. "Children need days like that. Freedom."

"They are everything to me." She said as she sat across from him. "Everything I do is for them."

"I know." His features softened as he leaned forward slightly, his attention narrowing onto her. "I see it. The way you've built this life for them. The sacrifices you've made."

Something in his expression caught her. It was an understanding that went deeper than simple observation. "You speak as if you know something of sacrifice," she said carefully, watching his face for a reaction.

He remained quiet for a moment, staring into the empty cup before him. Then he drew a long breath and smoothed his cravat with a steady hand. "I was engaged once."

Nell went still, her fingers tightening on her cup. He'd never mentioned a fiancée, and she had only heard about her from Mrs. Pemberton's gossip.

"Jasmine." He spoke the name as if it still carried a physical weight, his gaze dropping to the scarred wood of the table. "We were engaged for four years. I thought we were happy. I thought we would finally marry once I had established my practice and could give her the life she deserved." He paused, his jaw tightening into a hard, pained line. "I thought wrong."

"What happened?" Nell leaned closer, her cup forgotten between her palms.

"She left." His expression remained a carefully maintained mask. "It's been almost eight months. She went with a French count who promised her Paris. Adventure. A life more exciting than the one I could provide."

"I am sorry." Nell reached out like to touch his hand, then

hesitated, her fingers fluttering before coming to rest on the table instead. "The words feel inadequate."

"She said I was too dull for her." A ghost of a bitter smile flickered across his face as he looked up. "Too steady. Too predictable. She wanted passion and romance, and I gave her security and routine. Four years of waiting, and in the end, I was not enough."

Nell's throat tightened. She recognized this wound; it was the pain of being made to feel insufficient, of giving everything only to be told it was not what was desired. "You are not dull." She squared her shoulders, meeting his eyes without blinking. "You are kind and steady. Those are not flaws, Dr. Hartley."

He looked up at her, his features softening with surprised gratitude.

"Some people don't know how to value what they have until it's gone." Nell smoothed a stray lock of hair behind her ear.

"No." Something shifted in his expression, a sudden gravity settling over him. "They don't."

The kettle began to whistle, breaking the silence. Nell rose to tend to it, pouring the steaming water over the tea leaves, grateful for the task.

She poured the tea in the cups and settled. "Here you go, Mr. Hartley."

"Edmund." He traced the grain of the wood with a thumb, his posture relaxing into a new kind of intimacy. "Please. Call me Edmund."

"Edmund." Nell tested the name, her fingers tightening around the handle of her cup the way to steady herself. It felt strange and dangerously intimate. "Then you must call me

Nell."

His smile reached his eyes this time, softening the weary lines of his face. "Nell." He reached across the table, his hand covering hers. His palm was warm and entirely undemanding.

She didn't pull away. Instead, she let herself lean into the comfort of the gesture, exhaling a breath she'd held for three days. It was simple. It was safe.

The front door opened, the bell clattering against the glass. Heavy, purposeful footsteps crossed the shop floor, eating up the distance between the entrance and the kitchen doorway. Nell's blood went cold. She knew those footsteps.

Lord Westmore filled the doorframe, his broad shoulders blocking the light from the shop. His misty eyes swept the scene, taking in the tea, the quiet intimacy, and Edmund's hand still covering hers. A shadow cut across his face, dark and dangerous.

Nell snatched her hand back, her pulse spiking. She felt a hot flush of guilt, which immediately turned to fury, though she had nothing to be ashamed of.

"Lord Westmore." Edmund rose smoothly, offering a polite, professional nod. "Good morning to you."

Dominic didn't look at him. His eyes remained fixed on Nell, tracing the colour in her cheeks and the teacups that spoke of a shared morning. "I appear to be interrupting."

"Not at all." Edmund's expression remained unruffled as he gathered his gloves. "I was just checking on Mrs. Ashford after her ordeal at the lake."

"How… Thorough of you." Dominic's attention finally shifted to Edmund, assessing and overtly hostile.

The two men regarded each other across the small kitchen. Hartley stood calm, his hands relaxed at his sides, while Westmore remained coiled, a spring of tension in every line of his body.

Edmund turned back to Nell, his expression warming despite the crackling atmosphere. "I should be going. I have patients to see."

"Of course." Nell rose, grateful for his presence even as her heart hammered against her ribs. "Thank you for checking on me, Edmund."

"It was my pleasure." He took her hand and raised it to his lips, pressing a brief, proper kiss to her knuckles. "Nell."

He said her name deliberately, his eyes sliding to Westmore to ensure the familiarity was noted. A stubborn tension pulled at Dominic's face, his gloved hands curling into fists.

"Edmund," Nell managed, offering a small dip of a curtsy with a composure that belied the frantic thrum of her pulse.

Edmund gathered his medical bag and crossed to the doorway, pausing just inches from Dominic. "I shall call again soon."

"I should like that." Nell lifted her chin, her gaze unwavering.

He nodded politely to the viscount. "Lord Westmore."

Dominic remained silent, watching the doctor depart with eyes like flint. The front door opened and closed, the bell ringing out a final, lonely note as Edmund's footsteps faded down the street.

Nell turned back to the worktable and began clearing the tea things, needing the distraction of labor. The china clinked sharply as she stacked the cups on a tray.

"Edmund." Dominic spat the name like a curse. "You call him Edmund now."

"We are friends." She kept her back to him, focusing on the dregs of tea. "Friends use Christian names."

"Friends." He paced a short line near the hearth, his boots clicking rhythmically on the stone. "How pleasant for you both."

"Was there something you needed, my lord?" She kept her expression flat, though her hands wouldn't stay steady.

"You know why I am here." His eyes dropped to her hands, tracking the slight tremor in her fingers.

"I am afraid I don't." She picked up the tray and turned from him, desperate for distance. "Excuse me. I have work to attend to."

She walked toward the back storeroom, that cramped space crammed with flour sacks and sugar barrels where the air always sat thick and warm. His footsteps followed, unhurried and certain, the floorboards groaning beneath his weight.

"Since the lake, I haven't had a single night's peace." He spoke from directly behind her, close enough that his breath stirred the loose hairs at her nape. "Not one."

"And why should that concern me?" She set the tray on a shelf with a jarring rattle and turned to face him—then lost whatever she'd meant to say next. He was too close. Near enough that she could see the flecks of silver in his grey eyes. "I need to get back to work. If you'll excuse me."

"You felt it." His tone dropped low, almost hoarse. "At the lake. When I held you."

Heat flooded her face and throat. "I don't know what you are talking about." She smoothed the front of her apron with fingers that would not stop shaking.

"Liar." The word came out almost gentle, which made it worse. He stepped fully into the room, and the door swung half-closed behind him. Sandalwood and rain—that was what he smelled of, and the storeroom was too small to escape it. "You felt what you do to me. What you have always done to me. And it terrifies you because your body told the same story mine did."

"That was —" She broke off, her mouth working around a word she couldn't find, the memory of his hardness against her hip burning through every sensible thought she'd built in the three days since.

"My body saying what my pride won't let me." He closed the distance between them by another half-step, his boots scraping the worn stone floor. "And I am done pretending otherwise."

"Stop." The word cracked down the middle as it left her. She stepped backward until her spine met the sturdy wooden shelf, jars clinking softly behind her.

"I have tried." His ashen eyes burned into hers with a raw, agonizing honesty. "Two weeks of staying away. Two weeks of telling myself I don't care about you."

"But you *don't* care about me. Why should you?" She lifted her chin, fury finally eclipsing her fear. "Your words, my lord. Nothing of consequence. That's what you called me to your friends."

He flinched like she'd struck him across the scar. "I was trying to protect you," he said, reaching out to grip the edge of a shelf near her head, effectively pinning her in place.

"From what?" Her eyes flicked briefly to his white-knuckled grip on the wood before snapping back to his face.

"From me." He stepped closer, so close she could feel the heat radiating from his chest. "From what the ton would say if they thought I was interested. Your reputation would be destroyed by their gossip."

"So you destroyed it yourself instead." She held on to the shelf to steady her shaking frame. "You made me feel like dirt beneath your boots. All to protect me. How very noble of you, my lord."

"I apologize." He stepped closer until he was looming over her, the individual stitches in his silk waistcoat coming into sharp focus as he crowded her space. "I know what I did. I have hated myself for it every day since."

"Good." She tried to slide along the shelf to escape his shadow, but he tracked her movement, caging her with his body without yet making contact.

"Does he make you feel like this?" He searched her eyes, his words dropping to a rough, gravelly rasp. "Your Edmund."

"Like what?" She breathed, her pulse skidding wildly as she pressed her spine against the wood.

"Like you are burning." He braced one hand on the shelf beside her head, his arm creating a barrier she couldn't pass. "Like you cannot breathe. Like you'd rather fight than walk away."

"Edmund is kind." She spat the words, her eyes flashing with defiance. "He is gentle. He would never behave with such insolence. He would never..."

"He would never set you on fire." Dominic finished for her, his focus dropping to her mouth with a hunger he didn't bother hiding. "He would never make you feel alive."

"I don't want to feel alive." The words tore out of her, ragged and desperate. She shoved at his shoulders, her palms meeting the unyielding wall of his chest. "I want to feel safe. I want peace. I want..."

"You want what you cannot have with him." He crowded her against the shelf, the soft flour sacks yielding at her back while his body remained hard and hot against her. "You want someone who sees the fire beneath all that armor. Someone who is not afraid of it."

"You know nothing about what I want." She turned her face away, her breath coming in short, jagged gasps.

"I know you haven't stopped thinking about me either." His mouth hovered just above hers, his warmth ghosting over her skin. "I know because I see it in your eyes, in the way you look away."

"You are delusional." She whispered the insult, though she didn't pull back.

"Am I?" His breath brushed her lips, teasing the sensitive skin. "Then why is your pulse racing? Why are your hands shaking? Why do you look at me like you cannot decide whether to run or—"

"Or what?" She lifted her chin, refusing to cower even as her knees threatened to fail her.

"Or this." The words were a mere vibration against her mouth.

He kissed her.

She should have pushed him away. She should have screamed or brought her knee up hard. Instead, as his mouth moved over hers with a hot, demanding hunger, her resolve shattered. His hand fisted in her hair, tilting her head back to deepen the contact, pressing her into the shelf until she felt every rigid line of him through her muslin dress.

She kissed him back.

Her hands fisted in his wool coat, dragging him closer. Her mouth opened under his, hungry and furious, while he let out a low, desperate groan that vibrated through her very bones. His hands found her waist, pulling her against him until there was no space left.

A flour sack tumbled from the shelf beside her head, bursting softly and coating the floor in white dust. Neither of them noticed.

His hands slid down her sides, gripping her hips to lift her onto the edge of the shelf. More sacks shifted and fell as she wrapped her legs around his waist. He stepped between them, the rigid length of him straining against his breeches as he pressed into her. His hand found her ankle beneath her skirts, sliding up her calf and over her knee with agonizing slowness.

She should stop him. Should shove him away, slap his face, remind him who he was and who she was.

His fingers traced along her inner thigh, and every logical thought in her head turned to smoke. "Tell me to stop." His breath was scorching against her ear. "Say the word and I shall walk out that door."

She said nothing. She simply tilted her pelvis toward him, opening wider.

"Nell." His expression was wrecked as he pulled back just enough to look at her, his chest heaving. "I need you to say it. Yes or no."

"Yes." The word ripped out of her. "God help me. Yes."

His fingers found the slit in her drawers, discovering the slick, aching heat of her. She bit down on her own hand to keep from crying out, her eyes fluttering shut.

"So wet." A dark growl escaped him as his fingers slid through her folds. "Is this for me?"

She couldn't answer. She couldn't think. His thumb circled

the bundle of nerves at her center, and her whole body jerked in his arms.

"Answer me." He pressed harder, rubbing slow, maddening circles. "Is this for me, Nell? Or do you get like this for your kind, gentle Edmund?"

"I hate you." She whimpered, her hips rocking instinctively against his hand. "I hate you so much."

"I know." He slid a finger inside her, and her back arched off the shelf. "But you are going to come for me anyway."

He worked her with devastating skill. One finger became two, stretching her and crooking forward, yet his thumb kept up its relentless rhythm, driving her higher and higher.

"Look at me." He gripped her chin, forcing her eyes to meet his. "I want to see your face when you shatter."

She couldn't look away. His eyes held hers with a predatory intensity; and her whole body wound tighter, a coil of tension nearing its breaking point.

"That's it." His features darkened with a primal focus. "Let go. Give it to me."

She shattered. Her teeth sank into her fist to muffle her scream, her body clenching around his fingers in wave after wave of release. He worked her through the climax, slowing his strokes and drawing out every last tremor until she finally collapsed against his shoulder, boneless and gasping for air.

For a long moment, neither of them moved. Her forehead remained pressed against his shoulder, her breath hot through his linen shirt, but then, he withdrew slowly, and she shuddered at the sudden, hollow loss of him. He raised his hand to his mouth, his eyes burning into hers, and licked his fingers clean.

"Sweet." The word was a rasp, ruined by the friction of the moment. "Even sweeter than I imagined."

A wire pulled taut inside her and gave. She grabbed the lapels of his coat with both fists and dragged his mouth down to hers. She kissed him hard, tasting herself on his tongue. Dominic groaned into her mouth, his hands gripping her hips to pull her flush against his frame.

She bit his lip. It was a hard, vicious snap that drew the metallic taste of copper into her mouth.

He jerked back with a sharp hiss of pain. Blood welled on his lower lip before dripping down his chin—and she stared at him, her breathing ragged, every breath tearing out of her. The taste of him sat heavy on her tongue.

"Don't come here again." The words shook, yet she fixed him with a steady, freezing glare. "Ever."

He touched his lip, looking at the blood on his fingertips before shifting his regard back to her. She looked magnificent amidst the chaos of fallen flour sacks, wrecked and furious. He smiled. It was a slow, dangerous expression, his teeth stained pink. "I'm afraid I can't promise that, Mrs. Ashford."

He inclined his head in a small, formal gesture, a gentleman acknowledging a lady in a drawing room, and walked out of the storeroom. She heard his heavy footsteps cross the shop floor. She heard the front door open and the bell chime one final time as it closed.

He was gone.

She sat on the shelf, surrounded by the ruins of her work, her thighs still trembling and the ghost of his blood on her tongue.

The front door banged open. Nell flinched, her heart beating faster. She stumbled out of the storeroom on legs that felt like water, smoothing her skirts with frantic hands. Daphne stood in the kitchen doorway, her face flushed pink from the autumn wind and her delivery basket swinging empty on her arm. Her eyes swept over Nell, noting the disheveled hair, the high colour in her cheeks, and the swollen curve of her lips.

"I just passed Lord Westmore in the street." Daphne said with piercing curiosity. "His lip was bleeding quite profusely."

Nell said nothing. She moved to the worktable and gripped the edge until her knuckles turned white, needing the solid wood to keep from collapsing.

"He was smiling." Daphne set down her basket and moved closer, her eyes narrowing into slits. "Bleeding and smiling like a cat who had caught a particularly fat mouse. What happened, Nell?"

Nell looked at her friend, seeing the question burning there. She couldn't give the answer. Not to Daphne. Not to anyone.

"I don't know." She heard the words fall from her lips, and the lie soured in her mouth. "I don't know what I did."

But she did know. She knew exactly what she'd done.

Dominic made it halfway down the lane before he tasted blood.

He stopped, pressed the back of his hand to his mouth. It came away red. He stared at it, then pulled his handkerchief from his coat and scrubbed his chin clean. The cut on his lip he could do nothing about—swollen and visible, a brand she'd left on him with her teeth.

He couldn't walk through the village square like this. Not with her shop sitting at the end of the street and every tongue in Cresswell ready to wag. One whisper that the viscount had stumbled out of Nell Ashford's storeroom with blood on his face, and the damage would fall on her. Never on him. Men like him collected scandal like dust on a coat sleeve. Nell would lose everything.

He cut down the alley between the smithy and the saddler's, taking the back lane toward the churchyard. His collar turned up, his stride quick.

But beneath the caution, his blood still roared.

He could still feel her. The way she'd shattered around his fingers, biting into her own fist to keep quiet. The way she'd grabbed his collar and kissed him like she meant to wreck him—then done exactly that with her teeth.

Don't come here again. Ever.

He smiled against the sting of his split lip.

She could bar the door. She could spit fire and threats and tell him to keep his distance until her voice gave out. It wouldn't change what he'd felt—her body arching into his touch, not away from it. Her mouth opening under his, hungry and furious and honest in a way her words refused to be.

He would not be careless with her name. He would not parade through the village or let the gossips sharpen their knives on her reputation. She had children, a livelihood, a standing in this place that one reckless moment could gut.

But he was done pretending he didn't want her.

He touched his lip again, the pain bright and grounding. She'd marked him, and he intended to earn every scar that followed.

Chapter Eleven

The morning air bit sharp against Nell's cheeks as she walked toward the grocer's, her basket swinging empty at her side.

Lily had woken in the night, coughing. It was that wet, rattling sound that made Nell's heart seize every time she heard it. Edmund's tonic helped; it always helped. However, the cough had returned with the weather, and Nell knew from bitter experience that tonics alone were insufficient. Her daughter needed building up. She required warmth, nourishment, and rest.

Soup was the remedy. That was what Nell's mother had always made when someone was poorly. Chicken broth with root vegetables, simmered low and slow until the kitchen filled with steam and the whole house smelled of comfort. *Good for the lungs,* her mother used to say while stirring the pot. *Good for the soul.*

Nell had been making soup for her children since before they could walk. Some traditions were worth keeping.

She'd been avoiding thinking about him. She tried to push

away the memory of the storeroom, of the shelf digging into her back, and the taste of blood on her tongue. She tried to forget the way he'd smiled when she bit him, the way she'd given him exactly what he desired.

The avoidance didn't work.

She thought about him constantly. She woke in the night with her lips tingling and her body aching for something she refused to name. She caught herself staring at the storeroom door during quiet moments, remembering the force of his body against hers and the desperate sound he'd made against her mouth. Two days had passed, and she could still taste him.

The grocer's shop was warm and dim, smelling of dried herbs and sawdust. Nell gathered what she needed. She selected carrots, onions, and a parsnip that was slightly soft but suitable for broth. The butcher next door had chicken, and she managed to haggle him down a penny on a piece that was smaller than she liked but would have to do.

Daphne was with the children this morning while Martha was fitting a dress for Mrs. Pemberton. Nell could almost see Martha now, pins held between her teeth and a measuring tape draped around her neck. These were the women who helped Nell survive, day after day, holding her fragile life together with their capable hands.

She counted her coins carefully outside the butcher's, tucking them back into her purse with the familiar ache of never quite having enough. The shop did well, better than she'd dared hope when she first opened those doors five years ago, but there was never extra. Every penny was spoken for twice over.

Coming out of the grocer's, her basket heavy on her arm and her mind wandering to broth and the ghost of a kiss, she nearly collided with a passerby on the pavement. "Oh!" Nell stumbled back, clutching her basket to her chest to steady the contents. "Forgive me, I was not looking where I stepped."

Lady Philippa Westmore stood before her, silver hair gleaming beneath a deep blue bonnet. A maid hovered at a respectful distance behind her, though the older woman's face lit up with surprised delight.

"Mrs. Ashford!" Philippa clasped her gloved hands together near her chin. "What a happy accident. I was just thinking about you."

Nell dipped into an awkward curtsy, her heavy basket making the gesture feel graceless. "Lady Philippa. Good morning to you."

"None of that." Philippa waved away the formality with a brisk, impatient motion of her hand. "I have been meaning to call at your shop, but my nephew has been..." She paused, her lips pressing together in a thin line. "Difficult. I haven't had a moment to myself."

Her nephew.

Heat crept up Nell's cheeks before she could catch it, and she fixed her attention on a point somewhere past Philippa's shoulder, praying the older woman wouldn't notice the flush.

"Provisions?" Philippa eyed the carrots peeking out of Nell's basket with open curiosity, her head tilting. "You are not baking today?"

"Soup." Nell shifted the crush of the basket to her other arm, her muscles straining under the weight. "My daughter is unwell, and I am making broth."

Philippa's expression shifted, genuine concern replacing her curiosity as she stepped closer. "Unwell? The little girl you mentioned at Sir Huxley's?"

"Lily, yes." Nell found herself answering honestly, smoothing the edge of her cloak with restless fingers. There was something about Philippa that invited confidence—a warmth beneath her aristocratic bearing and a directness that felt more like friendship than condescension. "She has asthma, and the damp weather makes it worse."

"Poor child." Philippa shook her head, her brow creasing with a heavy sigh. "My friend's boy had the same affliction—it is a dreadful thing to watch them struggle for breath. Is she being treated?"

"Dr. Hartley has been very attentive." Nell adjusted her grip on the wicker handle, the weave biting into her palm.

"The good doctor." Philippa's eyes sharpened slightly, a knowing flicker appearing in their depths as she tilted her head. "Yes, I noticed he was quite attentive at Sir Huxley's."

Nell didn't know how to respond to such an observation and changed the subject instead, gesturing vaguely toward the end of the street. "She is resting today—my lodger is sitting with her."

"Your lodger?" Philippa prompted, raising a curious eyebrow.

"Martha. She's a friend and a seamstress." Nell tucked a stray strand of hair behind her ear, her fingers lingering there as though they needed something to do. "She rents a room above the shop and helps with the children when I am working."

"A seamstress, a doctor, and a loyal assistant." Philippa's voice softened as she reached out to touch Nell's sleeve, studying Nell's face with something that looked almost like admiration. "You have built yourself quite the little household,

Mrs. Ashford. But I suspect the weight of it still falls squarely on you."

"I manage." Nell lifted her chin, her spine lengthening as she claimed every inch of her height. "We manage."

"Of course you do." Philippa studied her for a long moment, her expression settling into something both gentle and resolute. "But even capable women deserve an afternoon's rest now and again."

"My lady?" Nell's brow furrowed in confusion.

"You must come to Bramwell Park for tea tomorrow." Philippa stated it as though it were the most natural suggestion in the world, smoothing the front of her elegant pelisse with one gloved hand.

Nell's stomach dropped through the cobblestones. Bramwell Park—his house, where he lived and slept, where he probably sat in some grand study at this very moment turning over the same memories she couldn't bury.

"I couldn't possibly." The words came out too fast, tripping over themselves as she took a step backward. "Lily is unwell, and I couldn't leave her bedside."

"Bring her." Philippa waved a hand as though Nell had raised no objection at all, her silk scarf fluttering in the autumn breeze. "The gardens are sheltered from the wind and quite mild even in this season—the country air will do her lungs a world of good."

"My lady, that's very kind, but..." Nell's grip tightened on the basket handle until the wicker creaked. "Bramwell Park is Lord Westmore's estate, and I couldn't presume to intrude upon his hospitality."

Philippa laughed, a warm and resonant sound that turned

heads on the pavement. "My dear, I practically raised that boy and have been managing his household since he was in short coats." She adjusted her bonnet with a confident pat. "He won't mind."

He will mind, Nell thought. Or worse—he wouldn't mind at all.

"Bring your son as well." Philippa continued, steamrolling over Nell's hesitation as she counted off the benefits on her gloved fingers. "Children need room to run, and the grounds are extensive—thirty acres, if you can believe it. Far too much space for one man and his elderly aunt."

"Tomorrow is Sunday." Nell seized on the excuse, her eyes brightening as she finally found a foothold. "It is the one day we all have together—Martha, the children, and myself. I couldn't break our little tradition."

"Bring her too." Philippa decided with a nod, as though the matter were already settled and entered into a ledger. "And Miss Wells—we shall make it a proper outing, tea on the terrace if the weather holds."

"Lady Philippa, truly..." Nell began, shaking her head.

"I have been rattling around that great house with only my nephew for company, and the man has all the conversational charm of a stone wall." Philippa took Nell's arm and began steering her down the pavement, her grip gentle but inexorable as she leaned in with a conspiratorial glint. "You would be doing me a kindness, Mrs. Ashford. Truly."

A kindness—she was framing it as a favour to herself, and Nell looked at the woman's earnest face and realized how terribly clever she was.

"Tomorrow at two." Philippa released her arm and patted her hand with brisk affection. "I shall send the carriage for you."

"Lady Philippa, I really must decline..." Nell tried one last time, reaching out as though to catch the invitation before it solidified into fact.

"Two o'clock." Philippa was already walking away, her maid hurrying to keep pace. She called back over her shoulder without slowing. "Don't make me come fetch you myself, Mrs. Ashford—I will, you know, and I am not above causing a scene in the middle of the village."

Nell stood on the pavement with her basket heavy on her arm and her heart heavier still, watching the older woman disappear around the corner with the satisfied stride of a general who had won a battle without drawing a single weapon.

She could still refuse—could send a note in the morning claiming Lily had taken a turn for the worse. Philippa would understand, and Philippa would forgive.

But Philippa had been kind, genuinely kind, in a way that had nothing to do with rank or obligation. And she was right about the children. Lily had been cooped up for weeks, trapped between the shop and her sickbed, watching the world through rain-streaked windows while her brother worked too hard and carried burdens too heavy for a boy of nine. They deserved an afternoon of freedom and beauty and something that was not merely survival.

And perhaps he wouldn't be there—perhaps he would be out riding or visiting tenants or called away to London on business that couldn't wait.

Nell didn't believe it for a moment.

He would be there. Standing too close, saying too much, watching her with those steely eyes that saw everything she was trying to hide. She could still see that wicked smirk—

blood on his teeth and not a shred of shame on his face, as though she had given him exactly what he wanted.

Don't come here again. Ever.

She'd spat those words at him in her own storeroom, and now she was going to willingly walk into his house, accepting his aunt's invitation, drinking his tea. The irony was enough to choke on.

She knew she was a fool—for agreeing, for not running, and for wanting, despite everything, to see him again.

God help her.

Chapter Twelve

The carriage arrived at two, just as Lady Philippa had promised. Nell climbed in first. Daphne followed, then Martha holding Lily's hand, and finally Oliver, who scrambled up the steps with the coiled energy of a boy trapped indoors too long. The yellow dress whispered against Nell's legs. It was borrowed from Martha and altered to fit her curves, chosen this morning with shaking hands. She'd told herself she hadn't worn it for him, but she was lying. The knowing sat heavy in her chest as the carriage lurched into motion.

"A real estate, Mama!" Lily pressed her face against the window, her breath fogging the glass. "With gardens and everything!"

"Sit properly." Nell tugged her daughter back onto the seat, smoothing the girl's pinafore with hands that wanted to shake. "You will smudge the glass, Lily."

"I don't care about smudges." Lily sat, but she kept bouncing, her spectacles sliding down her nose the way they always did when she was excited. "Do you think there will be a lake? Sarah Martin said rich people always have lakes."

Oliver pressed himself against the opposite window, his dark eyes fixed on the countryside rolling past. "I thought Sarah Martin was a liar." He muttered the words, though he didn't pull his gaze from the scenery.

Bramwell Park appeared around a bend in the road, and the carriage went silent.

Golden stone glowed warm in the autumn light. Ivy climbed the walls in carefully maintained cascades, and the windows caught the sun, throwing it back like scattered coins. The house rose three stories with wings extending on either side, and gardens swept down toward what was, indeed, a lake glittering silver in the distance. Lily's mouth fell open, her spectacles sliding forgotten to the tip of her nose—and Oliver's studied indifference cracked. His jaw went slack, though he clamped it shut when he caught Nell watching.

"Blimey." Daphne breathed the word, so low Nell could scarcely hear it against the rattle of the wheels.

Lady Philippa waited on the front steps, her silver hair gleaming in the sunlight. She descended as the carriage rolled to a stop, reaching for Nell's hand before the footman could offer his.

"You came!" Philippa clasped Nell's fingers between her own, her face creasing into a delighted smile. "I was half afraid you'd send your regrets."

"I considered it." Nell stepped onto the gravel drive, acutely aware of how her borrowed dress swished around her ankles and how out of place she must look against the grandeur of the house.

Philippa laughed, a warm, genuine sound that echoed off

the stone facade, and linked her arm through Nell's with the easy intimacy of an old friend. "I like you, Mrs. Ashford. You say what you mean—yet come, all of you. Tea is ready on the terrace, and Cook has outdone herself with the scones."

The entrance hall swallowed them whole. Marble floors veined with grey stretched in every direction, and portraits of stern-faced Westmores stared down from heavy gilt frames. A chandelier the size of Nell's entire kitchen hung overhead, its crystals winking in the light that poured through tall windows. Nell felt small beneath it. She felt the yellow dress shrink against her skin. Every coin she'd ever counted and every hour she'd ever worked seemed to press down on her shoulders.

"It's like a palace!" Lily spun in a slow circle, her neck craned back as she gaped at the chandelier.

"It's drafty." Philippa steered them toward a corridor, her hand warm on Nell's arm. "But it has its charms. Come, the terrace is this way."

They passed through rooms filled with furniture older than Nell's grandmother and carpets that had surely cost more than her shop earned in a year. This was where he lived, Nell thought. Where he slept. Where he'd grown from a boy into the complicated man who haunted her dreams.

"Lord Westmore is…?" Nell bit her lip, the question escaping before she could catch it back.

"Around somewhere." Philippa waved a hand toward the interior of the house, her rings flashing. "He has been impossible all morning. He is snapping at servants and pacing the halls like a caged wolf. I told him to make himself useful or make himself scarce."

Nell's pulse kicked hard against her throat.

They emerged onto a back terrace that overlooked the

grounds, and Nell stopped breathing. The gardens spread below them like a painting, manicured lawns swept toward the lake, and ancient oaks cast pools of shadow. And in the distance, rising dark and mysterious, stood a hedge maze with walls that had to be twelve feet tall.

"It goes on forever!" Lily grabbed Nell's hand and squeezed hard enough to hurt, her whole body vibrating.

"Is that a lake?" Oliver asked excitedly but then cleared his throat, trying to recover the dignity befitting a boy of nine.

"Thirty acres." Philippa settled into a chair near the tea service with a contented sigh, smoothing her skirts. "Though I confess I have never walked all of it myself."

"Can we go see it?" Lily started pulling toward the terrace steps, her eyes fixed on the glittering water.

"After tea." The voice came from behind them, low and rough and achingly familiar.

Nell's spine locked straight.

Dominic stepped onto the terrace through a door half hidden by climbing roses. No cravat today. His collar hung open, showing a triangle of tanned skin at his throat. His shirt-sleeves were rolled to the elbow, baring forearms roped with muscle, and his dark hair looked as though he'd been running his hands through it in frustration.

He stopped a few feet from the group, his hands loose at his sides, and let his eyes move over them one by one. His attention landed on Lily, and something in his face shifted. He took in her spectacles, crooked as always, and the outline of a book pressing through her pocket.

"What is that?" He nodded at her pocket. He skipped the patronizing lilt adults usually reserved for children, speaking as if to an equal.

Lily's free hand flew to cover the bulge, her cheeks flushing a deep pink. "It's my book, sir."

"What book?" He took a slow step toward her.

"The Castle of Otranto." Lily lifted her chin, bracing for the laughter that so often followed the discovery of her reading tastes.

Dominic paused as he surveyed the small girl. "A Gothic story? It's a bit dark for a Sunday afternoon, is it not?"

His eyebrow rose a fraction of an inch. "Walpole." He tilted his head, studying her with a look that bordered on genuine respect. "You like being frightened?"

Lily blinked behind her spectacles, clearly thrown by his knowledge of the author. "I like the mystery," she said and looked into his eyes, trying to gauge whether he was truly interested or merely humoring her. "And the castles."

"Our library has a first edition of Udolpho." He jerked his chin toward the house, his focus never leaving her face. "Have you read it?"

"Three times." Lily's grip on Nell's hand tightened until her small fingers ached. Nell could feel the excitement thrumming through her daughter's body like a live wire.

"You can hold it before you leave." Dominic adjusted his stance, stating it as an absolute fact rather than a casual offer. The matter was settled. "If you're careful."

Lily's mouth dropped open, her spectacles sliding down her nose unheeded as she looked up at her mother with eyes the size of saucers.

Dominic turned his attention to Oliver, who stood apart with his arms crossed over his narrow chest. The boy was guarding his territory, sizing up this stranger with the suspicion of a sentry. "Do you like to fish?" Dominic's expression remained neutral as he studied the boy's rigid posture.

Oliver's chin jutted forward, his jaw tight. "No," he muttered, staring back.

"Ever wanted to?" Dominic leaned back, resting one hand on the stone balustrade in a posture of easy unconcern.

Oliver shrugged. He seemed determined to show how little he cared for anything a lord might offer. "I don't know anyone who fishes. I've never gotten the opportunity to try it."

"The lake holds pike." Dominic nodded toward the glittering water, his tone remaining strictly matter-of-fact—as though discussing the weather rather than trying to win over a hostile child. "Nasty brutes, some of them. I once saw one take a man's bait, rod, and half his dignity in a single strike."

Oliver's eyes flicked toward the lake despite himself. Nell saw a spark of interest flare across his face before he shuttered it away. "So?"

"So nothing." Dominic matched the boy's studied indifference with a shrug of his own.

Oliver narrowed his eyes, his feet planted firmly on the terrace. "You don't have to be nice to us, you know." His chin lifted, a challenge aimed squarely at the man towering above him. "Just because we're here doesn't mean we need minding."

"Oliver." Nell's warning was sharp.

Dominic held up a hand to still her, his eyes never leaving the boy's. "I am not minding you." His expression gave nothing away. "I am telling you about the pike. What you do with the information is your own affair."

Oliver searched his face for mockery or some hidden agenda and found none. Slowly, his arms uncrossed and his shoulders dropped half an inch. He didn't smile, but the rigid armour of his posture began to crack.

Finally, Dominic turned to Nell.

His eyes dropped to her yellow dress, tracing the line of her shoulders with a heat she could feel on her skin. They traveled lower, lingering on the curve of her bodice until her breath hitched in her throat. When he finally looked back up, his expression was a mask of composure, but his eyes burned.

"Mrs. Ashford." The greeting was a low scrape, rough at the edges as he bowed his head.

"Lord Westmore." Nell folded her hands in front of her. She pressed her nails hard into her palms to keep herself from reaching up to touch her heated cheeks.

They settled around the tea table, which was laden with more food than Nell's family ate in a week. Scones piled high with clotted cream and jam, tiny sandwiches with the crusts cut off, seed cakes, ginger biscuits, and a towering arrangement of fruit that looked too beautiful to eat. Lily devoured three scones in rapid succession, cream smearing the corner of her mouth. Oliver picked at his food with studied disinterest, even as a pile of sandwiches accumulated on his plate. Martha sat quietly beside Philippa, her seamstress's eyes cataloguing every stitch of the older woman's gown while she nibbled a ginger biscuit with the careful restraint of someone unaccustomed to being waited on. Daphne kept shooting Nell significant looks across the table, her eyebrows climbing toward her hairline whenever Dominic spoke. Nell ignored every single one of them.

Dominic answered Lily's endless questions about the library with a patience that made Nell's chest ache. He explained which shelves held which genres and described the reading alcove with the best light. "I shall show you the section devoted to gothic novels before you leave," he promised, reaching for the teapot.

"The east wing is haunted," he said, his face perfectly serious and his chilling eyes solemn as a judge's. "A lady in grey. She walks the halls at midnight, weeping for her lost love."

Lily leaned forward over her half-eaten scone, her spectacles sliding down her nose, utterly captivated. "Have you seen her?" She whispered.

"Once." Dominic held her stare without blinking. "When I was your age. The sound of her crying woke me from a dead sleep."

"He's lying." Philippa set down her teacup with a delicate clink, her eyes twinkling with suppressed laughter. "He made up that story to scare his cousins when they came to visit. He made poor Margaret cry for an hour."

Dominic shrugged, reaching for another sandwich with complete unconcern. "They deserved it. Margaret put a toad in my bed."

Lily giggled, the sound bright and unexpected. She clapped a hand over her mouth the way the laugh had escaped against her will. "I would have put two toads."

"I like you." Dominic's mouth twitched at the corner. It was the closest thing to a smile Nell had seen from him, and something in his face softened in a way that made her heart clench.

An hour passed. The afternoon sun was warm on the terrace. The children relaxed in his presence with a speed that surprised Nell, and Lily chattered about books and ghosts and castles while Dominic listened with apparent interest. He asked questions that showed he was actually paying attention rather than merely tolerating her. Oliver gradually thawed enough to ask about the pike in the lake. He wanted to know how big they grew, how to catch them, and whether Dominic had ever been bitten.

Nell kept her eyes on her tea, on the gardens, or on her children, looking anywhere but at him. Even so, she felt him watching her like heat from a fire, tracking her movements and lingering on the bare skin of her shoulders. Every time he shifted in his chair, she grew painfully aware of the movement, for every time he spoke, his rough voice seemed to vibrate through her very bones. She didn't look at him. She couldn't. If she looked, everyone would see what she was feeling, and she was not yet ready to name those emotions, even to herself.

"The grounds." Dominic pushed back from the table and rose to his full height, his frame towering over the party and momentarily blocking out the sun. "I shall show them to you."

The children scrambled up from their chairs before Nell could speak. Lily grabbed Oliver's hand and dragged him toward the terrace steps, already chattering about the lake and whether there might be toads hiding in the garden.

"Everyone come." Philippa accepted Martha's offered arm and rose more slowly, her joints creaking audibly in the quiet afternoon. "These old bones stiffen if I sit too long."

They set off across the lawn, the grass soft and springy beneath their feet. Dominic led the way with the children flanking him like eager lieutenants. The women followed at a more sedate pace, Philippa leaning on Martha's arm while Daphne walked beside Nell, her eyes fixed suspiciously on the viscount's broad back.

Philippa's voice dropped to a murmur meant only for Nell's ears. "He is not usually like this, you know."

Nell kept her gaze fixed on her children's retreating backs, her pace steady. "Like what?"

"Social." Philippa watched her nephew crouch to show Lily something in the grass, perhaps a flower or an interesting beetle. "Since the war, he barely speaks to anyone outside the household staff. He rarely leaves the house except to ride alone across the moors. I have been quite worried about him."

Nell said nothing. She simply pressed her lips together, not trusting herself to speak.

At the lake, Dominic crouched at the water's edge with Oliver beside him. He pointed toward a dark, languid shape moving through the depths beneath the overhanging willows. "See that shadow?" The question drifted across the still air, carrying a low, patient quality. "That's a big one. Three feet at least."

Oliver picked up a flat stone from the shore and flung it at the water with all the force his thin arm could muster. It sank immediately, vanished by the depths without a single bounce, though the boy's face fell.

"Flatter." Dominic scanned the stones at his feet, selected one that was thin and smooth, and held it out on his open palm. "Sideways. Like this." He demonstrated the motion with a sharp, controlled flick of his wrist, catching the air at just the right angle without releasing the stone.

Oliver took the stone and tried again, his brow furrowed in a knot of concentration. The stone took two bounces before it sank, while his whole face lit up with a rare, brilliant smile. He turned to Dominic, his eyes wide with wonder. "Two!"

"Not bad." Dominic gave a single, approving nod, his

expression remaining neutral even as a subtle warmth flickered in his eyes. "Not bad for a first try."

Nell watched from a distance, her ribs feeling too tight for her lungs. She knew it in her soul: her dead husband would never have crouched in the dirt to teach a boy anything. He had never looked at another person as worth knowing—only worth using.

This was dangerous. It was dangerous for him to be kind, to be human, and to treat her children like they mattered. It had been easier when he was cruel; easier to hate him and easier to resist.

Lily had wandered toward a patch of wildflowers blooming in the shade of an ancient oak. Martha crouched beside her, helping the girl gather a small bouquet of purple asters and goldenrod. Daphne stood nearby with her arms crossed, watching Dominic with narrowed eyes that promised violence if he stepped wrong.

The maze loomed ahead of them, its dark green walls rising like a fortress against the pale autumn sky.

"What is in there?" Oliver nodded toward the entrance, the question intended to sound casual even as his eyes danced with curiosity.

"Paths." Dominic straightened, brushing the lakeside dirt from his trousers with a brisk swipe of his hands. "It's easy to get lost if you don't know the way."

"Do you know the way?" Oliver stepped closer to the towering hedges.

"Every inch." Dominic's piercing eyes moved to Nell and held her gaze, a dark, knowing weight behind the words. "I spent half my childhood in there. Hiding from tutors, from my mother, and from anyone who wanted to make me do something I didn't wish to do."

They stood near the entrance where the hedges were thick enough to block out the sky. A breeze stirred the leaves, a dry whispering sound that felt like secrets Nell couldn't understand.

Philippa lowered herself onto a nearby bench with a grateful sigh, fanning herself with one hand. "I think I'll stay here for a while. You young people go on. Explore and enjoy yourselves."

"Let's play hide and seek." Dominic threw the suggestion out to the group, his posture relaxed while his eyes remained locked on Nell's face.

Everyone turned to look at him in surprise. "The grounds are perfect for it." His mouth curved just slightly at the corner. "There are plenty of places to hide."

Philippa raised a silver eyebrow at her nephew. "Everyone?"

"Not you, Aunt." That ghost of a smile deepened as he glanced toward her. "You can sit here and judge who hid the best."

"How generous of you." Philippa settled deeper into the bench, her eyes dancing with amusement.

"Martha seeks." Dominic turned to the seamstress, who was startled at being singled out by the master of the house. "She has sharp eyes. A one hundred count, if you please. The gardens and the maze are fair ground."

Martha blinked her dark eyes in confusion. "Me, my lord?"

"You will find everyone fastest." Dominic stepped toward the edge of the lawn, signaling the start of the game.

Lily squealed with excitement, bouncing on her toes while

her bouquet of wildflowers was clutched and forgotten in her hand. Oliver tried desperately to look bored, but he failed miserably as a grin tugged at the corners of his mouth.

Martha crossed to the ancient oak tree and pressed her palms over her eyes, her tone carrying clear across the garden. "One… Two… Three..."

Everyone scattered.

The children sprinted toward the rose garden, Lily's laughter trailing behind her like ribbons in the wind. Daphne ducked behind a nearby hedge, her russet dress disappearing into the greenery. Philippa waved cheerfully from her bench, calling out that she would pretend to be invisible as she settled her skirts.

Dominic vanished. One moment he was standing near the maze entrance, and the next he was simply gone, swallowed by the landscape as if he'd never been there at all.

Nell stood frozen on the lawn, her heart hammering against her ribs. The maze loomed before her. Its entrance was dark and inviting, promising secrets. Before she could think, and before she could talk herself out of it, she was running toward it.

Inside the maze, the hedges swallowed sound.

The walls rose twelve feet above her head, blocking out the sky and turning the world into a tunnel of green shadows and dappled golden light. The air was cooler here, damp with the scent of earth and growing things. Her footsteps on the gravel path seemed to echo strangely, coming back to her from directions that didn't make sense.

She turned left. Then right. Then left again. Every path looked the same, with green walls pressing close on either side and gravel crunching underfoot. Glimpses of sky were visible only directly overhead. Every turn led to another identical passage, another choice, and another opportunity to lose herself completely. She was lost already. She'd known she would be.

"...forty-five... forty-six..." Martha's voice drifted faintly through the hedges, muffled and directionless.

Nell kept walking, her pulse quick in her throat, as she searched for somewhere to hide. She looked for a corner, a nook, or a hollow in the hedge—anywhere Martha wouldn't think to look.

Dead end. She spun on her heel and doubled back, her yellow skirts swishing sharply against the hedge.

Another dead end. A stone bench was tucked into an alcove, but it was too obvious and too easy to find.

"...sixty-two... sixty-three..." She counted under her breath, fingers pressing into the counter.

Martha's voice was fainter now, the numbers blurring together, and panic began to rise in Nell's chest. She should have stayed in the garden, but she should have hidden behind a hedge like Daphne. She should never have run toward this green labyrinth that seemed designed to swallow her whole.

Footsteps sounded behind her. They were quick, purposeful, and closing fast—and she spun around, her heart slamming against her ribs.

Chapter Thirteen

Dominic rounded the corner, moving through his maze with the easy confidence of a man who knew every inch of it. He knew every turn and every secret passage because this was his. All of it belonged to him.

"You are going the wrong way." He came to a halt, a glint of amusement dancing in his grey eyes while they gleamed in the dappled light.

Nell pressed a hand to her heaving chest, her lungs working hard to catch her breath. "I am trying to hide," she whispered, her gaze searching the jagged lines of his face.

"Not there." He moved past her, close enough that his arm brushed hers and sent heat racing up her spine. She caught the scent of sandalwood and clean male sweat. "Martha will find you in minutes."

"Then where shall I go?" Nell turned to follow his shadow.

"Come." He took her hand without asking permission. His fingers wrapped around hers, firm and certain, as he pulled her after him.

She should pull away. She should demand he release her

and march back to the rose garden where safety lay in being seen. She didn't.

He led her deeper into the maze, moving with the surety of long familiarity. They moved through a gap between two hedges that looked like a solid wall until she was standing directly in front of it. "Through here." He pushed branches aside, holding them back with a protective arm so they wouldn't scratch her face. He pulled her after him into the darkness.

She ducked under his arm, her shoulder brushing his chest —a contact that sent a bolt of heat through her.

"One hundred!" Martha's voice was faint and far away, barely audible through the thick walls of the hedge. The game had begun.

They emerged into an alcove completely hidden from the rest of the maze. Dappled sunlight filtered through the leaves overhead. "No one knows this place." Dominic released her hand and stepped back, finally putting distance between them. "I made this path when I was twelve. I cut through the hedge with a knife I had stolen from the kitchen."

Nell stared at him, her pulse hammering against her ribs. Her hand still hummed from the warmth of his touch. "You brought me here." She struggled to find a steady note, her words wavering. "Why?"

"Because Martha would have found you." He stood between her and the entrance, his broad shoulders blocking the only way out. He kept his glacial eyes fixed on her face, unblinking and intense. "And I didn't want the game to end."

"The game." She echoed him, her throat tightening as the reality of their isolation settled over her.

"Come here." He stepped back, a sharp nod directing her toward the center of the alcove.

She should refuse. Should demand he take her back to the garden, to her children, to the safe and sensible life she'd built. She should… Instead, she moved toward him on legs that felt like they might buckle.

He circled behind her, a sudden surge of heat radiating against her back. His hands found her shoulders, positioning her so she was facing the dense, green wall of the hedge. "No one can find us here." His mouth brushed her ear, his breath stirring the fine hairs at her temple. "Not Martha. Not Daphne. No one."

"That's supposed to make me feel safe?" She intended the remark to cut, but it emerged as a breathless rasp as she stared into the leaves.

"No." His teeth grazed her earlobe in a sharp, sudden spark of contact. "It's supposed to make you honest."

"Honest about what?" Her eyes fluttered closed, her head tilting instinctively away from the heat of him.

"About what you want." His hands slid down her arms, his touch light yet possessive. "When no one is watching."

Her mouth went dry.

"You wore yellow." His fingers traced the edge of her neckline, skimming the sensitive skin of her bare shoulders. "You look like sunlight. Like everything I shouldn't want."

"Stop." Nell tried to force some steel into her tone, but the word broke in the middle. Her hands hovered uselessly at her sides, fingers twitching against her skirts.

"Stop what?" Dominic stepped in front of her and leaned in until his shadow swallowed her whole.

"Whatever you are doing to me," she whispered, stepping back until the hedge pressed firm against her spine.

"I haven't even started." His hands found her waist, fingers pressing into the soft fabric as he pulled her closer. "But I want to. God, Nell. I want to worship you."

"This is madness." She looked away from his piercing gaze, her lungs forgetting how to breathe.

"Yes." His eyes burned into hers, reflecting the dappled sunlight.

"I hate you." She spat the words, though her fingers betrayed her by curling into the fine fabric of his coat.

"I know." A jagged line of pain flickered across his face.

"You called me nothing." The words spilled out, hot and bitter, as she tried to shove against his chest. "Nothing of consequence."

His teeth locked, the scar whitening against his tan. "Because I have felt like nothing my whole life. And when you looked at me like I was just a man, not a monster—" He stopped, swallowing hard as he searched her expression. "I panicked. I ruin everything."

She stared up at him, her anger faltering at the raw honesty in his tone.

"Tell me you don't want me." He cupped her face, his thumbs stroking her cheekbones with unexpected tenderness. "Tell me, and I shall take you back. I shall never touch you again."

She opened her mouth to say it, her lips trembling. The words wouldn't come.

"Tell me, Nell." Her name scraped from his throat as he tilted his head closer.

"I cannot." It was thinner than a breath, her eyes fluttering closed.

"Why not?" He pressed, his forehead dropping to rest against hers.

"Because it would be a lie." She hated herself for meaning it, her breath hitching in her throat.

Something in him snapped. He kissed her, hard and hungry. His hands fisted in her hair, tilting her head back to expose the line of her throat. She kissed him back with all the fury she'd been swallowing for weeks, all the want, and all the hate. Then, he dropped to his knees.

She stared down at him. This tall, powerful man was kneeling before her in the dirt, looking up at her as if she were holy.

"What are you—" She began, but the question died as she gripped his shoulders for balance.

"I have thought about this every night." His hands found her ankles beneath her yellow skirts, his fingers wrapping around bare skin. "I have woken up hard and aching with your name on my lips."

"Dominic." His name caught in her throat as she felt the cool air on her legs.

"I want to taste you." His hands slid higher, over her stockings and past her garters. "I want to bury my face between your thighs and make you forget your own name."

"Someone could see," she gasped, heat flooding her face as she glanced toward the maze path.

"No one will hear you but me." He ducked beneath her skirts and disappeared into the yellow silk.

She couldn't see him now. She could only feel his breath

hot against her inner thigh and his hands gripping the back of her left leg. He lifted her. Her leg came up, and he draped it over his shoulder, opening her wide to the quiet alcove. She grabbed the stone bench behind her, her knuckles going white as she strained to stay upright.

"Dominic." She gasped his name again, feeling off-balance and terribly exposed.

"Hold tight." His response came muffled through layers of fabric. "I am going to ruin you."

His fingers found the slit in her drawers and parted the linen. There was a shock of cool air, then a sudden, localized heat. His tongue dragged through her folds, one long, slow stroke that made her knees buckle.

"Christ." He groaned against her flesh, the vibration shooting straight to her core. "You are already dripping."

"Please." The word escaped before she could catch it, her head falling back against the hedge.

"Please what?" He licked her again, maddeningly slow. "Tell me."

"I don't know." She shook her head blindly, her fingers clawing at the stone.

"Yes, you do." His tongue circled her pearl without quite touching it. "Say it."

"More." Her hips rocked instinctively toward his face. "I need more."

"More of what?" He pressed a kiss to her inner thigh, pointedly avoiding the center of her ache. "This?"

"No." She whimpered, her breath coming in shallow stabs.

"Then what?" He gave her another kiss, higher but still not high enough. "Use your words, Nell."

"Your mouth." She was begging now, shameless and desperate. "On me. Inside me. I don't care. Just, please."

He sealed his lips over her and sucked. She screamed, her hand flying to her mouth as her teeth sank into her own palm. He didn't stop. He sucked, licked, and devoured her like he would die without the taste. Her thigh clenched around his shoulder, her heel digging into the sturdy muscle of his back.

"Let me hear you." He growled against her skin. "No one is listening but me."

"I cannot." A sob tore from her throat as she struggled to remain quiet. "Someone will hear."

"Let them." He spread her wider with his thumbs, his tongue plunging inside her. "Let the whole world hear what I do to you."

She stopped trying to be quiet. The sounds that came out of her were no longer words, but broken moans and his name, repeated like a prayer. He ate her like a man possessed, his tongue everywhere at once.

"You taste like mine." A low, guttural groan escaped him between licks. He worked her with a desperate, wrecked focus. "Like you were made for my mouth."

"Ahhhh." She was shaking so violently her standing leg threatened to buckle. "I cannot—I am going to—"

"Not yet." He pulled back slightly. She let out a broken sob at the sudden, agonizing loss of friction. "Not until I say."

"Please." Tears pricked her eyes and spilled over, hot and frantic. "Please, I need..."

"What do you need?" His thumb pressed against her entrance, circling the sensitive skin with maddening precision but refusing to enter. "Tell me."

"You." The word ripped from somewhere deep inside her,

raw and unguarded. "Inside me. Your fingers. Your tongue. Anything. Please. I shall do anything."

"Anything?" He asked from under her skirts.

"Yes." She was beyond pride and beyond shame. "Yes. Anything. Just make me come. Please. I am begging you."

"Good girl." He slid two fingers inside her, crooking them forward, as his mouth returned to her center.

She shattered. There was no warning and no slow build. Just white-hot pleasure ripping through her as her inner walls clamped down on his fingers. Her whole body convulsed so hard she would have collapsed if his shoulder were not holding her up.

Kept licking, kept sucking, kept fucking her with his fingers while she screamed into her fist and sobbed his name and came so hard she forgot where she was, who she was, forgot everything except his mouth and his hands and the pleasure that wouldn't stop cresting.

"One more." He commanded against her damp skin, his pace relentless. "Give me one more."

"I cannot." She was crying now, tears streaming down her face. "It's too much."

"You can." His fingers curled, hitting the spot that made her see stars. "You will. For me."

His tongue flicked her, fast and relentless, while his fingers drove deep. She broke again, harder this time, a scream tearing from her throat that she couldn't muffle. He worked her through the peak, finally gentling his strokes. He used soft, soothing licks to ease her down until she was boneless and trembling, held up only by the strength of his shoulder beneath her thigh.

He withdrew his fingers slowly. Nell whimpered at the sudden loss of him, her body sagging forward.

He emerged from beneath her yellow skirts, his face glistening in the dappled light and his eyes dark with a savage satisfaction. He rose to his full height, steadying her by placing his large hands firmly on her waist.

"Sweeter than anything you've ever baked." He choked the words out, lungs burning as his chest rose and fell in jagged rhythms.

She stared at him and found she couldn't speak. Her whole body continued to tremble, aftershocks rippling through her like waves on the lake. No one had ever done that to her. Not Gabriel, who had taken and taken and never once thought to give, and certainly not the fumbling boy she'd kissed at sixteen.

"Nell." He cupped her face, his thumbs moving to wipe the lingering tears from her cheeks. "Are you all right?"

"I didn't know." The words came out broken and full of wonder as she leaned into his touch. "I didn't know it could be like that."

Something fierce crossed his features, an expression tender and furious all at once. "It can." He pressed his forehead to hers, both of them breathing the same cooling air. "It should. Every time. You deserve to be worshipped."

She laughed, a wet and shaky sound that died in the quiet alcove. "I am a baker. I make tarts."

"You are everything." He said it simply, like it were a fact of nature, his gaze never wavering from hers.

She didn't know what to say. She didn't know what to do with him kneeling in the dirt to pleasure her, looking at her as if she'd hung the moon herself.

"The others." Nell finally found the breath to speak, the words emerging as a hoarse rasp as she forced her spine to straighten.

"They are still playing." He smoothed the front of her skirts, his hand moving with a care as he checked to see if her legs would hold her weight. "We should go back." He stepped back, giving her room to move. "Can you walk?"

"I don't know." Her fingers remained white-knuckled, still clutching the edge of the stone bench for support.

A flash of dark pride crossed his features, a shadow of satisfaction in his eyes. "Good."

He helped her to the bench, letting her rest until the worst of the trembling subsided. When he finally offered his hand, palm up, she took it. He led her through the maze on unsteady legs, her body still humming, haunted by the ghost of his mouth against her skin. They emerged behind the rose garden where the terrace was visible in the distance—yet he stopped, his hand dropping to his side.

"Go back that way." He nodded toward the terrace, his features showing indifference. "You got lost. Martha never found you."

"And you?" Nell smoothed her hair with a frantic, nervous hand.

"I shall come from the other side." He released her, and she felt the loss like a splash of cold water. "I shall follow a few minutes after."

She should go. The children were waiting. She remained rooted to the spot. "What are we doing?" Her eyes were wide and searching as she looked up at him.

"I don't know." He shook his head, his jaw tightening into a hard line. "I only know I cannot stop."

"Neither can I." The admission felt like a defeat, her gaze dropping to the grass.

"Go." His hands curled into fists at his sides, his knuckles pale. "Before I drag you back into that maze and spend the rest of the afternoon between your thighs."

Heat flooded her face in a sudden, scorching wave. She went.

She moved toward the terrace and the world she'd left behind. Martha looked smug with victory while the children were flushed and laughing. Daphne watched Nell approach, her eyes sharp and knowing.

"Mama!" Lily ran toward her, pigtails flying. "We thought you were lost forever!"

Nell smoothed the girl's hair with trembling hands, her heart in her throat. "The maze. I got completely turned around."

Daphne's eyes swept over her. She lingered on the flushed cheeks, the swollen lips, and the way the dress sat slightly wrong on Nell's shoulders. Her expression hardened, every trace of warmth gone. Martha watched as well, her dark gaze missing nothing.

"I couldn't find you anywhere." Martha folded her arms, her delivery as bland and flat as milk. "Or Lord Westmore."

"The maze is treacherous." Philippa remarked from her bench, fanning herself with a placid, rhythmic motion. "Dominic used to disappear in there for hours as a boy."

Dominic appeared several minutes later, rounding the corner of the house. He looked casual and unhurried, not a single hair out of place.

"Where were you?" Philippa's silver eyebrows rose in a silent, aristocratic demand.

Dominic shrugged, crossing the terrace to pour himself a glass of lemonade with a steady hand. "The far end of the grounds. I simply lost track of the time."

Daphne's eyes narrowed to thin slits.

"We should go." Nell reached for Lily's hand, her movements jerky and desperate. "The children are tired."

"But the book!" Lily pulled back, her face crumpling. "He said I could hold it!"

Dominic set down his glass and nodded toward the house. "The library. We shall visit it before you leave."

The library was a cathedral of leather and gold. Lily gasped and spun in a slow circle, her spectacles fogging with the heat of her excitement. Dominic crossed to a glass-fronted case and withdrew a single volume. He walked to where Lily stood and placed it carefully in her small, shaking hands.

"Careful." His posture softened as he guided her fingers, his movements uncharacteristically gentle. "It's older than this house."

Lily held it like a holy relic. When the carriage was called, Philippa embraced Nell like an old friend, but Dominic stood apart. He kept his hands clasped behind his back, his glacial eyes fixed on Nell's face with an intensity that made her skin prickle.

In the carriage, as Bramwell Park shrank behind them, Daphne leaned in close. "Your dress was crooked when you came back. And your lips are swollen." Daphne folded her arms, one brow rising.

Nell stared out the window at the rolling countryside, her reflection ghostly in the glass. "I fell in the maze."

Daphne said nothing for a long moment, her gaze heavy. "You are a terrible liar, Nell."

Nell pressed her forehead against the cool glass and closed her eyes. She could still feel his hands on her and his fingers inside her, though god help her, she wanted to go back.

Chapter Fourteen

Nell woke before dawn, as she always did, but this morning was different. This morning, she hadn't slept at all.

Every time she closed her eyes, the ghost of his weight returned. She could still feel the phantom pressure of his hands at her waist and how he made her tremble with pleasure. When sleep finally teased the edges of her mind, his commands would echo back—low, desperate, and jagged—shattering her resolve. She'd find herself tangled in the sheets, legs pressed tight to stem the ache, biting the pillow to swallow a name she wasn't supposed to say.

She was sore in places she'd forgotten could ache. Her lips felt tender, her thighs ached where he'd knelt between them, and when she pressed her fingers to her neck in the grey pre-dawn light, she could feel the raised welts where his teeth had marked her skin.

The yellow dress hung on the wardrobe door where Martha had placed it last night. Its cheerful colour seemed to mock her in the dimness; she couldn't look at it. She couldn't think about what she'd done while wearing it, what she'd let him do, or what she'd wanted him to do. She turned her back on it and dragged herself out of bed, her legs unsteady beneath her. Her whole body felt like it belonged to someone else.

The kitchen was cold and dark, and she welcomed it. She welcomed the familiar rhythm of lighting the ovens, of measuring flour and salt and yeast, and of pushing and folding the dough until her arms ached and her mind went blessedly blank.

Push, fold, turn. Push, fold, turn.

But her hands remembered different things now. They remembered the texture of his hair between her fingers, the heat of his mouth on her core, and the strokes of tongue as he made her come undone.

The children were still asleep upstairs, along with Martha, and the house was quiet in that heavy way that came before dawn. It was a time when the world held its breath and waited for the sun. Nell was alone with her thoughts—it was dangerous territory, the most dangerous territory she knew. What had she done? What was she doing?

The shop bell rang. It was too early for customers, as the sun was barely cresting the horizon, and Nell's hands stilled in the dough, her heart lurching against her ribs.

Daphne stood in the doorway, her face set in hard lines and her arms crossed tight over her chest. She wore her cloak still fastened at the throat, like she'd thrown it on and come straight here without bothering to properly dress.

"We need to talk." Daphne's voice was flat and brooked no argument as she tightened her jaw.

Nell's stomach dropped through the floor. She wiped her floury hands on her apron, her fingers trembling against the coarse fabric. "Daphne, I—" She stopped, the words dying in her throat.

"Not here." Daphne jerked her chin toward the back of the shop, her expression hard and unyielding. "The storeroom. Now."

The storeroom was where Dominic had first kissed her. He'd pressed her back against the shelves and pleasured her with his fingers that had left her shaking. The irony was not lost on Nell as she followed Daphne through the kitchen, for her legs felt wooden beneath her, and her pulse hammered against her windpipe.

Daphne closed the door behind them and turned to face her, her dark eyes sharp in the dim light filtering through the small window. "I am not stupid, Nell." She stood with her back to the door, her frame blocking the only exit.

Nell pressed her back against a shelf of flour sacks, putting distance between them. Her hands gripped the rough burlap for support. "I never said you were." The response was a mere breath of sound, barely audible over the hum of the shop.

"Both of you were missing from that garden party." Daphne ticked the points off on her fingers, her tone low but intense. "Both of you came back flushed and out of breath. Your dress sitting crooked on your shoulders, his lip bleeding that time at the shop—don't think I forgot that. And Martha couldn't find either of you in that maze, no matter how hard she looked."

Nell remained silent, her throat too tight for words as she stared at her friend.

"And the way he looks at you." Daphne's posture slackened, some of the anger draining away to reveal the raw worry beneath. She uncrossed her arms slowly. "Like you are the only person in the room. Like everyone else might as well be furniture."

Still Nell held her peace, trying to remain steady.

"Tell me I am wrong." Daphne stepped closer, her stare boring into Nell's face for any sign of a denial. "Look me in the eye and tell me nothing happened in that maze."

Nell opened her mouth to lie. She wanted to protect herself, to protect her children, and to maintain the careful fiction that she was a respectable widow. She should never do something so foolish as to let a viscount put his hands on her in a hidden alcove. The words wouldn't come.

"I don't know what is happening." The confession spilled out of her. Her composure fractured, and she let her hands fall uselessly to her sides. "I don't… I cannot explain it. I hate him. I do. He called me nothing, and he humiliated me in front of the whole village, and he is arrogant and reckless and everything I should despise. But when he is near me—" She paused, her breath hitching.

"You forget to hate him." Daphne finished the thought quietly, her shoulders dropping.

Nell didn't answer. She just nodded.

Daphne let the silence sit. She uncrossed her arms, reached over, and squeezed Nell's hand once — hard — before letting go.

"He is a viscount, Nell." Daphne's head tilted as she studied her friend's face. "With a title, an estate, and a family that will have opinions about who he brings home."

Nell's fingers curled around the edge of the shelf. "I know what he is."

"And you are a widow." Daphne held up a hand before Nell could interrupt, ticking off each word like beads on a string. "A widow with two children. Running a bakery in a village where the grandest thing is the church steeple. You think his family will welcome that with open arms?"

Nell said nothing. Her jaw tightened.

"Then there's the money." Daphne leaned against the opposite shelf, arms crossing again. "You count pennies, Nell. He's never had to count anything in his life. That kind of difference — it doesn't just disappear because two people fancy each other."

"I am not some fool who thinks —" Nell started.

"And he is younger than you." Daphne cut her off, not unkindly, her dark eyes steady on Nell's. "Nearly six years younger. The ton will count every single one of those years, and they will not be generous about it."

Nell pressed her back harder against the shelf. The thoughts she'd been avoiding all night crashed over her — each one landing heavier than the last. Widow. Common. Poor. Older. Mother of two. She'd known all of it, every impossible obstacle, since the moment his hand had lingered on hers a breath too long. She simply hadn't let herself line them up in a row like this, where she couldn't look away.

"I am not saying anything you haven't already thought." Daphne's expression softened, and she reached out and took Nell's hands between her own. "I just want you to be careful. He can walk away from this and lose nothing. You can't."

Careful. The word echoed in the small space, bouncing off the flour sacks and sugar barrels.

"He called you nothing once." Daphne spoke softly, her thumb rubbing across Nell's knuckles with a rhythmic, grounding pressure. "At the festival. In front of Mrs.

Pemberton and Sir Richard and anyone else who was listening. Because someone asked about you and he panicked."

Nell drew a shuddering breath, her throat aching as she stared at a stray dusting of flour on the floorboards. "I remember."

"I am not saying he meant it." Daphne shrugged, her hands tightening their hold on Nell's fingers. "But he said it. Without thinking. Without considering how it would make you feel. He panicked, and he was cruel."

Reckless, Nell thought. She looked away, her gaze snagging on the heavy iron scales. He'd panicked and lashed out because he didn't know how else to handle the heft of his station. What else might he say without thinking? What else might he do on impulse when the pressure of the ton became too much?

"Just be careful." Daphne squeezed her hands once more. "You have children to think about. You don't want to end up as his… mistress."

She went silent, letting the drag of the word hang between them. She didn't have to say more.

Nell's mind was already spinning, cataloging every objection and every obstacle that made this union a madness. This could destroy the life she'd built so carefully from the ruins of her marriage. She was thirty-four years old, six years his senior, a widow with two children and flour permanently embedded under her fingernails. The ton would never accept her. They would call her a fortune hunter, a scheming widow who had trapped a young lord with common charms and a baker's body. They would whisper behind their fans and laugh behind their hands. Eventually, inevitably, Dominic would hear them, and he would start to wonder if they were right.

"I will." Nell managed the words through a throat gone tight, returning the squeeze of Daphne's hands. "I will be careful."

Daphne pulled her into a hug, a quick and fierce embrace of sharp elbows and protective love. Then she moved toward the door, slipping out of the storeroom to open the shop and leaving Nell alone with the ghost of his hands on her skin.

This had to stop. Whatever madness had seized them both, it had to end before it destroyed them.

The morning slipped past her familiar routines.

Lily came downstairs in her nightgown, as she chattered about the library at Bramwell Park. "He had a first edition of *Udolpho*, Mama. And Lord Westmore promised I could come back to see it again."

"Can we, Mama?" Lily tugged at Nell's stained apron, her eyes appearing enormous behind her smudged lenses. "Can we go back? He said I could hold it again if I was careful, and I was very careful, was I not?"

Nell busied herself with the bread, keeping her face turned away as she kneaded the dough with unnecessary force. "We shall see, sweetheart."

Oliver was quieter than usual when he appeared, but there was a lightness to him that Nell hadn't seen in months. There was a softness around his eyes and a looseness in his shoulders that had long been absent. He ate his breakfast without his usual sullen silence, looking up with a spark of eagerness when Lily mentioned the lake.

"There are pike in that lake." Oliver spoke casually, pushing eggs around his plate as if the information were a mere trifle. "Big ones. Lord Westmore showed me where they hide."

Nell's hands stilled on the dough, her heart tightening at the boyish hope in his tone.

Martha appeared in the kitchen doorway, her dark eyes moving over Nell's face with quiet assessment. She said nothing, she rarely did, but her silence spoke volumes. Nell knew the woman had understood everything at Bramwell Park and had drawn her own conclusions about the missing viscount, the flushed baker, and the crooked yellow dress.

The shop opened at eight, and customers came and went in the usual morning rush. Mrs. Potts requested her weekly order of seed cakes. Old Mr. Thornton fumbled for coins to pay for his daily loaf, but the vicar's wife sent her maid for scones to serve at a ladies' meeting. Nell smiled and served and made change, her hands moving through the familiar motions while her mind churned.

Mid-morning brought Mrs. Potts, her neighbor from the haberdashery next door, bustling through the door.

"The usual, dear." Mrs. Potts set her coins on the counter, her eyes bright with the gleam of someone holding a secret. "And did you ever catch that nice doctor?"

Nell paused in the act of wrapping the loaf, her brow furrowing as she looked up. "The Doctor came?"

"Yes, Dr. Hartley." Mrs. Potts leaned across the counter, delighted to be the bearer of news. "He came by yesterday afternoon while you were out. Stood at your door for ages, poor man, knocking and waiting and knocking again. I told him you had gone to Bramwell Park for tea with Lady Philippa."

Nell's heart stuttered, and she gripped the edge of the wooden counter until her knuckles turned white.

"He came twice." Mrs. Potts nodded vigorously, her bonnet ribbons bouncing with the movement. "Once around two o'clock, then again near four. Seemed quite determined to see you."

Nell finished wrapping the loaf and handed it across the counter, her movements stiff and mechanical. "I didn't know."

"Well, now you do." Mrs. Potts tucked the bread into her basket and patted Nell's hand with a fleeting touch. "Lovely man, that doctor. Very respectable. And handsome, too, in that steady sort of way."

She bustled out, the bell chiming behind her. Nell stared at the closed door with a hollow feeling in her chest—Edmund had come to see her. Twice. While she'd been at Bramwell Park, letting another man put his hands on her body.

Chapter Fifteen

Noon brought the lunch lull, the shop emptying as the village retreated to their own kitchens for their midday meals. The bell chimed, and Nell looked up from the counter she'd been wiping to find Dr. Hartley standing in the doorway. He held his hat in his hands, his warm smile already forming as he caught her eye.

"Nell." He stepped inside, his brown eyes crinkling at the corners in a way that spoke of genuine kindness. "I hope I am not intruding."

Nell set down her cloth and smoothed the front of her apron, suddenly conscious of the flour on her sleeves and the wisps of hair escaping her pins. "Not at all. I heard you came by yesterday."

"Yes, I did." He admitted the fact with a slightly sheepish duck of his head, his fingers turning the stiff brim of his hat. "Mrs. Potts told me you were at Bramwell Park."

Nell clasped her hands in front of her, her fingers interlacing tightly as she searched for a neutral expression. "Tea with Lady Philippa."

"So I gathered." He moved closer to the counter, his expression gentle as he searched her face. "I hope it was pleasant."

Pleasant. One word for it. Nell's cheeks heated at the memory of the library, and she dropped her gaze to the scarred wood of the counter. "It surely was eventful, Dr. Hartley."

"Edmund." He corrected her softly, setting his hat aside and leaning forward to catch her gaze. "Please. I thought we'd established that."

Nell's fingers twisted in the fold of her skirt, the wool bunching beneath her touch. "Edmund."

He studied her face for a long moment, his brown stare steady while his hands rested flat on the counter. "Nell. May I speak plainly?"

Her heart stuttered, knowing the gravity of what was coming, and she gripped the edge of the counter for support. "Of course."

"I have enjoyed our friendship." He leaned toward her, the space between them narrowing until she could see the golden flecks in his eyes. "Very much. More than I can say. But I find myself wanting… more."

She'd known this was coming. She'd seen it building in the warmth of his gaze and the frequency of his visits. She'd felt it in the way he found excuses to touch her hand or brush her shoulder. She'd known, and she'd done nothing to discourage it, because Edmund was safe and kind and everything a sensible woman should want.

"I know I am not a young man." He pressed on, his posture straight even as a slight tremor took his fingers. "Thirty-nine next spring, with grey in my hair and lines on my face."

Nell gripped the edge of the counter, her knuckles turning white against the dark wood.

"You know about Jasmine." A shadow crossed his face, his fingers curling against the grain of the wood as if bracing against an old wound. "I told you about her. How she left a month before we were to marry."

"I remember." The words were a ragged friction in Nell's throat, her chest aching with a sudden, sharp sympathy.

"I tell you this because I want you to know." He reached across the counter and covered her hand with his own. His palm was warm and steady, his touch entirely undemanding. "I have been where you are. Alone. Rebuilding. Afraid to trust again after someone destroyed your faith in love."

Nell's throat tightened. She shook her head, her breath hitching as she tried to find the air to interrupt. "Edmund—"

"I can offer you my name." He squeezed her hand gently, his brown eyes pinning hers with a quiet, fierce intensity. "I can offer you my home. Stability. Security. I would be a man who would treat your children as his own, who would love them like they were born to me. Not someday, not when circumstances permit. Now. Today."

It was everything she should want. It was everything that made sense.

"You deserve someone who sees your worth." He leaned in closer, his thumb tracing a slow, rhythmic path across her knuckles. "Someone steady. Reliable."

Steady. The opposite of reckless.

"I am not asking for an answer today." He released her hand and stepped back, giving her space to breathe as he smoothed his coat. "I know this is sudden. I know you need time to think. I am only asking you to consider it."

Nell's throat felt too tight for words, and she pressed her hand to her chest to still the fluttering there. "I don't know what to say."

"Say you will think about it." He picked up his hat from the counter with a gentle smile. "That's all I ask."

Nell drew a shaking breath and nodded, her gaze fixed on the sincerity in his face. "I will think about it."

"I shall call again soon." He settled his hat on his head, his eyes lingering on her face with a warmth that felt like a shield. "If that's all right."

Nell managed a smile that felt fragile and thin on her lips. "I should like that."

He nodded once, that quiet smile still playing at his mouth, and walked to the door. The bell chimed as he left. Nell stood alone behind her counter, staring at the empty doorway.

Two paths. One safe, one fire—one that made sense, one that burned.

She was still standing there, still staring at nothing, when the bell chimed again. Her heart stopped.

Chapter Sixteen

Dominic filled the doorway, his broad shoulders blocking the afternoon light. His grey eyes found her immediately, burning with a restless energy. He looked as though he hadn't slept. There were shadows under his eyes and a harsh tension in the set of his jaw. His cravat was tied carelessly, as if he'd pulled it together without the aid of a glass.

"Lord Westmore." Nell's throat tightened, making the words come out as a strangled rasp. Her hands once again found the edge of the counter, gripping the wood for support. "The shop is—"

"I saw Hartley leaving." He stepped inside and closed the door behind him with a definitive click. His movements were deliberate, his hand reaching for the sign hanging in the window and flipping it to CLOSED.

Nell's spine went rigid. She pressed back against the shelves of cooling bread, the warmth of the loaves seeped through her dress but did nothing to chill the fear in her chest. "You cannot just—"

"I can." He moved toward her, eating up the distance with long strides. "I am."

"Someone will see." Nell's hands curled into fists at her sides, her heart hammering against her ribs.

"Let them." He stopped at the counter, looming over her. A muscle jumped in his jaw as he searched her face with eyes the colour of a stormy sea. "What did he want?"

Nell lifted her chin, refusing to cower beneath the solid mass of his stare. "That is none of your concern."

"Everything about you is my concern." The words were scraped from somewhere deep in his chest. He braced his hands on the counter, leaning in until they were mere inches apart. "What did he want, Nell?"

"He made me an offer." She held his gaze. "A good one."

A spark lit within him, edged with cruelty and possession. His fingers curled against the wood until his knuckles blanched, mirroring the tension that seized his frame. "What kind of offer?"

"The kind that makes sense." Nell forced the words out past the constriction in her throat. "Stability. Security. A father for my children. His name. Today, if I want it."

His face drew taut, at the word *today*, his expression fractured into a look of pure, jagged jealousy.

"And what did you say?" His words had thinned to a rough rasp. He leaned in further, making her skin prickle.

Nell clasped her hands in front of her to hide their trembling. "I said I would think about it."

He stood there for a moment, utterly still, his hands curled into white-knuckled fists at his sides. Then he moved. He rounded the end of the counter, invading her space and coming so close she could smell the scent of sandalwood and feel the heat radiating from his body.

She didn't back up. She held her ground, her spine as straight as a poker.

"You are considering him." He threw the words at her not as a question, but as an accusation, the pain in his expression raw.

"Of course I am considering him." She kept her features schooled into something steady, though her hands remained locked together so tight her fingers ached. "He is everything I *should* want. Kind, steady, respectable. And he is free to offer it. No complications, no scandal, no whispers behind fans about the scheming baker who trapped a viscount."

"*Should*." He latched onto the word. His eyes turned to slits as he tilted his head. "Not do. Should."

Nell's lips pressed into a thin line until they ached. "It's the same thing."

"It's not." He stepped closer still, towering over her. His breath was warm on her face. "Should is what other people want for you. Do what you want for yourself." Nell went still.

Nell pressed her back against the wooden shelf behind her, her heart hammering like a trapped bird. "Perhaps they are the same for me."

"They are not." The statement landed between them with the pressure of cold iron. He leaned in until the world narrowed to the lines of his face and the heat of his breath against her skin. "I know what you want, Nell. I felt it yesterday. In that maze. When you came apart against me."

"That was a mistake." She forced the words out, even as her body betrayed her. Heat pooled low in her belly at the memory, her cheeks flushing a deep, telltale crimson.

"No." He spoke the word with a fierce conviction, his hands coming up to bracket her against the shelf without quite touching her. "That was the first honest thing either of us has done since we met."

Nell went still. She pressed her palms flat against his chest, feeling the frantic thud of his heart through the fine wool of his coat to hold him at bay. "Dominic—"

"Marry me." He blurted the words, like the breath had been knocked from him.

The request hit her like a physical blow, driving the air from her lungs. She stared at him, her mouth falling open as her hands froze against the heat of his chest.

"What?" She barely recognized the thin, reedy sound of her own voice.

"Marry me." He said it again. His hands finally made contact, gripping her shoulders to hold her in place. "Be my wife."

She kept staring, waiting for the mocking smile that would tell her it was a joke, a jest, or some cruel game of the aristocracy.

He was not smiling.

Nell shook her head, her fingers curling into the fabric of his coat as if to anchor herself. "You are mad."

"Probably." He didn't soften his expression, but his grip on her shoulders tightened. "But I am also in love with you."

The breath left her body in a soft whoosh.

"I love you." He said it as though the confession were being ripped from him, like every word cost him something vital. He leaned forward, his forehead dropping to rest against hers. "I have tried not to. God knows I have tried. But I cannot stop thinking about you. I cannot stop wanting you. I cannot imagine my life without you in it."

Nell's hands trembled against his chest. She shook her head again, the movement brushing her brow against his. "You barely know me."

"I know enough." He pulled back just far enough to look at her, his thumbs brushing across the fabric on her shoulders. His expression was raw and entirely open. "I know you are the strongest woman I have ever met. I know you built a life from nothing. I know you'd die for your children without a second thought. I know you make me feel like I am worth something for the first time in my miserable life."

Nell pressed her hands harder against his chest, trying to create a desperate distance. "Dominic—"

"Marry me." The words were raw with desperation. His hands slid from her shoulders to cup her face, his palms warm against her skin. "I will give you everything. Bramwell Park. Money. Security. Your children will want for nothing. They shall have the best education, the finest clothes, everything they have ever dreamed of. I will adopt them legally, and give them my name. They will be Westmores, with all the rights and privileges that entails."

It was everything. It was more than she'd ever dared to hope for in her darkest hours. And she couldn't say yes. Nell closed her eyes, drew a long breath, and pulled his hands away from her face. "No."

He went utterly still. The colour drained from his face, and his hands fell limply to his sides. "What?"

"No." She spoke firmly, forcing the word past the ache in her chest. She opened her eyes to meet his. "I cannot marry you."

His brow furrowed. Confusion and pain crossed his face. "Why not?"

"Because it would destroy us both." She pressed her back against the shelf, needing the support as her legs shook beneath her heavy skirts.

"I don't understand—" He reached for her again, but she held up a hand, palm out, to stop him.

"I am a widow, Dominic." She pressed her hand flat against his chest to hold him back, her composure brittle as old plaster. "A common widow with two children and a bakery that barely keeps us fed. And you are a viscount."

"I don't care about—" He tried to step closer, but she shoved against him with a sudden, sharp strength.

"The ton will care." She cut him off, her jaw set in a hard, uncompromising line. "They will call me a fortune hunter. Every ball, every dinner, every drawing room — I will be the joke they tell behind their fans."

"I don't care what they think." He caught her hand against his chest, trapping it there so she could feel the steady, insistent beat beneath his ribs.

"You say that now." She shook her head, her throat tight as she struggled to pull free. "But I count pennies, Dominic. I measure flour by the ounce and stretch every shilling until it screams. You have never had to count anything in your life. That kind of distance between two people — it doesn't disappear because you want it to."

"Money means nothing to me—" Dominic protested.

"Because you've always had it." She wrenched her hand free. "That is exactly my point."

He stood there, breathing hard, his fingers empty.

"And I am six years older than you." She pressed on before

he could reach for her again. "Six years. The ton will count every one of them, and they will not be kind about it. When your friends sit around their clubs and laugh about the viscount who married an old widowed shopkeeper who..."

"Stop." His voice cracked on the word.

"I cannot stop." She wrapped her arms tight around her middle. "Because you won't think about this, so someone has to. I have Oliver and Lily depending on me. Two children who have already survived so much — I cannot do this to them."

The words landed like a blow. She saw him flinch, saw the colour leave his face, and she pressed on anyway because stopping now would mean losing her nerve entirely.

"There is more." The admission tore out of her, the truth she had never spoken aloud. A tremor ran through her frame. "Lily nearly killed me. The birth was so difficult the doctor said another pregnancy could —"

She stopped. Drew a jagged, shaking breath. Her free hand pressed hard against her stomach. "I might not be able to give you an heir, Dominic. And the viscountcy needs one. The title, the estate, the legacy your family has held for generations — it all ends if you choose me."

"I don't need an heir." He spoke fiercely, reaching out to cup her cheek.

Nell turned her face away, jaw clenching. "You are a viscount. Of course you need an heir."

"I don't care about the legacy." He tried to turn her face back toward him, but she pulled away entirely, stepping sideways until her shoulder brushed a stack of cooling tins.

"You will." She saw the future stretching out before her, clear and terrible. "When the wanting fades. When you look across the breakfast table and see a woman with grey in her hair and a body that has carried children and a name that brings you nothing but whispers. You will care then."

"It won't fade." He followed her, his breath coming in jagged, desperate hitches, his fingers hovering just inches from her sleeve. "What I feel for you — it won't fade. I have never felt anything like this."

"It always fades." She thought of Gabriel — of promises made and love that had curdled into contempt. She held up both hands, palms out, to keep him at bay. "You are reckless, Dominic. You followed me into that maze without caring who saw us. You are proposing right now because you saw Edmund leaving and you panicked — not because you have thought any of this through."

"That is not true." His jaw set like iron, his hands falling to his sides.

"Is it not?" She held his gaze, arms wrapped tight around her ribs. "You saw him leaving my shop and you panicked. Just as you panicked at the festival. You act on impulse, on feeling, without considering what comes after. And I cannot build a life on impulse. Dominic, I cannot afford to be reckless."

"Nell." He reached for her one more time, her name breaking in the back of his throat.

"My answer is no." The words fell between them, heavy and final. She stepped back, well out of his reach. "I am sorry. But no."

He stared at her as though she had spoken a language he did not know, his arms hanging at his sides.

"You are saying no." The light in his pale eyes went dull, his tone flat.

"I am saying no." Nell repeated.

"I am offering you everything." A raw, wounded sound escaped him. He spread his hands wide, gesturing around the humble shop. "My name. My home. My heart."

"I know." She held her ground, refusing to let a single tremor show, though the effort cost her everything she had. "And I am saying no. Because you can walk away from this and lose nothing, Dominic. Your title stays. Your fortune stays. Your reputation stays. But if I say yes and it falls apart — I lose everything. My shop. My standing. My children's future. I cannot gamble with their lives because your heart is racing."

He went very still.

"So that is it." He stood emptied of everything but a quiet, echoing pain. His hands fell to his sides. "You would rather have him. The safe choice."

"I would rather have sense." She held him there, her vision burning and her throat aching with the effort not to break. "I would rather have a future I can count on."

"And I cannot give you that." His mouth went hard.

"No." The word came out soft. Air forced through a chest that felt as if it might split.

He stayed there for a long moment. He did not move. He took in her face as if he meant to learn it by heart. Then something shut behind his eyes. The warmth went out. The vulnerability vanished behind walls that rose in an instant.

"I see." The lord returned as the man retreated, his words clipped and frosty. His spine went rigid, his posture regaining its aristocratic stiffness. "I understand perfectly."

He turned and walked toward the door, his stride stiff and his shoulders set. He didn't look back. He paused with his hand on the handle, his back to her. "I hope he makes you happy." The parting shot sounded like ice cracking on a winter pond. "I hope sense keeps you warm at night."

The door slammed behind him. The bell jangled, harsh and discordant, before settling into a mocking silence.

Nell stood alone in the middle of her shop, surrounded by the scent of yeast and flour and the silence of her own breaking heart. She'd done the right thing, for she knew she had. Her hands were steady as she crossed to the door and flipped the sign back to OPEN, even if her heart was not.

The afternoon passed in a blur of familiar routines. Customers came and went. Nell smiled and served and made change, her hands moving through the motions while her mind drifted somewhere far away.

Daphne returned from her errands at half past three. She set down her basket of thread and ribbon and took one look at Nell's face. Whatever she saw there made her go quiet, and she set to work without a word.

She didn't ask until closing, when the shop was empty and the door was locked. They stood alone in the kitchen, putting away the unsold loaves.

"What happened?" Daphne asked, concerned. She stilled her hands on a loaf of bread, waiting.

Nell wiped down the counter with methodical rhythmic strokes. "Lord Westmore came by."

"And?" Daphne set the bread down, looking at her intently.

Nell kept wiping, her movements mechanical and repetitive. "He proposed."

Daphne went absolutely still, her hand frozen in midair. "He did what?"

"He proposed marriage." Nell didn't look up, her tone remaining flat. "He said he loved me. He offered me everything. Bramwell Park, money, his name for the children."

Daphne sucked in a sharp breath and stepped closer to the counter. "Nell—"

"I said no." Nell set down the cloth and finally looked up, meeting Daphne's shocked gaze.

Silence filled the kitchen, broken only by the crackle of the fire in the hearth.

"You said no." Daphne repeated the words slowly, testing whether they could possibly be true. Her brow furrowed in confusion. "To a viscount."

"To a man who doesn't think before he acts." Nell folded the cloth, her movements precise and sharp. "To a future that would destroy us both."

Daphne was quiet for a long moment, arms crossed tight over her chest as she processed the heaviness of it. "And Dr. Hartley?"

"He offered, too." Nell hung her apron on its hook by the door, keeping her back turned. "His name. Today. No complications."

"What did you tell him?" Daphne's voice was soft, treading carefully.

"That I'd think about it." Nell smoothed her skirts with brisk, clipped movements, as if she could press the turmoil out of the fabric.

Daphne nodded slowly. When Nell finally turned around, she found her friend's dark stare tracking every shift in her expression. "Are you all right?"

"I'm fine." Nell straightened her spine, her expression settling into a practiced, porcelain blankness. "I made the sensible choice."

"That's not what I asked." Daphne stepped closer, her hand grazing Nell's arm in a silent plea for honesty.

Nell didn't answer. She couldn't—because the truth was a luxury she couldn't afford, and she was so tired of lying to Daphne, to herself, and to a world that saw only a sensible widow who always did the right thing.

Chapter Seventeen

The ride back to Bramwell Park rushed past in trees and pounding hooves. Her final refusal beat against his skull with every strike of the horse's feet.

My answer is no. Dominic didn't remember the journey. He didn't remember urging his horse faster, nor the wind cutting at his face or the branches whipping past his shoulders. He only remembered her steady eyes as she refused him. He'd offered her everything. His name. His home. His heart. She had said no as though the choice were simple, as though it cost her nothing.

Bramwell Park appeared through the trees, a grey stone monolith with empty windows that looked like hollow eyes. It was a mausoleum of memories and silence, yet he'd grown up in this house. He'd learned to walk in its corridors and had hidden from his father's rages in its dark corners. Now it loomed before him like a prison, and he rode toward it with something black and terrible building in his chest.

He dismounted in the stable yard and threw the reins at a groom without a word. His boots hit the gravel with a sharp crunch as he strode toward the house. He moved through the entrance hall, past Graves, who took one look at his face and pressed himself against the wall in silent retreat. He took the stairs two at a time, his pulse hammering and his hands shaking, running from a rejection he couldn't escape because it lived inside him.

He reached his study and slammed the door behind him hard enough to rattle the paintings on the walls.

Silence pressed in from all sides, punctuated by the ticking of the clock on the mantel and the crackle of the fire in the grate. He stood in the middle of the room, breathing hard, his fists clenched at his sides and his whole body trembling with a volatile energy he couldn't name.

She'd said no.

Because he was too young. Too reckless. Too impulsive. Because his feelings would fade. She spoke as if he were some boy with a passing fancy, some green youth who didn't know his own heart.

The rage came then, hot and sudden. It roared up from somewhere deep in his gut like a wave crashing against jagged rocks. His arm swept across the desk before he could stop it. Papers flew into the air, and the crystal inkwell shattered against the floor in an explosion of black.

It was not enough.

He grabbed the edge of the mahogany bookshelf and pulled with all his might. His muscles screamed with the effort as books cascaded down around him in a waterfall of leather and parchment. They were first editions his father had collected, volumes that had been in his family for generations. He didn't care. He snatched the crystal decanter from the sideboard—expensive and irreplaceable—and hurled it at the wall with every ounce of his strength. Glass exploded. Brandy dripped down the wallpaper like amber tears.

Still, it was not enough.

His fist connected with the wall, the impact jarring his shoulder. Once. The plaster cracked beneath his knuckles. Twice. Blood bloomed across his skin, staining the white wall. Three times. Four. He kept hitting until his hand was a ruin of split skin and shattered bone, until pain screamed up his arm and he could no longer lift his limb.

He slid down the wall, his back scraping against the ruined plaster, and drew his knees up to his chest. Blood dripped from his hand onto the carpet, pooling in the cracks between the floorboards.

She'd said no. And he'd nothing left to give.

The study was destroyed. Books lay scattered across the floor like fallen soldiers, their spines cracked and their pages torn. Glass glittered in the firelight—the remnants of the decanter, the shattered inkwell, and a vase he didn't remember breaking. Brandy soaked into the expensive wool of the carpet, filling the air with its sharp, sweet scent. The wall bore the imprint of his fists, plaster crumbling and blood smeared across the cream-coloured surface.

He didn't care. He couldn't feel anything except the hollow ache in his chest where his heart used to be.

The door opened. He didn't look up.

Footsteps crossed the room, careful and measured. Someone was picking through the debris with the practiced ease of one who had seen far worse. He heard the rustle of silk as a visitor settled into the one chair that remained upright.

"Well." Philippa's voice was dry as autumn leaves,

carrying no judgment and no surprise as she observed the carnage. “I see we are redecorating.”

Dominic kept his focus on his bloody knuckles, watching the slow drip of crimson onto the carpet. “Go away, Aunt.”

“No.” The chair creaked as she settled deeper into the velvet cushions, her skirts rustling around her ankles. “I don’t think I will.”

She let the quiet sit. She had always been good at waiting, and she was as patient as stone and as immovable as a mountain.

“She said no.” The words scraped out of him like shards of glass, tearing at his throat. He didn’t move a muscle.

Philippa’s hands folded in her lap, her tone remaining carefully neutral. “Who said no to what?”

He let out a laugh that was hollow and broken, echoing off the ruined walls. He tipped his head back against the plaster until it bruised. “Nell. I proposed. She refused.”

Philippa stayed quiet for a long moment. She took in the room. “You proposed marriage.” She spoke each word with care. Her silver brows rose. “To the baker.”

Dominic looked up at last. His jaw set. “Yes.”

“Today.” Her head tilted to the side as she studied his disheveled appearance.

“Yes.” He dropped his gaze back to his ruined hand, watching the blood well up from his split knuckles.

Philippa studied him for a long moment, her expression unreadable. “Did she give reasons, or did she simply refuse?”

“Reasons.” He laughed again, the sound as bitter as wormwood, and began listing them on his uninjured fingers. “She is a widow. She has children. She counts pennies while I have never wanted for anything. She is older. The ton will eat her alive. She cannot give me an heir. And my feelings —" He spat the next words like something foul. "My feelings will fade. As if I am some boy with a passing fancy who will forget her in a fortnight."

Philippa listened without interrupting, her hands still folded in her lap, her face giving nothing away.

"She thinks I proposed because I saw Hartley leaving." Dominic's voice turned bitter. His bloody hand curled into a fist despite the white-hot pain. "Because I panicked. Because I was jealous."

"Did you?" Philippa's voice stayed gentle, but it pressed. Her stare stayed sharp.

"I—" He stopped. The word caught in his throat. He let his head fall back against the wall. He shut his eyes. "Perhaps. I saw him leaving her shop with that smile on his face, and I just… I couldn't stand it. Not the thought of her with him. Not the thought of her choosing him."

"So you proposed on impulse." It was not an accusation. It was a fact delivered in the calm tone she used when he was being foolish. She smoothed a stray thread on her sleeve.

Dominic opened his eyes. He held her stare. His jaw tightened with defiance. "I proposed because I love her."

"Both can be true." Philippa spoke gently, her head tilting as she studied his face. "You can love her and still have proposed rashly. One doesn't preclude the other."

Silence fell between them again, broken only by the crackle of the fire and the distant, rhythmic ticking of the clock.

"She is not entirely wrong, you know." Philippa gestured toward the destruction surrounding them—the shattered glass, the scattered books, and the blood on the wall. "This is what you do when you are hurt. You destroy things. You lash out. You make the world match the chaos inside you."

Dominic stared at his bloody hand, watching the slow drip of crimson onto his trousers. "I know."

"The ton would be unkind to her." Philippa maintained her unwavering focus on him, her fingers laced together in her lap —a picture of aristocratic composure. "A widow. Older than you. No connections, no fortune, and no family name to protect her. They would tear her apart, and you know it."

"I don't care about the ton." He growled the words, his good hand curling into a fist against his thigh.

"You can afford not to care." Philippa said. "You are a viscount. They can whisper about you all they like, and it won't touch you. But she? My dear boy, she cannot afford your indifference to society's opinion."

Dominic stilled. His mouth opened, then closed. He looked down at his hands — whole, titled, wealthy hands that had never built anything, never stretched a shilling, never held a child through a fever while wondering if the flour would last the week. For the first time, he had nothing to say.

Philippa rose from her chair, her joints creaking with a dry protest, and crossed the room to where he sat slumped against the wall. She looked down at him for a long moment, then lowered herself to the floor beside him with a grunt of effort. Her silk skirts pooled around her on the blood-spotted carpet.

"Let me tell you something, nephew." She took his injured hand in both of hers, turning it over to examine the damage. Her touch was surprisingly gentle despite the age in her fingers. "Something I have learned in my sixty-eight years on this earth."

Dominic watched her face, his breathing slowing as he waited for the blow or the wisdom.

"You cannot force love." She began cleaning his wounds with a linen handkerchief pulled from her sleeve, dabbing at the blood with careful precision. "You cannot demand it, or chase it, or wrestle it into submission. Love is not a horse to be broken or a battle to be won."

"Then what am I supposed to do?" The words cracked, sounding raw and desperate in the hollow room. He didn't pull his hand away.

Philippa looked up from his mangled knuckles. Her attention settled on him with quiet certainty. "If she is meant to be yours, she will come back to you. Not because you chased her. Not because you hammered down her door. But because you became the man worth coming back to."

"And if she doesn't?" He whispered the question, his throat tight.

"Then you will survive it." Philippa wrapped his hand in the bloodied handkerchief, tying it off with practiced efficiency. She patted his knee before beginning the slow process of rising to her feet, her knees popping with the strain. She paused at the door and looked back. "But remember — fate favours the man who has done the work to deserve it."

She stood over him, her silver hair gleaming in the dying firelight. Her expression softened with a sharp stab of genuine sympathy.

"Give her time, Dominic. Give her space." She gestured at the wreckage surrounding them, one silver eyebrow arching in a silent reprimand. "Let her see who you are when you are not chasing her, not demanding things from her, and not destroying rooms because you didn't get what you wanted. And if it's meant to be, if she is truly yours, she will find her way back to you."

She left him there, sitting in the wreckage of his study. His hand throbbed in time with his heartbeat, and her words echoed in the heavy silence.

Fate favors the man who's done the work to deserve it.

He looked at his bloody knuckles. He looked at the shattered glass and the destruction he'd wrought simply because a woman had dared to refuse him. Philippa was right. Nell was right. He was reckless. He destroyed things when he was hurt. He'd proposed because he was jealous, without thinking about what it would cost her or considering anything except his own desperate need to claim her before someone else could. That was not love. That was possession.

If he truly loved her, if he wanted to deserve her, he needed to become someone different. He needed to be steady. Reliable. He needed to be a man who didn't destroy rooms when he was hurt or make reckless proposals out of jealousy.

He looked at the ruin surrounding him, the books he'd scattered and the wall he'd bloodied. This was who he'd been—but it was not who he would remain. He would give her time. He would give her space. He would let fate do whatever fate intended.

He pushed himself to his feet, found a clean cloth, and wrapped his hand more securely. Tomorrow he would start. Tomorrow he would begin becoming the man who deserved her, whether she ever chose him or not.

Chapter Eighteen

Five days passed.

They were five days of bread and customers and smiles that didn't reach her eyes. They were five days of lying awake at night, staring at the ceiling as his words drifted through the shadows, refusing to fade. *I love you.*

Nell moved through her routine like a ghost. She rose before dawn, kneading dough until her arms ached, serving customers with the mechanical efficiency of one who had stopped feeling anything at all. She was hollow. She was a shell of a woman going through the motions of a life she no longer recognized.

She'd made the right choice. She told herself that every morning when she woke and every night when she couldn't sleep. It was the sensible choice. It was the choice that would protect her children, her reputation, and her fragile, hard-won independence.

Edmund called twice during those five days. Once he brought her a book he thought she might enjoy, and once he invited her to walk with him along the river. She was pleasant to him. She was even warm. She gave him a hope she didn't feel, because it was easier than explaining the truth. She couldn't feel anything anymore. The numbness had spread through her like frost, leaving her frozen from the inside out.

Market day dawned grey and damp, matching her mood. Nell pulled her cloak tight around her shoulders and made her way through the village to the grocer's. Her basket was over her arm, and her mind was drifting somewhere far away.

"Lord Westmore has a guest at Bramwell Park." Mrs. Pemberton savoured each word like a sweet on her tongue, leaning closer until Nell could smell her heavy lavender water. "A lady. Lady Catherine Thorne. She arrived three days ago. They were seen riding together through the village yesterday morning. Very attentive, from what I hear."

It hadn't even been a week since he proposed to her, since he told her he loved her.

Nell kept her face carefully blank, though her heart buckled. She adjusted the clasp of her cloak with numb fingers. "How nice for him."

"They took tea at the inn afterwards." Mrs. Pemberton continued her assault. "Sat by the window where everyone could see. Laughing together. Such a handsome couple."

Tea at the inn. By the window. Where everyone could see. As if he wanted the village to watch.

"There's to be a ball." Mrs. Pemberton delivered the final blow with evident relish, her hand pressing to her chest in a gesture of mock excitement. "Friday evening. In Lady Catherine's honour. All the best families have been invited."

A ball.

His feelings had certainly faded with a dizzying speed, Nell thought bitterly. One refusal and he'd moved on to the next woman the way Nell had never existed. It was like he'd never knelt before her in that hidden alcove and touched her as if she was the most precious thing in the world.

She'd been right about him. He was infatuated. Nothing more. Then why did it feel like her heart was being crushed beneath a heavy weight?

"Excuse me." Nell gathered her basket and stepped around Mrs. Pemberton, her spine straight and her head held high. "I have a shop to run."

She walked away before the woman could utter another word. Her footsteps remained steady on the cobblestones, her expression giving nothing away.

She wouldn't cry. Not here. Not ever. Not over a man who had forgotten her in less than a week. She'd made the right choice, and he'd proven it.

So why did she want to scream?

She rounded the corner near the butcher's shop and walked straight into something solid, warm, and devastatingly familiar.

Dominic.

Her basket dropped from numb fingers. Apples rolled across the cobblestones, bright red against the grey stone. She stumbled back. Her heart slammed against her ribs. She froze as she took him in. He looked different. He looked rested. He looked calm. Clarity sat in him. His jaw sat loose. His scarred face showed none of the ruin she expected. He wore a simple coat and no hat. His dark hair sat rough from the wind. He regarded her like a stranger he meant to acknowledge with manners.

Where was the wrecked man who swore he loved her?

Where was the desperation? Where was the intensity? Where was the need?

"Mrs. Ashford." He stood straight, hands clasped behind his back.

She matched him. Her chin lifted. Her hands clenched at her sides. "Lord Westmore."

Neither moved. The apples kept rolling across the stones until one stopped at the toe of his boot.

"I hear congratulations are in order." The words escaped before she could stop them. They sounded like broken glass.

His lids lowered. A small muscle jumped in his jaw. "Congratulations?"

"Lady Catherine." She practically spat the name, her arms winding tightly over her chest as though to hold herself together. "A ball in her honor. How quickly you've moved on."

A shadow passed across his face—a brief shadow of surprise, or perhaps hurt—but he didn't rise to the bait. He didn't crowd her against the wall the way she expected, though he didn't demand that she listen.

"Lady Catherine is—" He started to speak, but his gaze drifted toward the horizon, his expression carefully blank.

"I don't want to hear it." She cut him off, dropping to her knees to gather the scattered fruit. Her hands trembled so violently the apples thudded against the wicker of the basket. "I don't need explanations. You are free to court whomever you please."

"Nell." The name was a low, ragged plea, a crack finally appearing in his careful facade as he took a half-step toward her.

"Mrs. Ashford." She corrected him, the syllables sharp and

biting. She straightened her back and clutched her basket, eyes flashing. "We should maintain propriety."

He fell silent, studying her face. The face that always seemed to see too much. She waited for the anger. The old Dominic would have demanded her attention. He would have refused to let her walk away

He didn't.

"As you wish." He gave a short, controlled nod. He bent down, picked up the last apple that had rolled near his feet, and placed it carefully in her basket. His fingers didn't touch hers. "Good day, Mrs. Ashford."

He walked away. He simply walked away with a steady stride and straight shoulders, never once looking back. She stared after him, her basket clutched to her chest, as confusion and fury warred within her.

Where was the fire? Where was the reckless man who had chased her and refused to let go? This calm, composed stranger was not the Dominic she knew.

She should be relieved. She was not.

That evening, a knock came at the door. Nell looked up from the bread she was wrapping, her brow furrowing in confusion. The shop was closed, the children were already upstairs with Martha, and the streets outside were growing dark.

"I will get it." Daphne crossed to the door. She pulled it open to reveal a young man in Bramwell Park livery.

"Messages for Mrs. Ashford, Miss Wells, and Miss Finch." He held out three cream-coloured envelopes, each sealed with heavy black wax. "From Bramwell Park."

Daphne's eyebrows shot toward her hairline as she took them, closing the door with the nudge of her hip. She crossed the shop and handed one to Nell, keeping the other two. Nell broke the seal with trembling fingers and unfolded the heavy paper.

Lord Westmore requests the honour of Mrs. Ashford's company at a ball given in celebration of Lady Catherine Thorne. Friday evening, the 12th of November. Eight o'clock. Bramwell Park.

Daphne was already tearing open her own. "Well." Daphne looked up from her own invitation, her dark eyes wide. She tapped the paper against her chin. "Lady Philippa invited me specifically. There's a note. She says she enjoyed our conversation at the tea."

Nell stared at the elegant script, her mind racing. He'd invited her after everything, even after she'd refused him. After he'd walked away from her in the street without a backward glance, and why? To torture her? To make her watch him with another woman?

She should refuse.

"You have to go." Daphne spoke firmly, reading the protest on Nell's face. She set her invitation on the counter. "We all do."

Nell shook her head, her jaw tightening. "I most certainly don't."

"If you don't go, everyone will know why." Daphne crossed her arms, her expression shifting into one of grim practicality. "They will say you are pining. Jealous. They will say you cannot bear to see him with another woman."

She was jealous. She was desperately, achingly jealous, but no one needed to know that.

"Edmund could take you." Daphne's head tilted to the side as she calculated the social move. "Show everyone you've moved on as well."

Moved on. To what? To whom?

The next day, Edmund called.

"I received an invitation to the Bramwell Park ball." He stood in the middle of her shop, his hat held respectfully in his hands. His brown eyes were warm and earnest, lacking the stormy fire she had grown used to. "I wondered if you might do me the honor of attending with me."

She should say no. She should stay far away from Dominic and the disaster waiting to happen.

"Yes." The word escaped her lips before she could catch it. She smoothed the front of her apron with precise movements, her own response sounding strangely distant, as if spoken by someone else. "I would like that."

Edmund smiled—warm, safe, and everything she should want. He took her hand and pressed a gentle kiss to her knuckles. Nell felt nothing. Nothing except a cold, growing dread.

Friday evening arrived like a sentence being carried out.

Martha had sent her regrets that afternoon—a headache that had settled behind her eyes and refused to shift, leaving her pale and apologetic in the doorway of her room. She would stay with the children, she insisted, waving away Nell's offer to remain home with a firmness that brooked no argument. She pinned Nell's hair up in loose curls with a green ribbon before retreating to bed, her parting gift one last tug on a stubborn curl and a quiet "you look lovely" murmured through the pain.

Nell wore the same green silk dress she'd worn to the harvest festival—the one Dominic had seen her in before everything fell apart. She tried not to think about that as she smoothed the fabric over her hips. Daphne appeared in a deep burgundy gown borrowed from a cousin, her cheeks flushed with excitement she wasn't bothering to hide.

Edmund's carriage arrived precisely at half past seven. He handed both women down with the practised ease of a man who had been raised to mind his manners, looking at Nell's dress with warm appreciation as he tucked her hand into the crook of his arm. Daphne walked on his other side, her burgundy skirts rustling against the gravel drive.

Bramwell Park blazed with light. Every window glowed, music drifted across the dark gardens, and carriages lined the drive. It looked like something from a fairy tale, a palace of golden stone and glittering glass.

Nell's stomach turned at the sight of it. She squeezed Edmund's arm, seeking an anchor in the storm of her own making.

She'd been here only a week ago. She'd been in the maze. She'd been in his arms.

Nell forced the memory aside, her breath catching. The entrance hall was crowded with guests. They were the finest families in the county, their jewels sparkling under the chandeliers and their voices carrying through the vast marble space. Nell felt their eyes on her immediately. She felt the whispers starting like a physical weight and felt herself shrinking beneath the cold pressure of their scrutiny.

She didn't belong here. She was a baker among lords and ladies. She was a woman with flour permanently embedded under her fingernails, merely pretending she had any right to walk these hallowed halls.

Philippa intercepted them near the entrance to the ballroom. Her silver hair gleamed beneath a diamond tiara, and her smile remained gracious as she greeted each guest in turn.

"Mrs. Ashford, how lovely you could join us." Philippa clasped Nell's hands briefly. "And Miss Wells. I am so pleased. You must find me later to discuss that cardamom recipe you mentioned at tea."

"Lady Philippa." Daphne dropped a deep, respectful curtsey, her cheeks flushing a bright pink with pleasure.

Philippa turned to Edmund with equal warmth, her silk skirts rustling. "Dr. Hartley. How good of you to escort our village ladies this evening. The refreshments are just through there, and I believe the first dance has already begun."

The ballroom took Nell's breath away. Chandeliers dripped with crystals that fractured the light into a thousand diamonds. A string quartet played in the corner, and couples were already swirling across the polished floor. The walls were lined with hothouse flowers, their perfume heavy and cloying in the warm air. Servants moved through the crowd with silver trays of champagne, their movements silent and precise.

She saw him immediately.

Dominic stood near the far wall. He was devastatingly handsome in black evening clothes that emphasized his broad shoulders and lean waist. His dark hair was combed back from his face, and he was smiling—and he was actually smiling at something the woman beside him had said.

Lady Catherine.

Nell's stomach turned to ice. The woman was young, younger than Nell by at least ten years, with golden hair piled artfully atop her head. She had a face that belonged on a porcelain doll. She was beautiful in that effortless way that Nell had never been. She was all delicate features and graceful lines, and her hand rested on Dominic's arm with familiarity.

"Shall we dance?" Edmund's voice came from somewhere far away. He placed a warm, steadying hand on her elbow.

Nell tore her gaze away from the couple across the room, her throat feeling as though it were constricted by wire. "Yes. Please."

Anything would be better than watching them.

They joined the other couples on the floor. Edmund led her through the steps with steady competence. He was a good dancer. He was reliable and predictable. She barely felt his hands on her waist or his fingers wrapped around hers as they moved in time to the music.

She was watching Dominic. She watched him smile at Lady Catherine. She watched him lean close to hear something the girl said, his dark head bowing toward her golden one. She watched his hand cover hers where it rested on his arm.

He hadn't looked at Nell once since she'd arrived.

Good, she told herself, forcing her gaze back to Edmund's kind, familiar face. *This is for the best.*

The dance ended, and Edmund excused himself to fetch her a glass of lemonade with a polite bow. Nell found a spot near the potted palms where she could stand without being too conspicuous. Her fan fluttered against the heat of the crowded room, the silk ribs clicking with every movement.

The next dance began, and she watched from the sidelines.

Dominic and Lady Catherine took the floor together, moving through the steps with practiced grace. His hand rested on the small of her back. It was the exact spot where it had rested on Nell's back in the maze. Lady Catherine tipped her golden head back and laughed at something he whispered.

Nell's fan snapped shut in her grip with a sharp, wooden crack.

She was jealous. The realization hit her like a blow to the stomach. It stole her breath and made her hands shake against the silk of her skirts. She was jealous of this beautiful young woman with her perfect golden curls and her porcelain skin. She was jealous of every smile he gave her, every word he spoke, and every moment of attention that should have been…

Should have been what? Nell had refused him. She'd told him no. She'd sent him away. She had no right to be jealous; she had no claim on him whatsoever.

And yet.

She watched Lady Catherine lean closer to whisper in his ear. She watched his face soften with what looked like genuine affection, and she wanted to march across the ballroom and tear them apart with her bare hands. It was madness. She barely recognized the woman she'd become.

The dance ended. Dominic escorted Lady Catherine to the edge of the floor. He bent and kissed her gloved hand. Then he released her. Nell could not bear to watch. She looked away. She tried to steady her breath.

She was still standing there, still seething, when a shadow

fell across her. He had moved beside her with the silence of a predator, his first words warm against the top of her ear.

"Mrs. Ashford." The greeting landed flat, stripped of warmth.

She spun around, her heart lurching into her throat. He was suddenly there. He was close enough to touch, and his steely eyes were fixed intently on her face. He'd crossed the entire ballroom without her noticing, and now he stood before her with one hand extended, his palm up.

"May I have this dance?" His expression was carefully neutral, giving nothing of his thoughts away. He remained perfectly still.

She should refuse. She should claim exhaustion, or a twisted ankle, or any of a dozen excuses that would keep her away from the heat of him. She should protect herself from the wanting that clawed at her chest every time he came near.

"Shouldn't you be dancing with Lady Catherine?" The words came out sharp and bitter before she could stop them. She gestured toward the golden haired girl with a jerky movement of her fan. "She seemed to be enjoying your company quite thoroughly."

A glint surfaced in his ashen eyes. It might have been surprise, or perhaps a dark satisfaction, but his expression remained bland. "Lady Catherine is dancing with Sir Richard Wentworth. I believe she finds him amusing."

"How fortunate for Sir Richard." She snapped her fan open, using the rhythmic motion to hide the flush creeping up her neck.

"One dance." He kept his hand extended toward her, as patient as stone. "The host should attend to all his guests. I am merely being attentive."

People were watching. Nell could feel their eyes on her like a physical weight, and she could hear the whispers rising like the hum of a disturbed hive. She could well imagine what they were saying about the baker who had dared to show her face at a viscount's ball.

She placed her hand in his, her jaw tight and her posture rigid. "Very well."

He led her to the floor, his grip firm but not possessive, his every movement controlled. The music began. It was a waltz, slow and intimate, and his hand settled on her waist—he was warm through the silk of her gown, his palm large and steady.

They moved together like they had been dancing their entire lives, perfectly matched in rhythm and step. He was taller than her by more than a foot, and she had to crane her neck to see his face, but somehow the geometry of it worked. Her body fitted against his like it remembered exactly where it belonged.

She hated that. She hated how right it felt, and she hated herself for the betrayal of noticing.

"Lady Catherine is very beautiful." Nell fixed her focus on the neat knot of his cravat. Her smile stayed sweet with a bite beneath it. "Young, too. What is she? Twenty? Twenty-three?"

His hand tightened almost imperceptibly on her waist, the sudden pressure pulling her a fraction of an inch closer. "Nineteen actually."

"Ah." Nell looked up at him then, her expression razor-sharp. "Still. She is practically a child, and I am sure the ton approves. It's much more appropriate than a thirty-four-year-old baker."

His mouth went rigid as he stared down at her. "Nell."

"Mrs. Ashford." She corrected him, her words short and

clinical. She shifted her gaze toward the other dancers, effectively shutting him out while they moved in perfect, agonizing rhythm. "We agreed on propriety, did we not?"

"You agreed on propriety." He finally looked at her, and she saw a dark frustration simmering in their depths. He guided her through a turn with effortless strength. "I agreed to nothing."

"How quickly you've moved on." She continued, ignoring his protest, her fan dangling from her wrist as they turned. "Not even a week after proposing to me, and you've already found a replacement. I suppose I should be flattered that you waited even that long."

"Is that what you think?" He leaned in until his forehead nearly brushed hers, his words vibrating with a dangerous, low-thrumming intensity. "That I have moved on?"

"What else am I supposed to think?" She tilted her chin back, meeting his stare with eyes that burned. For a fleeting moment, she let the mask slip, allowing him to see the raw, jagged jealousy she could no longer suppress. "You are hosting a ball in her honor. You are walking arm in arm through your gardens. You are smiling at her the way she hung the moon in the sky."

"You are jealous." The realization seemed to please him. His stare sharpened, and his hand moved instinctively, pressing more firmly against the small of her back to pull her a fraction closer.

"Don't be ridiculous." The denial snapped between them, far too fast to be believed. She jerked her gaze away, her heart hammering a frantic rhythm against her ribs.

"You are." A sense of wonder smoothed out the rough edges of his expression. He didn't look away, tracking the way the flush deepened across her cheeks and down the curve of her neck. "You are jealous of Catherine."

"I am not." She held herself perfectly still, daring him to argue.

His thumb moved. It was a small circle on her waist which made her lost her train of thought entirely as the heat of the contact bloomed through her. "You refused me." He said it quietly, his iron eyes burning into hers with an intensity that made her lightheaded. "You told me no. You said my feelings would fade."

"They clearly have." She shot the words back, her chin lifting in defiance. "Given how cozy you've been with Lady Catherine."

"And yet here you are." His hand shifted lower on her back, far too low for propriety, and pulled her closer until her body was pressed flush against his chest. "Seething with jealousy."

"I am not seething." She panted the words, her hands trembling where they rested on him.

"You are." His lips curved just slightly. It was not quite a smile, but it was close enough to one to be dangerous. "Your eyes are practically shooting sparks. It's magnificent."

She tried to pull away, but his arm was like iron around her waist. "Let go of me."

"Not until you admit it." He held her firm, his steely eyes burning down into hers from his great height.

"Admit what?" She glared up at him, her jaw tight and her neck craning.

"That you are jealous." He pulled her closer still, until she could feel the heat of him through every layer of silk and cotton. "That you hate seeing me with another woman. That you want me, even though you told yourself you didn't."

"People are watching." She hissed the words, her cheeks flaming as her fingers curled into the fine wool of his shoulder.

"Let them." His cold eyes never left hers. They were dark with a hunger that made her knees weak. "Let them all watch."

"You have lost your mind." She aimed for a dismissive scoff, but the words hitched in her throat, coming out thin and breathless. Her traitorous body leaned into his warmth of its own accord, seeking the very heat she claimed to reject.

"Oh, have I?" He bent low, his mouth hovering near her ear, his breath hot against her sensitive skin. "You showed up in that dress looking like every dream I have had for the past five days. And then you stood there glaring at me while I danced with Catherine, as if you wanted to murder us both."

"I didn't." She started to protest, her face burning hotter than the ovens in her shop.

"You did." His hand pulled her tighter still, flush against him in a way that was utterly scandalous. "And it's taking every ounce of control I haven't to drag you out of this ballroom and show you exactly how little I have moved on."

Her breath caught. Her fingers dug into his shoulder hard enough to bruise the muscle beneath.

"Dominic." His name escaped her like a prayer or a curse.

"Don't." He tensed, throat tight, bending until his breath warmed her forehead. His smoke eyes were bright with something that looked almost like pain. "Don't say my name like that. Not here. Not when I cannot touch you the way I want to."

The music ended.

They stood frozen in the sudden silence, their bodies still

pressed together. The ballroom had gone quiet around them—far too quiet—and Nell became acutely aware of the stares and the fluttering fans of society matrons leaning toward each other with gleaming eyes.

Everyone was watching. Everyone had seen.

Dominic released her abruptly. He stepped back, his face shuttering as the mask slammed back into place, for the hunger in his eyes vanished so quickly she might have imagined it.

"Thank you for the dance, Mrs. Ashford." He spoke with a cold formality. He clasped his hands behind his back, his spine rigid. He acted like nothing had happened.

He turned on his heel and walked away without waiting for a response. He disappeared into the crowd, leaving her standing alone in the middle of the dance floor with her heart slamming and the bitter, hot taste of jealousy still burning on her tongue.

Chapter Nineteen

Nell couldn't breathe.

The room felt too hot, too crowded, and far too full of whispers. She needed air. She needed to get away from the music and the lights and the burning memory of his hand on the small of her back.

Edmund appeared at her elbow, his brown gaze tracing the lines of her face with deep concern. "Nell? Are you all right?"

"I need air." She was already moving, pushing through the crowd with her skirts rustling, not waiting for his response. "Just a moment."

She didn't look back. She didn't care if she was being rude. She pushed through the press of bodies and fled down a quiet hallway, away from the music and the light and the eyes that followed her everywhere. A door appeared on her left. She opened it and slipped inside, closing it firmly behind her and pressing her back against the wood.

The study was quiet and dark. It was lit only by the fire burning low in the grate, casting shadows that danced across the rows of leather-bound books. She leaned against the door, breathing hard, her hands pressed flat against the timber.

What was wrong with her?

She'd made the right choice. Dominic had Lady Catherine now. She was a beautiful, young, and appropriate woman who would give him heirs and grace his arm at balls without ever embarrassing him in front of the ton.

But his hand on her waist had been so steady. His body had been pressed against hers, and he'd said her name like a prayer and a curse. He still wanted her — she'd felt it in the heat of his gaze — and God help her, she still wanted him.

She crossed to the window and stared out at the dark gardens. Her reflection appeared ghostly in the glass. The maze was visible in the moonlight, its green walls edged in silver and its secrets hidden in deep shadow. That was where he'd touched her. Where he'd made her come apart and told her she was his. She pressed her forehead against the cool glass and closed her eyes.

Back in the ballroom, Dominic watched her disappear down the corridor with something twisting painfully in his chest. He should let her go. He should stay away and maintain the careful distance he'd been building for five days. But he couldn't.

He was already moving toward the hallway when he heard the voices. They were sharp and malicious, carrying from behind a cluster of potted palms. Mrs. Pemberton was there with two other ladies, their heads bent together and their fans fluttering.

"Did you see them dancing?" Mrs. Pemberton's voice dripped with venom. "Quite the display. I am surprised they didn't simply couple right there on the floor."

"Shameless." A second woman chimed in, her chin lifting as she fussed with the strand of pearls at her throat. A tight, pinched quality entered the conversation. "A baker at a ball. Who does she think she is?"

"A scheming widow." Mrs. Pemberton laughed, the sound like breaking glass, and she tapped her chin with her fan. "First she traps Dr. Hartley with her sad story, and now she is after the viscount. Though heaven knows what she thinks she can offer a man of his standing."

"She is too old for Lord Westmore." The third woman sniffed, her nose wrinkling with distaste as she looked toward the refreshments. "And those children of hers. No one even knows who the father was."

"Probably some traveling merchant." Mrs. Pemberton tittered behind her fan, her shoulders shaking with mirth. "Or worse. A groom, perhaps. A footman."

Dominic's blood turned to ice. He stepped around the palms and into their view, his hands clasped behind his back and his expression carved from stone. All three women froze. Their fans stopped mid-flutter and their faces drained of all colour.

"Ladies." He didn't raise his volume, yet the single word seemed to suck the warmth from the hallway. He tilted his head with a predatory slowness, pinning them under a stare that held all the warmth of a winter grave. "Forgive me—I could not help but overhear."

Mrs. Pemberton's smile faltered, her hand flying to her

chest like to shield her heart. "Lord Westmore, we were simply..."

"You were insulting a guest in my home." He took a single step forward. The three women moved as one, retreating until the wall stopped them, their eyes rounding with a sudden, sharp fear. "A woman worth more than the three of you combined."

"I didn't mean..." Mrs. Pemberton's fan rattled against her stays, her words stumbling over one another.

"Mrs. Ashford built a business from nothing." He severed her protest mid-sentence, the words landing with the sharp, clean edge of a blade. He stood his ground, a towering shadow that seemed to shrink the space around them. "She raised two children alone, without help or support. She works harder in a single day than any of you work in an entire year. And she does it with more grace and dignity than I have ever seen in a London ballroom."

The three women stood silent and frozen, their mouths hanging open.

"If I hear her name in your mouths again." He stepped closer still. "If I hear so much as a whisper about her, or her children, or her reputation, you will find yourselves unwelcome in every home in this county. Every ball. Every dinner party. Do I make myself clear?"

They nodded, mute with terror.

"Then enjoy the rest of the evening." He turned on his heel and walked away. He didn't care who had heard or what they thought.

He didn't see Daphne standing behind a nearby pillar. Her dark eyes were wide and her face was slack with shock. But

Daphne saw him. She heard every word. And for the first time, she didn't know what to think about Lord Westmore.

Dominic found the study door and stood before it. His hand rested on the handle, and his heart pounded against his ribs, but he should stay away. He was trying to be steady and reliable, not reckless. He opened the door anyway.

She was standing at the window with her back to him, silhouetted by the moonlight. The green silk of her gown hugged her curves. Her hair was coming loose from its pins, and dark tendrils curled against the pale skin of her neck.

"Please, go away." She didn't turn. Her shoulders stayed rigid, her attention fixed on the window as if he weren't standing there at all.

"No." Dominic stepped inside and shut the door behind him. The key turned in the lock, the final click sharp in the quiet room.

"Dominic." Her fingers curled into fists at her sides as she started to turn.

"Don't." He crossed the room. He did not look away from her. "Don't tell me to go. Don't tell me to be sensible. I have been sensible for five days." He let out a rough breath. "It is killing me."

She turned to face him. The firelight caught the anger in her face. "Then go back to your Lady Catherine." Her chin lifted in challenge. "You looked perfectly content with her."

"I don't want Lady Catherine." He stopped a few paces away, his hands hanging loose, his concentration fixed entirely on her.

"You certainly seemed to." Nell's mouth twisted.

A broken laugh tore out of him. He dragged a hand through

his hair and shook his head. "I was pretending. I've been pretending since the moment you refused me." His gaze sharpened. "Pretending I'm fine. Pretending I've moved on. Pretending I don't see your face every time I close my eyes."

She lifted a hand between them, palm out, as though she could physically stop the words from reaching her. "Stop."

He didn't. He moved closer, close enough that the warmth of him reached her, close enough for the faint scent of lavender in her hair to hit him square in the chest. "I can't. I've tried. God knows I've tried. You're under my skin. In my blood. I don't eat. I don't sleep. I don't think about anything else."

Her hand fell. "You haven't even known me that long."

"I know enough." The words landed hard. "I know you're braver than anyone I've ever met. I know you'd die for your children. I know you taste like honey and fight like fire." His chest rose with a heavy breath. "You make me want to be better, Nell. Just to deserve you."

She shifted back a step, then another, until cold glass pressed against her spine. "You have Lady Catherine."

"Lady Catherine is Alistair's sister." The words were blunt. "Alistair Thorne. My best friend and the man whose life I saved at Waterloo." His mouth tightened. "She's been like a younger sister to me since I was twenty. She's visiting. That's all."

Nell searched his face, her lips parting like she expected the lie to reveal itself. "Your best friend's sister?"

"Yes." He closed the distance again, close enough to see the frantic pulse at her throat.

"Not your..." The rest dissolved into silence.

"Not anything." He stepped closer still, until there was

barely a breath between them. "There's no one else. There never will be. Just you."

She shook her head, even as her gaze dropped—traitorously—to his mouth. "I don't believe you."

"Then don't." He lifted his hands and cupped her face, tilting it up. His thumbs brushed along her cheekbones reverently. "But understand this—I'm yours. Whether you want me or not."

Her hands came up to his wrists, gripping without pushing. "You can't just say things like that."

"I can." His thumb traced the curve of her lower lip, his breathing uneven. "I'm done being careful. Done pretending. You're the only thing that matters."

His name slipped from her mouth before she could stop it.

"Refuse me again." His forehead dipped closer to hers, his composure finally cracking. "Send me away. Marry your doctor." His gaze swept hers. "But never doubt that I love you."

Her whole body trembled—anger, want, fear tangled together. Tears brightened her eyes as he leaned in, the last inch between them vanishing.

Her hand flew up.

The slap cracked through the room.

He didn't flinch. He didn't step back. He only stood there, staring at her, his cheek already flushing beneath the imprint of her hand.

"Stay away from me." She kept her hand raised, unsure whether she might strike him again. Panic flickered sharp and sudden in her eyes. "I mean it. Stay away. Please."

She reached past him and fumbled with the lock, yanking the door open and fled. He didn't follow. He stood alone in the study, his hand eventually rising to press against his burning cheek, watching the empty doorway.

Nell ran. She moved down the hallway and through the crowd, not caring who saw or who whispered. She couldn't breathe. She couldn't think.

Daphne intercepted her near the entrance hall. "Nell? What happened?"

"We are leaving." Nell didn't stop or slow. She kept moving toward the grand doors. "Now."

Edmund stood near the entrance, his hat already in his hands. He saw her face and stepped forward, his brow furrowing with immediate worry. "Nell?"

She pushed past him, lungs burning as she sought the cold night air. "I need to go home."

The walk home passed in silence, their boots crunching along the dark, rutted lane. Nell stared straight ahead, her arms wrapped tight around herself while her hand still tingled from the impact of the slap.

"Nell." Daphne fell into step beside her, her breath clouding in the cold air. "What happened in that study?"

"Nothing." She lied and kept her gaze fixed on the road ahead.

"You are shaking." Daphne reached out and caught her elbow.

"I am fine." She was not. She felt like her heart had been flayed open.

"He loves you." Daphne said it quietly, as if stating a fact that could no longer be disputed. "You know that, do you not?"

"He doesn't know what he wants." Nell closed her eyes, her throat aching with the effort not to sob.

"He defended you tonight." Daphne's voice took on a

strange, wondering quality. "To Mrs. Pemberton and her coven. I heard every word."

Nell's eyes flew open, and she turned her head sharply toward her friend. "What?"

"They were saying horrible things." Daphne continued. "About you. About your children. About where they came from and why you didn't belong at that ball."

Nell's stomach turned to ice.

"And he stopped them. He told them you were worth more than all of them combined. He threatened to ruin them, to make them unwelcome in every home in the county, if they ever spoke your name again." Daphne shook her head, still processing the scene. "I have never seen anything like it, Nell. He meant every word."

Nell stared at her, her blood rushing against her ribs. "He defended me?"

"Like God help anyone stupid enough to try it again." Daphne nodded slowly. "Like anyone who hurt you would have to answer to him personally."

Nell's throat closed.

"It doesn't matter." She forced the words out, turning back to face the dark road. "It doesn't change anything."

Daphne said nothing. She just kept walking.

But the silence gave Nell nowhere to hide. He had told her about Lady Catherine. Plainly, repeatedly, with nothing hidden. And she had chosen not to hear it because believing him meant admitting she'd been wrong, and being wrong meant she'd thrown away something real.

. . .

That night, she lay awake in her narrow bed, staring at the ceiling as his voice echoed in the darkness.

Send me away. Marry your doctor. But don't ever doubt that I love you.

Nell closed her eyes tightly. She'd made the sensible choice; but sensible had never felt so much like breaking.

Chapter Twenty

One week.

Seven days had passed since the ball. There'd been seven nights of lying awake in the dark, staring at the ceiling and hearing his tone echo through the hollow chambers of her chest. *don't say my name like that. Not here. Not when I cannot touch you the way I want to.* There'd been seven mornings of dragging herself out of bed before dawn, of kneading dough until her arms ached, and of smiling at customers while something inside her slowly died.

He hadn't come. He hadn't sent a word. He hadn't done any of the things the old Dominic would have done. There were no dramatic appearances at her shop door, no passionate declarations, and no reckless pursuit of a woman who had slapped him and run. She'd told him to stay away. He was staying away.

She should be relieved.

Nell stood at the kitchen table in the grey pre-dawn light, working the dough with mechanical precision. Flour dusted her forearms and clung to the creases of her knuckles. She pressed the heel of her hand into the soft mass, folded it over, turned it, and pressed again. Her shoulders ached. Her back ached. Everything ached, and none of it had anything to do with the labor of baking.

Her hand had stopped tingling days ago. The phantom sensation of his cheek beneath her palm had finally faded, but she still felt the sharp crack of it in her dreams. She still saw the shock in his glacial eyes and the way he'd stood perfectly still while she fled.

The children came down as the sun crept over the horizon. Lily appeared first, her spectacles already crooked and her nightgown trailing behind her; Oliver followed, quieter than usual, watching Nell with eyes that saw far too much.

"Mama." Lily tugged at her dress, her small face pinched with worry as she looked up. "You've been sad all week."

Nell's hands stilled in the dough, and she forced a smile that felt like shards of broken glass on her lips. "I am fine, love."

"You are not." Lily pressed closer, her arms wrapping around Nell's waist while her spectacles fogged from the warmth of the kitchen. "You haven't laughed once. Not even when Oliver fell in the flour yesterday."

"I am just tired." Nell smoothed her daughter's wild hair back from her face, her throat aching with the effort to remain composed. "That's all. Just tired."

Lily didn't look convinced, but she let it go, retreating to the table where Martha was setting out breakfast. Oliver lingered a moment longer, his dark look reading Nell's face with unsettling intensity.

"Is it because of Lord Westmore?" He asked it quietly, so

Lily wouldn't hear, while he shoved his hands deep into his pockets.

Nell's hands trembled. She gripped the edge of the floured table to steady them. "Why would you think that?"

"Because you've been different since the ball." Oliver shrugged, his jaw tightening in a way that made him look far older than nine.

She opened her mouth to deny it, to tell him he was wrong, but the lie wouldn't form. "Go eat your breakfast." She forced the words past a throat that felt raw and tight, gesturing toward the table with an unsteady hand. "I will be fine."

He went, but his eyes lingered on her all the way across the room—a boy who had learned too young that his mother sometimes needed watching.

Daphne arrived at half past seven, her dark gaze sweeping over Nell's face with the knowing look she'd worn all week. She said nothing. She simply hung her cloak on the peg and tied her apron with brisk efficiency, and they fell into the familiar rhythm of the morning—ovens, dough, counters, customers—without a word about any of it.

The midday lull had just settled over the shop when Edmund walked through the door. He stood with his hat in his hands, turning the brim between his fingers. He looked tired—shadows sitting heavy beneath his brown eyes, lines carved around his mouth that hadn't been there a week ago.

"Mrs. Ashford." He nodded to Daphne, who was watching from behind the counter. "Might I speak with you? Privately?"

Daphne's gaze flicked to Nell, a silent question in her expression. Nell stepped forward with a nod.

"I will watch the counter." Daphne stepped aside, brushing her hand lightly against the edge of the table as she gestured for Nell to pass. Her shoulders relaxed, and she gave a small, encouraging nod. "Take your time."

Nell led Edmund through the kitchen to the storeroom. Every familiar corner stirred a memory, and she couldn't help the slight tightening in her chest as she thought of the countless times she had hidden here from the world.

"Edmund..." She started.

He raised a hand before she could say more. He leaned slightly forward, grounding himself, like to make her pause and listen. "Please. Let me speak first."

He set his hat aside on a barrel of sugar, his movements careful and precise. Then he turned to face her, his brown eyes meeting hers without flinching.

"I saw you that night." He said it quietly, without a trace of accusation, his hands now clasped firmly behind his back. "At the ball. Dancing with him."

Nell's stomach dropped. She pressed her back against the wooden shelf behind her, seeking support. "Edmund, I can explain..."

"You don't need to." He cut her off gently, taking a single step closer. "I have eyes, Nell. I saw how you both looked at each other. I saw how he held you, and how you ran afterward."

She couldn't deny it. She wouldn't insult a man of his character with lies. She stood there in silence, waiting for the anger that never came.

"I am not angry." He said it almost with a smile, his head tilting slightly as he studied her. "I am not even surprised, if I am honest."

Nell's brow furrowed, her confusion finally cutting through her shame. "You are not?"

"There has been something between you since the beginning." He shrugged, his shoulders lifting and falling in a slow, weary motion that seemed to age him a decade. "I saw it the first time I saw him in your shop. The way you looked at each other… It was like you wanted to either kill each other or kiss each other. I hoped it would fade. I hoped you'd choose sense." He leaned in, the distance between them vanishing until his words were a warm, heavy weight against her skin. "That you'd choose me."

"Why did you not come sooner?" The question escaped in a frantic rush, her nails biting into the soft flesh of her palms. "It has been a week."

"I needed time." Tension flickered across his face before he forced it to settle. "Time to think. Time to decide what I wanted to say. Time to decide what I wanted to ask." He looked at her, his expression stripped of its usual careful composure. "I spent seven days trying to convince myself that what I saw did not mean what I knew it meant. I tried to believe there was still a chance."

"Edmund." She tried to say more, but her throat tightened, the air catching against a sudden, sharp constriction.

"I need to know." He closed the final inch between them, his presence gentle but immovable. He reached out and gathered her hands in his, his palms steady and grounding. "I have been patient. I have waited. But I cannot wait forever, Nell. It's not fair to either of us."

Silence stretched between them. It was heavy and expectant, filled only by the distant sounds of the shop.

"I am asking for an answer." He squeezed her hands and earnestly searched her face. "Not about him. About me. Can you see a future with me? A life?"

She looked at him. He was a good, kind man with steady hands and warm eyes, for his love was comfortable and uncomplicated. He would never hurt her. He would never call her nothing in front of a crowd. Yet, he would never make her feel like she were burning alive, or the way her skin were too tight for her body, or as if she might die if he didn't touch her.

He would be safe. He would be steady and reliable. And she would never love him. Not the way he deserved.

"You are a good man." She said it softly, her fingers tightening briefly around his before she began to pull away. "The best man I know."

"But?" He heard it coming. His expression shifted, his shoulders squaring like bracing for a physical impact.

"But I cannot." Her throat closed around the words, and she had to force them out into the cool air of the storeroom. "I am sorry, Edmund. I cannot marry you."

He didn't flinch. He simply nodded, a slow and resigned movement, the way he'd known this was coming all along.

"Because of him." It was not a question. He let his arms fall to his sides.

"No." She shook her head, finally pulling her hands completely free and tucking them into the folds of her apron. "Because of me. Because I would be settling. And you deserve more than a woman who is merely settling for a life she doesn't truly want."

"You love him." He said it flatly, without inflection. He watched her with a piercing clarity.

She didn't answer. She couldn't. The words stuck in her throat like shards of broken glass.

"You don't have to say it." He released her and stepped back, reaching for his hat where it sat upon the sugar barrel. "I saw it that night. I saw the way you looked at him when you thought no one was watching."

"I refused him." The words scraped out of her, raw and ragged. She gripped the edge of a shelf until her knuckles turned white. "I told him no."

"I see." Edmund settled his hat on his head, his movements deliberate and graceful. "But refusing someone and not loving them are not the same thing."

"Edmund." She reached out a hand toward him, but he was already moving toward the door.

"I hope you find what you are looking for, Nell." He paused at the threshold, looking back at her with a gaze that held both sadness and a quiet acceptance. "I hope he makes you happy. Truly."

He left then. He moved quietly and gracefully, like the gentleman he'd always been. Nell stood alone in the storeroom, her whole body shaking with a chill that the kitchen fires couldn't warm.

She'd refused Edmund. She'd turned away the safe choice and the sensible choice. She'd rejected the man who would have given her stability, security, and a future she could count on.

And for what? A man she'd slapped and told to stay away? A man she hadn't seen in a week? She didn't love Dominic. She couldn't. She wouldn't. But she couldn't say yes to Edmund either. She couldn't condemn him to a loveless marriage, nor could she use his kindness as a shield against her own cowardice.

Daphne appeared in the doorway. "He is gone?"

"Yes." Nell replied.

"And?" Daphne leaned against the doorframe.

"I said no." Nell pushed past her, heading back toward the shop and the safety of her work. "I said no, and that's the end of it."

Daphne didn't follow. For once, she let Nell go without further questioning.

The day went by in a rush of customers, bread, and copper coins.

Nell smiled when she was supposed to smile, she spoke when she was supposed to speak. She moved through the motions of her life while, inside, she felt a hollow stillness. She didn't think about Dominic. She refused to. She didn't think about the ball, or his hand on her waist, or the way he'd bent low to breathe against her ear. She didn't think about the study, or the shock in his ashen eyes when she'd struck him.

She thought about nothing at all.

Night came, and the children went to bed. Lily went with her stack of books, and Oliver with his quiet, heavy watchfulness, yet Martha retired to her room. The shop grew quiet, and the fire crackled low in the hearth. Daphne lingered by the door, her cloak already fastened and her basket over her arm.

"You did the right thing." Daphne said it quietly as she looked at her friend. "With Edmund."

Nell looked up from the counter she was wiping, her hand stilling on the worn wood. "Did I?"

"You couldn't have made him happy." Daphne smoothed the silk of her gloves over her knuckles, her movements returning to their crisp, rhythmic precision. "Not when your heart is somewhere else."

"My heart is not..." Nell started, but the words died in her throat.

She couldn't finish the lie. She couldn't make her mouth form a denial that had felt so sturdy just a week ago. Daphne watched her for a long moment, something unreadable in her expression. Then she nodded once and slipped out the door, leaving Nell alone with the dying fire and the pressure of everything she couldn't say.

Morning came grey and threatening. The sky was heavy with clouds that pressed down on the village like a leaden hand. Nell woke with a headache pounding behind her eyes and a hollow ache in her chest that had become so familiar she barely noticed it anymore.

The shop opened slower than usual. The threatening weather kept the villagers in their homes, and by mid-morning, only a handful of customers had come and gone. The rain hadn't yet started. It simply hung there, waiting, like the whole world were holding its breath for a storm that was long overdue.

Nell worked in the back, her hands buried in dough as she fought to keep her thoughts at bay. By noon, the rain began. It was heavy and relentless. It pounded against the windows like rhythmic fists, drowning out all other sound and turning the village outside into a grey, watery blur. Thunder rumbled, low and ominous.

Lily appeared in the kitchen doorway, her spectacles fogged by the humidity. She pressed her small face against the glass of the window. "Mama, it's as if the sky is angry." She whispered the words with a touch of awe while watching a flash of lightning illuminate the distant hills.

Nell crossed the room to her daughter. She rested a gentle

hand on the girl's narrow shoulder. "It's only a storm, love. It will pass."

But something in Nell's chest tightened as she watched the deluge. It was a cold, twisting sensation that had nothing to do with the weather.

The afternoon dragged on. Few customers braved the downpour, and those who did hurried in and out with their hoods pulled low, barely pausing to exchange the usual pleasantries. Daphne dozed by the fire, her head nodding rhythmically against her chest. Upstairs, the children played quietly, their voices muffled by the constant drumming of the rain.

Nell was alone with her thoughts. It was dangerous territory. She was wiping down the counter for the third time, needing the movement to keep her mind from wandering, when the bell jangled. It was not the gentle chime of a customer—and it was something violent and urgent.

She looked up.

Lady Philippa stood in the doorway, soaked through to the bone. Her silver hair was plastered to her face and her fine silk dress was utterly ruined. Water pooled on the floor around her muddy boots—but it was her eyes that made Nell's blood turn to ice. They were wild and desperate, rimmed with a terrifying fear.

"Mrs. Ashford." Philippa was gasping for air, every breath a battle as she braced one hand against the doorframe for support. "You must come. Please. You must come now."

Nell's hand clenched around the cleaning cloth, her knuckles turning white. "Lady Philippa, what has happened?"

"Dominic." The name came out broken and ragged. Philippa lurched forward, grabbing Nell's arm with desperate, trembling fingers. "There has been an accident. His horse… The storm… he is hurt. Badly hurt."

The world seemed to tilt on its axis. The cloth fell from Nell's nerveless fingers and hit the floor with a soft thud.

"How badly?" Nell's hands trembled as she clutched the edge of the doorway, her fingers curling around the wood as if it could steady her.

Philippa's shoulders shook. Rain ran in rivulets down her face, mingling with tears she couldn't stop. She pressed a hand to her mouth, then let it fall. "The doctor is with him… but he won't… he keeps calling for you. Over and over." She swallowed hard, blinking rapidly. "Nell. Just Nell."

The sound of her name, whispered even through broken breath, struck Nell in the chest. He was calling for her… while he lay like that.

"I cannot..." Nell's lips parted, but her feet had already carried her toward the door. Her hands flew to the cloak hanging on the peg, tugging it free almost without thinking.

"The carriage is outside." Philippa seized her arm, her grip hard enough to leave marks. "Please. I have never seen him like this. I have never..."

"Daphne!" Nell's shout cut through the pounding rain.

Daphne was on her feet in an instant, sprinting toward them. Her skirts clung to her legs, soaked and heavy. "The children..." Her eyes darted, worried and frantic.

"Go." Daphne yanked the cloak from Nell's hands and wrapped it around her, fastening the clasp with precise, urgent fingers. She shoved Nell toward the door. "I will stay with them. Go."

The rain hit Nell like a wall, soaking through the cloak in seconds. Her body felt numb, yet her heart thudded wildly in her chest—yet Philippa's words echoed in her mind:*He keeps asking for you.*

She scrambled into the carriage without realizing she'd crossed the cobblestones. The horses strained against the storm as the wheels slid in the mud. Nell gripped the leather seat until her knuckles whitened, staring past the window at nothing, her breaths coming ragged and uneven.

Across from her, Philippa sat drenched, her skirts ruined and twisted, hands working frantically over and over like the motion could hold back the panic.

"What happened?" Nell finally forced the words past her lips, each one scraping raw against the chaos of the carriage's motion. She clenched her fists in her lap, trying to anchor herself. "Tell me… tell me what happened."

"He went riding this morning." Philippa's voice was hollow, her chilling eyes fixed on a point beyond Nell's shoulder. "Despite the weather. Despite everyone telling him not to go. He has been… restless. Ever since the ball."

Ever since the slap. Ever since she'd told him to stay away.

"Lightning spooked the horse." Philippa continued, wringing her hands until the skin was red. "It threw him. He hit his head on a rock. The groundskeeper found him in the mud, barely conscious."

Barely conscious. The words echoed through Nell's skull.

"He kept saying your name." Philippa finally looked at her. "Even when he didn't know where he was. Even when he couldn't remember his own."

Nell's eyes burned, but she bit her lip. She wouldn't cry.

"Why me?" The question escaped on a tremor of panic, sounding raw and desperate. "Why did you come for me?"

"Because he needs you." Philippa's answer was simple and

certain. "Because whatever is between you two… I have never seen him like this, and not even after the war. Not even after everything with Vivienne." Philippa stopped to draw a shaking breath. "He loves you. More than he has ever loved anything."

"I refused him." Nell whispered, her throat aching.

"I know." Philippa reached out, touching Nell's knee with a damp hand. "But you came anyway."

She had. Without a second thought. She'd heard his name and she'd run.

Bramwell Park appeared through the trees, every window blazing with light. Servants rushed through the courtyard with lanterns and umbrellas, looking like spirits in the gloom. They pulled up to the entrance, and Nell was out of the carriage before it had fully stopped. Her boots hit the gravel and her skirts dragged in the mud, but she didn't wait for help.

She ran.

The entrance hall was a scene of chaos. Servants rushed past with basins of water and armfuls of linens, their faces grey with worry. Nell pushed through them, following a frantic instinct; Graves appeared, materializing out of the crowd. His usually impassive face was tight with concern.

"Lady Philippa. Mrs. Ashford." He fell into step beside them, gesturing toward the grand staircase. "This way. The doctor is with him."

They climbed the stairs, past the silent portraits of Westmore ancestors and down a long corridor where the windows rattled in their frames. They stopped before a heavy oak door. Graves pushed it open.

Nell stepped inside.

The room was dim, lit only by candles flickering on the nightstand and a fire crackling low in the hearth. Heavy curtains muffled the storm to a distant rumble—a massive bed dominated the space, its dark wood posts rising toward the ceiling. The white linens were stained with a rust-coloured fluid that made Nell's stomach lurch.

And in the bed lay Dominic.

He was as pale as death. His dark hair was matted with blood, and a white bandage was wrapped clumsily around his head, crimson seeping through the fibers. His eyes were closed, his face slack, and his chest labored with shallow, uneven rhythms. He looked fragile—a ghost of the vital man who had once pinned her against a wall.

Edmund stood at the bedside. He was bent over Dominic's still form, two fingers pressed firmly to the pulse point at the man's wrist. He looked up as the door creaked, and a shadow of something far sadder than surprise crossed his face when he saw Nell.

"Mrs. Ashford." He didn't look up again, his attention returning to his watch as he counted the beats. He remained professional, clinical, and miles away. "You came."

"How is he?" The question felt far-off, a hollow rasp that seemed to echo from the end of a long tunnel.

"A concussion." Edmund straightened, setting Dominic's hand back upon the coverlet with a gentleness that was painful to watch. "Possibly worse. He has been unconscious since they brought him in. He rouses for a moment, but his mind is elsewhere."

Dominic stirred at the sound of the words. A low groan escaped him, his head turning restlessly upon the pillow as his features twisted with a sudden flash of pain.

"Nell." He mumbled the name, the word thick with a desperate, feverish longing. "Nell… please..."

Her heart cracked. It felt the way it had broken clean in two.

"He has been saying that for hours." Edmund's voice was quiet and carefully neutral as he adjusted the instruments in his medical bag. "Your name. Only your name."

"Nell." Dominic spoke again, thrashing now. His bandaged head tossed against the linen and his hands clawed uselessly at the heavy sheets. "Don't go… don't leave me… Nell..."

She couldn't breathe. She couldn't think. She could do nothing except move. She crossed the room in three quick strides and sat upon the edge of the bed, taking his hand firmly in both of hers.

His skin was cold and his fingers felt limp. But when she touched him, his expression changed. The tension in his jaw eased and his thrashing slowed. His whole body seemed to turn toward her, much like a flower seeking the sun.

"I am here." She whispered the words, squeezing his hand like she could pull him back to the surface. "Dominic. I am here."

He went still. The frantic movements stopped, and his eyes fluttered, half opening to reveal clouded, unfocused depths of grey. He stared at her as if he were not entirely sure she was real, like she might dissolve into the shadows if he were to blink.

"You came." A ghost of a smile touched his lips, weak and full of wonder. "I thought I was dreaming. I am always dreaming of you."

"You are not dreaming." She brought his hand to her cheek, pressing his cold fingers against her warm skin. "I am here. I am real."

His hand twitched in hers. It was weak, but it was there, trying to hold on to the anchor she provided.

"Don't leave." His eyes began to close again, the sheer weight of exhaustion pulling him back under. "Please… don't leave me..."

"I won't." The words came without thought or hesitation. She leaned closer to him. "I am not going anywhere."

He sighed. It was a sound that seemed to come from somewhere deep inside him, a final settling of his spirit. It was like he could finally rest, having received the permission he required. His breathing evened out, becoming deeper and steadier than it had been since the accident. His grip on her hand loosened, but he didn't release her.

She didn't let go.

Edmund watched from across the bed, his face a carefully maintained blank mask. Philippa stood in the doorway, one hand pressed hard against her mouth to stifle a sob while tears streamed silently down her cheeks. The room fell quiet, save for the rain lashing against the windows and the low crackle of the fire.

"He needs rest." Edmund finally broke the silence, the words clipped as he snapped his medical bag shut. "The next few hours will tell us more."

"Will he—" Nell couldn't finish. She looked down at the way her fingers were intertwined with Dominic's.

"I don't know." Edmund's reply was raw with a sudden, unexpected gentleness. He stepped toward the fire, the orange light catching the exhaustion in his face. "Head injuries are unpredictable. But he is strong. And he is calmer now than he has been all day."

Neither of them said the obvious reason why. Both of them simply knew.

"I should check the bandage." Edmund moved back to the head of the bed. "I must change the dressing."

Nell started to rise, intending to give him room to work, but Dominic's hand tightened on hers. It was a weak but insistent grip, an anchor he refused to let go of even in the depths of unconsciousness.

"Stay." The word was a ghost of a sound, barely a breath against the pillow. "Nell… stay..."

"I am staying." She settled back onto the edge of the mattress, her free hand smoothing the dark, matted hair back from his forehead. "I am not leaving."

Edmund worked around her, unwrapping the bloodied cloth and cleaning the wound with steady, practiced efficiency. But his eyes, when they briefly met hers across Dominic's prone form, held a painful clarity. He understood now why she'd said no that morning.

"You love him." He didn't ask; he simply stated it the way reading a final diagnosis.

She didn't deny it. She couldn't. "I didn't mean to." The confession was a mere thread of sound, an apology offered to the man she was hurting.

"No one ever does." Edmund finished wrapping the fresh linen and stepped back to gather his supplies. "I will return in a few hours to check his progress."

"Thank you." The words felt entirely insufficient for a man who had offered her his life and received only this revelation in return.

"Take care of him." Edmund fastened his bag, his posture

straight and his composure absolute. "He needs you more than he needs me at this moment."

He left then. He moved quietly, without looking back.

Chapter Twenty-One

Philippa brought a heavy chair upholstered in worn velvet and helped Nell settle beside the bed. The position was awkward, for Nell's arm had to stretch across the mattress to maintain her grip on Dominic's hand, but she cared nothing for her own comfort. Couldn't think about anything except the steady rise and fall of his chest, the warmth slowly returning to his fingers, the sound of his breathing in the quiet room.

"You should rest." Philippa stood beside the chair, her hand resting gently on Nell's shoulder. "I can sit with him for a while."

"No." Nell did not look away from Dominic's pale face. "I promised him I would stay."

Philippa remained quiet for a long moment, studying her. Then she nodded, a soft, knowing expression crossing her face.

"I will have them bring tea." She stepped toward the door, straightening her shoulders as if forcing herself to hold onto calm. "And something for you to eat."

Nell shook her head slightly, pressing a hand to her stomach as a wave of nausea twisted through her.

"Eat anyway." Philippa lingered at the threshold, one hand resting lightly on the doorframe as she looked back. "He will need you to be strong when he wakes."

When. Not *if.* Nell clung to the word like a lifeline, letting it anchor her as Philippa left.

At last, she was alone with him. She leaned over, studying his face now that the watchful eyes of the world had faded. In sleep, the sharp lines of his features softened, stripped of the armor he wore during the day. He looked younger this way. Vulnerable.

Her gaze traced the stark white ridge of the scar against his pale skin. Lower, she noticed the dark lashes resting against his cheeks and the rough shadow of stubble along his jaw. His lips were slightly parted, and his breath came slow and steady.

The room's quiet seemed to peel away the pressure of titles and reputation. This wasn't the powerful lord, the reckless rogue, for this was just Dominic.

"You idiot," she murmured, brushing her thumb along the knuckles of his hand, the motion tender but tinged with frustration. "Riding in a storm… what were you thinking?"

He didn't stir, his chest kept rising and falling in a calm rhythm.

Her hand clenched lightly in her lap. "You could have died." Her throat tightened, and she swallowed hard to push the words past the lump that caught in her throat. "You could have died, and I would have… I would have..."

She couldn't find the words for the void that would have opened beneath her feet.

"I was so scared." She admitted it to his sleeping face, the confession spilling out now that he couldn't truly hear it. "That's why I refused you. Not because you are reckless, or because of the ton, or because I cannot give you more children. It's because you terrify me."

He didn't stir, but his hand felt warmer in hers.

"You make me feel things I swore I would never feel again." The words were dredged up from a locked room in her heart. "After Gabriel… after everything he did to me… I promised I would never let anyone have that power over me again. And then you came along with your misty eyes and your reckless mouth, and I couldn't… I couldn't..."

She stopped to draw a shaking breath.

"But then Philippa came. She said you were hurt, and I couldn't think. I simply ran." She laughed, a wet and broken sound. "I didn't even hesitate. I didn't think of the children, or the shop, or what the neighbors would say. I just… came."

His hand twitched in hers. It was a small movement, but it was there.

"What does that mean?" She asked the quiet room and the flickering candles. "What does it mean when you run to someone without a single thought for yourself?"

She knew the answer. She'd known it all along, buried beneath the layers of fear, the denial, and the desperate need to protect herself from further ruin.

"I love you." She whispered the words, her lips brushing against his knuckles as she spoke into the quiet of the room. "God help me. I love you."

He didn't hear her. His breathing stayed even and his face remained peaceful, his hand resting still within hers. But she'd needed to say it. She needed it to be true in the air, even if only to herself.

The storm passed sometime in the night. Nell didn't notice when the rain stopped, nor when the thunder faded to a memory. She was watching him breathe, counting the rise and fall of his chest and tracking the colour as it slowly returned to his cheeks. She cataloged every twitch of his brow and every soft murmur he made in his sleep.

She didn't sleep. She couldn't.

Philippa came and went, bringing tea that grew cold in its porcelain cup and food that Nell didn't touch. The fire was stoked, the candles replaced, and blankets tucked more firmly around Dominic's still form. Servants moved in and out on quiet feet, speaking in hushed whispers and treating the sick-room like sacred ground.

Dawn arrived grey and pale, the light seeping through the gaps in the heavy curtains. Nell's back ached from her awkward position and her arm felt stiff from being stretched across the mattress all night. She didn't care. She could think of nothing except the warmth of his hand, the steady rhythm of his lungs, and the way his face looked in the growing light.

Edmund returned at first light. He carried his medical bag and his face was lined with exhaustion. He crossed to the bed and began his examination, checking Dominic's pupils with the light of a candle and pressing his fingers to the pulse at the man's throat. Finally, he unwrapped the bandage to inspect the wound.

"He is stable." Edmund spoke at last, rewrapping the linen with careful hands. "That's good. The swelling hasn't worsened."

"When will he wake?" Nell's voice came out hoarse and rusty from her long hours of silence. She cleared her throat.

"When he is ready." Edmund packed his bag and snapped

the latch closed with a sharp metallic click. "The body knows what it needs."

He paused at the door, looking back at her. He took in the dark circles under her eyes, her rumpled dress, and the way her hand was still clasped tightly around Dominic's.

"You haven't slept." He adjusted his coat, his gaze lingering on her tired form.

"I cannot." It was a simple, undeniable truth.

"He is lucky." Edmund said it in a low voice. Something unreadable crossed his face for a moment. "To have someone who refuses to leave his side."

"Edmund." She started to speak, not entirely sure what she wanted to say. Perhaps she meant to thank him, or perhaps to offer another apology for the pain she'd caused him.

"Don't." He held up a hand to stop her, his expression gentle and weary. "You don't need to apologize. I understand now. I think I always did."

He left then. The door clicked softly behind him, leaving her alone once more.

Nell turned back to Dominic, watching his face in the grey morning light. "Wake up." She whispered the plea, squeezing his hand like she could pull his consciousness back to the room. "Please. Wake up."

It happened slowly. A twitch came first. His fingers curled around hers with more strength than before. Then a groan followed, low and pained, as his head turned on the pillow. Movement stirred under his closed lids, as if he were fighting his way back through fog.

"Dominic?" Nell leaned closer. Her heart hammered against her ribs. "Dominic, can you hear me?"

His eyes opened. At first, they did not settle. He blinked against the pale light. Confusion clouded the grey.

"Where..." The word scraped out, little more than a dry friction against his teeth. He swallowed hard, his throat working with a visible, parched effort.

"Bramwell Park." She squeezed his hand, letting her fingers linger, and leaned close until the warmth of his body pressed against hers. "You're home. You fell from your horse."

He stared at her, disbelief etched across his face. "Nell?" The name hovered on his lips, fragile and searching.

"I'm here." She leaned closer, brushing her thumb over his knuckles, letting him feel her steady presence.

"You… you're here." His brow furrowed like the words themselves required effort. "But you… you told me to stay away."

"I know." Her thumb moved over his hand in a constant, soothing circle.

"You slapped me." A faint, almost incredulous smile brushed his lips.

She couldn't stop the twitch in her own. "You deserved it."

"Probably." His eyes closed briefly, then snapped open, trying to anchor himself to the moment. "Why are you here?"

"Philippa came for me." Her hand shook slightly as she kept it on his. She took a slow breath to steady herself. "She said you were hurt. She said you were saying my name."

"Always." His chest rose and fell with the word, his gaze sharpening, holding her with a mixture of wonder and need. "Always your name. Even in my dreams."

"Dominic..." She began, but he cut her off with a subtle tilt of his head.

"You came." Something like astonishment—or relief—softened his features.

"I came." She didn't move her hand from his, letting the grip anchor her.

"Why?" He searched her face, waiting for the answer she wasn't ready to give.

She swallowed, her lips pressed together. "Because I couldn't not come."

His hand tightened around hers, the pressure both urgent and grounding. "Say it again."

She repeated it, letting her chest rise with the words, though they came quietly. "I couldn't not come."

"No." His grip increased, steadying her. He didn't need to speak; the tension in his fingers said everything. He leaned toward her slightly, eyes unflinching. "What you said earlier. When you thought I was asleep."

Her stomach dropped. Heat and dread rushed through her. "You heard that?"

He blinked slowly, holding her gaze. "Say it again. Please. Nell. Say it again."

Her fingers trembled as they brushed his forehead, pushing a loose strand of hair back. She shook her head slightly and pressed gently, insistently, against his chest. "Rest. You need to rest."

"Nell." He tried to lift himself, wincing as the movement tugged at his injury.

"Later." Her hands held him firmly against the pillows. "We will talk later. When you are stronger."

His back teeth ground together, but the pressure of exhaustion claimed him. His grip on her hand loosened, though he didn't let go completely, while slowly, his eyelids fell, and his breathing evened as he drifted into deep sleep.

She stayed.

Hours later, Philippa found her still seated beside him, clutching his hand, her head resting lightly against the chair's back. The afternoon sun had turned watery, spilling pale light across the room.

"He woke." Nell's hand didn't move. Her gaze stayed fixed on him, unblinking. "He spoke to me."

Philippa sank into the chair opposite, pressing a hand to her chest. Relief washed over her in slow waves. "Thank God. I was so afraid."

"I know." Nell replied.

A comfortable silence settled between them. The worst of the fear had finally passed.

"He asked why I came." Nell said quietly, her eyes fixed on Dominic's sleeping face. "I didn't know what to tell him."

"Did you not?" Philippa's voice was gentle and knowing.

Nell finally looked at her friend. She saw the woman who had raised him and who understood the truth long before Nell had been willing to accept it.

"I was so determined to be sensible." The words tumbled out of her now. "I was so determined not to make the same mistakes I made with my late husband, Gabriel. I wanted to protect my children, and I wanted to build a life that no one could take from me. And then you came and said he was hurt, and I… I couldn't stay away."

"You love him." Philippa said it as if it were the most obvious fact in the world.

"I refused him." Nell's voice cracked.

"And yet here you are." Philippa gestured toward their

intertwined hands. "You've been here all night. You haven't let go of his hand once."

Nell looked down at their fingers. His large hand engulfed her smaller one, holding on even in his dreams.

"I don't know how to do this." It was a whisper, barely audible. "I don't know how to let myself..."

"You don't have to know." Philippa leaned forward. "You just have to stay."

Stay. It was a simple word, yet it felt like the most terrifying thing in the world. She looked at Dominic, his breathing steady and the colour returning to his face, and she'd come when he needed her. She hadn't hesitated.

Perhaps that was the only answer that mattered. She didn't let go of his hand.

Chapter Twenty-Two

The fire had burned to embers.

Nell sat in the chair beside his bed, her hand still wrapped around his. She watched the shadows shift across the ceiling, tracing the slow movement of light. Hours had passed since he'd briefly woken, since he'd asked her to say it again and she'd deflected, since exhaustion had pulled him back under. The clock on the mantel read half past two in the morning. The storm had long since passed, leaving nothing but silence and the occasional creak of the old house settling around them.

She should sleep. Her vision burned with exhaustion. Her back ached from the awkward position. Her body felt heavy with the weight of the day. Each time she started to drift, her mind dragged her back.

She replayed Philippa in the doorway of the shop. She saw the panic on her face. She saw Dominic lying pale and bloodied in this very bed.

He almost died.

The thought kept circling, a vulture that wouldn't land. He

almost died, and when he was fading, he'd called for her. Only her. Even when he couldn't remember his own name, he'd remembered hers.

She lifted his hand to her lips, pressing a kiss to his knuckles. His skin was warmer now, his breathing deep and even, but the colour had returned to his face. He would be all right—and Edmund had said so. He would recover.

But she'd come so close to losing him. So close to never—

His fingers twitched in her grip. She went still, her heart lurching. His hand tightened around hers, not the weak flutter from before, but something stronger and more deliberate. His head turned on the pillow, and a low groan escaped his throat.

"Dominic?" She leaned forward, searching his face in the dim light, her free hand reaching to touch his cheek.

His eyes opened. They were not unfocused and clouded like before, but clear and alert, grey as winter rain in the moonlight streaming through the curtains. He stared at her for a long moment, drinking her in like a man dying of thirst.

"You are still here." The words scraped out, dry from hours of silence. His fingers tightened around hers, a sudden, fierce pressure the way he were trying to anchor himself to the living.

"I said I would be." She squeezed his hand, her thumb stroking across his knuckles in a rhythmic, soothing motion.

He didn't look away from her face. His expression cracked open, a flash of determination or the stubborn set of his jaw that she'd come to know so well.

"You deflected earlier." He pushed himself up slightly on the pillows, wincing as the movement pulled at his injuries. "When I asked you to say it."

Her stomach dropped, and she pressed her lips together to keep them from trembling. "I know."

"Say it now." His iron eyes burned into hers, his hand pulling hers closer to the center of his chest. "Please, Nell. I need to hear it when I am not half-unconscious. When I can remember it properly."

She wanted to. God, she wanted to. The words sat on her tongue, burning to be spoken and aching to be released. But she couldn't. Not yet. Not like this.

"I cannot." She watched the flicker of hurt cross his face, and her heart cracked all over again. "Not until you know."

"Know what?" He tried to push himself higher on the pillows, his jaw clenching against the pain.

"Don't." She was on her feet instantly, her free hand pressing gently against his shoulder to ease him back down. "You will hurt yourself."

"Then tell me." He caught her wrist, his grip surprisingly strong. His thumb pressed against her pulse, feeling the frantic rhythm there. "Whatever it is. Tell me."

"It's not that simple." She shook her head, her hair falling loose around her face in a dark curtain.

"It's that simple." His thumb traced circles on the inside of her wrist. "You tell me. I listen. Nothing changes."

"You don't know that." She looked away, her chin trembling as she avoided his gaze.

"I know I love you." He tugged her wrist, pulling her attention back to him. "I know nothing you say will change that."

"You say that now." She pulled her wrist free, wrapping her arms around herself like a sudden chill had entered the room.

"I will say it forever." He reached for her hand again, his fingers gentle but insistent. "Sit. Please."

She sat, choosing the edge of the bed this time to be closer than the chair. Moonlight spilled through the window illuminating the bandage wrapped around his head.

Now or never. She drew a shaking breath.

"My name is not Ashford." The words forced their way out against her will. Her hands twisted in her lap, fingers tangling in the fabric of her skirts.

He went still beside her, his breath catching in his throat. But he didn't let go of her hand.

She stared at their joined fingers, unable to meet his eyes. "My name is Eleanor. Eleanor Whitmore. I changed it nine years ago. When I ran."

"Ran from what?" He stroked his thumb across her knuckles, watching her with a steady, patient intensity.

"From everything." She choked on the word and pressed her free hand to her stomach. "From who I was. From what I had done. From a dead man and a burning house."

They were both quiet for a long time. Then finally, Dominic broke the silence.

"Tell me." He squeezed her hand, an invitation rather than a demand.

She looked at him, this man who had proposed to her, who had defended her to the village gossip, who had called her name when he was dying. If she told him, he might hate her—he might look at her with disgust instead of love. But if she didn't tell him, she would never be free.

"I was seventeen when I met Gabriel Hyde." She turned to face the window, finding the glass easier to look at than his face. "My father was an esquire. Respectable. I was supposed to marry well and be a good, obedient daughter."

She paused, her shoulders hunching. "Gabriel was none of

those things. He was handsome. Charming. He said all the right things."

Dominic's hand tightened on hers, but he remained silent, allowing her the space to continue.

"I thought he loved me." She shook her head, the old shame rising like bile. "I was seventeen and stupid, and I believed every word he whispered." She shifted her gaze to the far corner of the room. "He asked me to elope. To marry in secret." She pressed her nails into her palms, the old shame rising like bile. "My mother begged me not to go. She pressed her jewelry into my hands and wept. She knew I'd need it. As for my father... He stood in the doorway and told me I was no longer his daughter. And I ran anyway."

Her fingers tightened around his. "We married in a small church with strangers for witnesses. My father disowned me that same week. My mother never wrote. I never heard from either of them again."

Dominic's thumb continued its steady, warm stroke across her knuckles.

"The first few months were not bad. Gabriel was attentive. We moved often because he said it was for work." Her expression turned brittle, the softness of the memory vanishing. "I didn't question it."

She pulled her hand from his and wrapped her arms around herself. "Then I learned what he really was."

The fire crackled, a sudden spark jumping in the hearth. She stared into the glowing wood.

"He'd lost badly at cards. He owed a man named Blackett more than he could pay." The name seemed to scrape her throat like broken glass. "Blackett came to collect. The man was thick-necked. Pig-eyed. Reeking of tobacco and sweat."

She could still smell him. She could still feel those heavy hands on her arms.

"Gabriel smiled at him. That charming smile I had fallen in love with." Her nails dug into her own arms through her sleeves. "And he gestured toward me like I was a horse he was selling."

The bed creaked. Dominic had gone rigid, his entire body tensing under the linens.

"He told Blackett I was his for the night. That we would be even." She forced the words out flat and distant, the only way she could bear to say them. "Payment for a gambling debt."

"Nell—" Dominic's words were a strangled rasp. He reached for her, his hand trembling slightly in the air.

"Blackett grabbed me. He started dragging me toward the bedroom." She didn't flinch from the memory. "I screamed. I begged Gabriel to stop him. He just poured himself a drink and watched."

Dominic's breathing had gone ragged, his chest heaving like he were the one struggling for air.

"So I fought." Something fierce flickered in her chest, a spark of the girl she'd been. "I clawed Blackett's face. Three deep gouges from his eye to his jaw. He was bleeding so badly he threw me to the floor and left."

"Good." The word ripped out of Dominic, savage and raw. His hands fisted in the sheets, knuckles white.

"Gabriel didn't think so." She touched her cheek, phantom pain ghosting across the bone. "He beat me until I couldn't stand. He said I had cost him. He said next time, I would do as I was told."

Dominic was shaking now. She could see it, the tremor in his shoulders and the vein pulsing at his temple.

"There were other nights." She kept her gaze fixed ahead, though her heart was hammering. "Other men he owed money to. I learned to lock myself in the cellar when he had that look in his eye. I never let them touch me, but there were nights I wasn't sure I'd manage it."

"I am going to kill him." Dominic didn't raise his volume, but the words carried a terrifying weight. He stared at the far wall like the surface of a frozen lake. "I wish he were alive simply so I could kill him again."

His jaw worked, his whole body vibrating with barely contained fury. He nodded once—a sharp, jagged movement—for her to continue.

"Twice I fell with child and lost them both." She pressed her hands flat against her knees, smoothing the fabric with slow strokes. "After the second, I went to an apothecary's wife in the village. She gave me herbs—pennyroyal and tansy—to keep from conceiving again. Gabriel found them." Her throat closed around the words, but she forced them through. "He beat me for it. And then he forced himself on me until I was with child again."

"I was pregnant, disowned, and married to a monster." She stared at her own hands as though they belonged to someone else. "There was nowhere to go."

"By the time I was eight months along, I learned that Gabriel had killed a man over card games. He was in hiding. I just knew I had to leave. Not for my own sake, but for the babies." She paused, her gaze flickering to the candle on the bedside table. "The midwife told me there were two. Twins. I hadn't known until then."

Dominic drew a sharp breath, his chest rising and falling beneath his linen shirt.

"I had saved money, coins snatched from the housekeeping. There was some of my mother's jewelry left" She began to pick at a loose thread on her shawl. "I just wanted to leave him before he came back from his hiding."

Her breath hitched, her throat seizing up.

"But luck was against me. Gabriel came home exactly the day I planned to leave." She flinched, her shoulders hunching at the memory. "He found my bag. He found the money and the note with directions to the coaching inn."

She wrapped her arms around herself, pulling her shawl tighter.

"He told me he would teach me what happened to wives who tried to leave." She looked down at her feet. "I don't remember exactly what happened next. It's all fragments." She leaned in close. "Him grabbing me. Falling. A candle on the dresser. And then fire."

"The curtains caught first, then the bedding." She flared her nostrils as if she could still smell the acrid smoke. "Gabriel was shouting, trying to put it out. And I just… I ran."

"I didn't look back." A sob finally broke through, and she squeezed her eyes shut. "I just ran until I could no longer breathe. The house burned to the ground." Her expression went vacant. "They found a body in the ruins, charred beyond recognition."

"Gabriel?" Dominic pushed himself up on the pillows, his brow still furrowed with a barely leashed rage.

She nodded then pulled her knees to her chest, making herself small. "Yes. I saw it." She forced the words out, her jaw trembling. "Saw what was left of him and the constable told me I was a widow."

"I went to an old friend, Margaret, a vicar's widow." She

stared into the dancing flames of the hearth. "But Gabriel's debts followed me. Collectors arrived at her door within weeks, demanding payment for a dead man's sins."

"I couldn't drag her down with me." She pulled her shawl closer to her neck. "So I sold the last of my mother's jewelry. I changed my name from Hyde to Ashford, and I vanished."

"I gave birth in a charity hospital." She placed her hand on her stomach. "I told them I was a widow, that my husband died in an accident."

"Lily almost killed me coming into the world." Her fingers curled against her belly like guarding a wound. "The doctor said it was a miracle I survived. That another pregnancy would likely..." She stopped and took a jagged breath. "That's why I told you I might not be able to give you children. It's not age, Dominic. It's damage."

"Four years I spent running from town to town." A hollow, mirthless laugh escaped her. "Then I found this village. I bought the shop and built something that was mine."

"I have been Nell Ashford for nine years." She brought her hand to her forehead, shielding her eyes. "Some days I forget Eleanor Whitmore ever existed."

"But she did exist." She turned to face him, letting him see the fear, the shame, and the desperate hope in her eyes. "She was seventeen and foolish, and she eloped with a monster because she thought his charm was love."

"That's who I am, Dominic." She forced herself to hold his gaze, her chin lifting despite the trembling of her lips. "A woman who was offered to men like livestock. A woman who left her husband to burn and felt nothing but relief. A woman who walked away from a corpse and never looked back."

"That's the truth. Every ugly piece of it." She finished, her hands going still.

The clock on the mantel ticked once, then twice. She stopped breathing, waiting for the blow.

"Come here." He held out his hand.

She didn't move, her whole body rigid with terror. "Did you hear what I said?"

"Every word." He held out his hand again, patient and steady, his fingers open in an invitation. "Come here."

"I might have killed a man." She pressed her back against the hard wood of the bedpost, her shoulders shaking with the force of the confession.

"You survived." He kept his hand extended, his expression calm and certain. "Come here. Please."

She crossed the distance slowly, like a creature approaching a cliff's edge. He took her hand when she finally reached him, pulling her down to sit on the bed beside him.

"You think this changes how I feel?" His thumb traced slow, soothing circles on her palm.

"It should." She stared at their joined hands, unable to meet his gaze.

"It doesn't." He lifted her hand to his lips and pressed a lingering kiss to her knuckles. "You were seventeen. You were trapped. You did what you had to do to survive."

"But I might have..." She broke off, the words dissolving into a jagged sob.

"You saved yourself." He gripped her hand tighter. "That's not murder. That's survival."

"The law wouldn't see it that way." She shook her head, trying to pull her hand back from his.

"The law doesn't know what it's like." He caught her hand

again, refusing to let her retreat. "To be trapped. To be beaten. To have no way out."

"You cannot just..." She tried to stand, her look probing the shadows for an exit.

"I can." He tugged her back down, pulling her into his space. "I can, and I am."

"Why?" The word tore out of her, ragged and raw, as she pressed her free hand against her mouth. "Why do you not hate me?"

"Because you are the bravest woman I have ever known." He cupped her face with his free hand, tilting her chin up to meet his eyes. "Because you built a life from nothing. Because you raised two children alone. Because you survived."

"I ran." Her composure fractured, and she tried to turn her head away.

"Running is not weakness." His hand slid to the back of her neck, holding her gently but firmly. "Sometimes running is the only strength we have."

Her eyes burned with unshed tears. She wouldn't cry.

"I have spent nine years hiding." She gripped his wrist, the confession spilling out in a rush. "Waiting for someone to recognize me. Waiting for Gabriel's family to come looking. Waiting for everything to fall apart."

"And now?" He stroked his thumb along her jaw, watching her with intense focus.

"And now you know." She met his gaze, finally letting him see the entirety of her soul. "Everything. Every ugly piece."

"There's nothing ugly about surviving." He pulled her closer, until their foreheads nearly touched.

"You cannot just forgive this." She placed her palm against his chest, feeling the steady thrum of his heartbeat.

"There's nothing to forgive." He covered her hand with his, holding it against his heart. "You told me the truth. That took more courage than anything I have ever done."

"Dominic." She struggled to speak, her breath hitching as she looked away.

"I love you." He spoke the words like a vow. "Eleanor. Nell. Whatever name you choose, I love you. I loved you before I knew this, and I love you more now that I do."

She couldn't breathe. She couldn't think. She could only stare at him, this man who should hate her, who had every reason to walk away, yet who was still holding her hand like she were the most precious thing in the world.

"You know my worst secret." She clutched his hand tighter, her knuckles turning white. "And you still..."

"Still love you." He finished for her, leaning forward to press his forehead against hers. "Still want you. Still need you."

"How?" The question was a broken, wondering whisper as she searched his face.

"Because you are you." His thumb traced her cheekbone, catching a tear she hadn't felt fall. "Because you are fiery and stubborn and maddening. Because you make me want to be better. Because when I was dying, yours was the only name I remembered."

The tears came then. She couldn't stop them anymore, and they spilled hot and fast down her cheeks.

"Say it." He urged her, pulling her closer until his breath was warm against her lips. "Now. When you know I know everything."

She looked at him, really looked, past the bandage and the bruises to the man beneath. This was the man who had defended her, proposed to her, and nearly died calling her name. He knew her darkest secret and loved her anyway.

"I love you." The words came easy now, freed from the pressure of secrets, and she cupped his face in her hands. "I love you, and it terrifies me."

"Why?" He leaned into her touch, his look tracing her face for the source of her fear.

"Because I loved Gabriel once." She stroked her thumb across his cheekbone, her gaze honest and raw. "Or I thought I did. And look how that ended."

"I am not Gabriel." He turned his head, pressing a firm kiss to her palm.

"I know." She traced the line of his jaw, careful to avoid the bandage at his temple. "I know you are not. But I am still scared."

"Of what?" He caught her hand and held it against his stubbled cheek.

"Of trusting this." She gestured between them with her free hand, a small, helpless motion. "Of letting myself believe it's real."

"It's real." He turned his head again, pressing another kiss to her palm. "I will prove it. Every day. For as long as you let me."

She stared at him, her heart cracking open. "You mean that."

"I have never meant anything more." He pulled her hand to his chest, pressing it against the steady beat of his heart.

"Dominic." She started, her breath hitching as tears threatened again.

"Say it again." He pulled her closer, his hand sliding to the back of her neck to anchor her. "I want to hear it again."

"I love you." She leaned into him, her forehead pressing against his. "I love you."

"Again." He breathed the word against her lips.

"I love you." She laughed, the sound wet and broken and free, her fingers threading through his dark hair. "I love you, I love you, I love..."

He kissed her, swallowing the words right out of her mouth. His lips were desperate against hers, his hand tangling in her hair to hold her steady. She gasped against his mouth, pulling back just enough to speak, her hands braced on his shoulders.

"Dominic, you are hurt." Her hands hovered over him, shaking.

"I don't care." He tried to pull her closer, wincing at the movement, his grip tightening on her waist.

"You will hurt yourself." She held him down to the pillows, her fingers curling into the fabric of his shirt.

"Then hurt me." His hands found her waist, large and warm through the fabric of her dress. "I need you. Please. I need..."

"Dominic." She tried to protest, even as her body leaned toward the heat of him.

"I almost died." The admission broke in the back of his throat, raw and jagged, his iron eyes dark with an unmasked hunger. "I almost died, and all I could think about was you. Your face. The memory of you. The way you taste."

"We shouldn't." She shook her head, even as her fingers curled into the linen of his shirt, grounding herself to him.

"I need to feel you." He pulled back just enough to look at her, his chest heaving the way he'd just run a mile. "I need to know you are real. That this is real. That I am not dreaming."

She should say no. He was injured and weak, and he needed rest, not the fire of this moment. But the way he looked at her—as if she were the only thing keeping him tethered to the world—decided it.

"Please." He exhaled the word against her lips, his hand cupping her cheek with a reverence that made her heart stall.

She kissed him, her mouth providing the answer he sought. He groaned against her lips—a sound of profound relief and desperate want—his hands pulling her closer.

"Slowly." The instruction was a soft breath against his mouth, her fingers tracing the sharp line of his jaw. "We do this slowly. Carefully."

"I don't want careful." He nipped at her lower lip, his hands sliding down her back to the small of her spine, pulling her flush against him.

"You are getting careful." She pulled back and met his eyes, letting him see the steel behind the softness. "Or you are getting nothing."

He laughed—a surprised, breathless sound that made his chest shake beneath her palm. "Stubborn woman."

"You love it." She traced a finger along his collarbone, feeling the fevered heat of his skin.

"I do." He reached for her, his fingers catching the fabric of her sleeve. "God help me, I do."

She rose from the bed, but his hand caught her wrist instantly, his grip tight with a sudden, sharp desperation.

"Don't go." He searched her face, panic flickering in the depths of his pupils.

"I am not going anywhere." She reached for the buttons of her dress with her free hand, her fingers trembling as she worked. "I am just… making it easier."

He went perfectly still, his eyes locking on her hands and tracking every movement. The buttons slipped free, one by one, for moonlight spilled through the window, silver and cold, painting her skin in pearl. She let the dress fall, the silk pooling at her feet with a quiet whisper.

Stays and chemise remained—but even those felt like a wall between them.

"Come here." The command was pure gravel, rough with a want that seemed to vibrate in the air as his hands reached for her.

She climbed onto the bed, careful to straddle his thighs without putting weight on his injuries. His hands found her hips immediately, large and trembling.

"You are shaking." She touched his face, tracing his jaw with her fingertips.

"I have wanted this for so long." He stared up at her, his thumbs pressing into the curve of her hips. "I didn't think you'd ever..."

"I know." She leaned down and brushed her lips against his. "I was afraid."

"And now?" He slid his hands up her sides, his touch reverent.

"Still afraid." She admitted, her breath mingling with his. "But more afraid of losing you."

He reached for the laces of her stays, his fingers fumbling in his eagerness.

"Let me." She helped him, loosening the ties and tugging at the fabric until the stays fell away.

He pulled the chemise over her head, his eyes never leaving her body. She was bare in the moonlight. He stared at her like he'd never seen anything so beautiful, his hands hovering just above her waist.

"You are perfect." He breathed, his palms finally settling on her skin.

"I am not." She tried to cover herself, arms crossing over her breasts as she curled inward.

He caught her wrists, gentle but firm, pulling her arms away. "Don't hide from me."

"I am not young." The words spilled out faster than she could think. "I've had children. My body isn't..."

"Your body is a miracle." He released her wrists, his hands finding her waist and the soft curve of her stomach. "You grew two lives inside you. You survived. Every mark on you is proof of that."

Tears threatened again, and she blinked hard. "Dominic."

"Let me worship you." He pulled her down toward him, his lips brushing her collarbone. "Please. Let me show you."

He kissed her throat, his touch soft and reverent, as if she were something sacred. Then he moved to her collarbone, his lips tracing the bone with a warm, gentle pressure, his breath hot against her skin. He moved lower still to the swell of her breasts, his hands cupping their weight while his mouth trailed heat across her flesh.

She arched into him, her fingers threading through his dark hair, careful to avoid the bandage. "Dominic."

"I have dreamed of this." He murmured the confession against her skin, his mouth trailing lower as his hands mapped the curve of her waist. "Every night since the maze. Sometimes even before."

"Before?" She gasped as his lips found the sensitive underside of her breast, her head falling back.

"Since the first time I saw you." He took her nipple into his mouth, sucking gently, while his hands tightened on her hips.

She gasped, her fingers tightening in his hair as her back arched off the linens.

"Since you threw that sovereign back at me." He switched to the other breast, his tongue tracing slow circles around the peak. "I knew then."

"Knew what?" She barely forced the words out, her breath coming in short, ragged gasps.

"That you'd ruin me." He looked up at her, his eyes dark as midnight and his lips swollen from her touch. "And I wanted you to."

She kissed him then, a hard and claiming thing. She poured everything into the contact, the love, the fear, and the desperate need that had been building since the first moment she'd seen him in her shop. Her hands found the hem of his shirt, tugging it upward. He hissed when she pulled it over his head, the movement jostling his injuries and forcing his jaw to clench against the pain.

"Did I hurt you?" She froze, her hands hovering uncertainly over his bare chest.

"Don't stop." He yanked her back down, his mouth finding hers again, hungry and desperate.

His chest felt warm and solid beneath her palms. The scar from Waterloo was a raised ridge beneath her fingers, and the bandages wrapped around his ribs served as a reminder of how close she'd come to losing him. She kissed the scar, tracing it with her tongue. He groaned, a deep and guttural sound, as his hips shifted beneath her and his hands gripped her thighs.

"I need..." His hands fumbled at her drawers, desperate and clumsy in his haste.

She helped him, kicking the silk away until she was finally bare against him. His hand slid between her thighs, and his pulse kicked when he found her already wet and ready for him. His fingers parted her slick folds with a trembling touch.

"God." He breathed the word, his eyes fixed on her face like memorizing her. "You are..."

"I know." She rocked against his hand, the need coiling tight in her belly. "I have wanted you too. Every night since the maze. Longer."

He slid a finger inside her, and she bit back a cry, her nails digging into his shoulders. "I need to taste you." He tried to shift beneath her, his hands gripping her hips to move her toward his mouth.

"No." She pinned him down, one hand flat on his chest to keep him still. "You will hurt yourself."

"Nell." He groaned in protest, his fingers still moving deep inside her.

"I said no." She reached for his breeches, her fingers working the fastenings with steady intent. "Tonight, you stay still. Tonight, I take care of you."

His eyes went black, his breath catching in his throat. "That might kill me faster than the fall."

"Then die happy." She freed him from his breeches, wrapping her hand around the hot, hard length of him.

He was straining, leaking at the tip, and when she tightened her grip, he choked out a sound, half groan and half sob, as his head fell back against the pillows.

"Nell… I cannot… I won't last." His hands gripped her hips, his whole body trembling with the effort of restraint.

"Then don't." She rose up, positioning herself over him

until she felt the blunt head of him pressing against her entrance.

She sank down slowly, taking him inch by inch. She let her body adjust to the stretch and the overwhelming sensation of finally having him inside her. He gripped her hips, his fingers digging in hard enough to leave marks, his teeth ground together until a muscle jumped in his cheek.

"God." He gritted out the word through his teeth.

She stilled for a moment, adjusting to his weight. He was bigger than she'd expected, thicker and more substantial.

"Are you..." He started to ask, his whole body rigid.

"I am fine." She breathed the reassurance, her hands braced on his chest. "Just… give me a moment."

He didn't move. He simply watched her, his chest heaving, every muscle taut, though then she moved, rolling her hips to test the friction. His head fell back against the pillows, his throat working as he swallowed.

"Oh, fuck!" He dragged her against him, his arms tightening like iron bands.

"Language, my lord." She almost laughed, rolling her hips again to hear him gasp.

"You try being polite when..." He choked as she lifted and dropped, his hands spasming on her hips. "Christ."

She found a rhythm, slow and deep, careful not to jostle his battered ribs. His hands slid up her body, cupping her breasts and thumbing her nipples.

"You are so beautiful." He breathed, staring up at her with eyes dark with want. "Look at you. Taking what you want."

"Is this what I want?" She ground down against him, watching his face contort with pleasure.

"God, I hope so." He surged up, capturing her nipple in his mouth and sucking hard.

She cried out, the angle shifting to hit something deep inside her that made stars burst behind her eyes.

"There." He held her hips, guiding her movements with a rough voice. "Right there."

"Dominic." His name came out broken and desperate.

"I have you." He thrust up, gentle yet relentless, his hands steadying her. "I have you."

The pleasure built, coiling tight in her belly.

"I am close." She gasped, her rhythm faltering as her thighs began to tremble.

"Look at me." He tilted her chin down with one hand, forcing her eyes to meet his. "Look at me when you come."

She met his gaze, grey and dark and full of love.

"Say it." He thrust deeper, a jagged catch in his throat. "Say it when you come."

"I love you." The words tore out of her, raw and uncontrolled. "I love you, I love..."

She shattered. The orgasm crashed through her in waves, her whole body shaking as her inner walls clenched around him. He followed her over the edge, a guttural groan of her name—both of her names—escaping as his hips jerked beneath her.

"Nell. Eleanor. God. I love you." The words tore out of him, ragged and desperate, his forehead pressed to hers.

She collapsed against his chest, careful even now of his injuries, her whole body trembling with aftershocks. They breathed together, hearts pounding in tandem, bodies still joined.

"Did I hurt you?" The question was a faint breath against his skin, punctuated by a kiss to his collarbone.

"Yes." He let out a breathless, broken laugh, his arms wrapping around her to pull her tight. "It was perfect."

"You are impossible." She nipped at his shoulder, smiling against the salt of his skin.

"You love it." He stroked his hand down her spine, a gesture both possessive and tender.

"I do." She pressed a kiss to his chest, right over his heart. "God help me, I do."

They lay tangled together, her head on his shoulder, his arm wrapped securely around her. Moonlight had shifted while they slept, shadows sliding across the ceiling, the fire reduced to ash in the grate.

"I meant what I said." His words rumbled deep in his chest beneath her ear, his fingers tracing slow, absent patterns on her bare back.

"Which part?" She mirrored the motion on his chest, her fingertip following the familiar ridge of his scar.

"All of it." His arm tightened, pulling her closer. "I love you. I want to marry you. I want to raise your children as my own."

"We can't talk about this now." She curled her fingers into the front of his shirt, as if she could physically hold the solid press of his words at bay.

"Why not?" He caught her hand and held it there, directly over his heart.

"Because you're injured," she whispered, her fingertip

tracing the edge of the bandage. "And exhausted. And possibly delirious."

"I've never been more clearheaded in my life." He lifted her hand to his mouth, his lips lingering on her knuckles.

"Dominic—" she began.

"I'm not asking for an answer." He kissed her hair, warm lips brushing her temple. "Not tonight. Just… know that I meant it. Every word."

Silence settled between them—comfortable now, safe.

"Eleanor," he murmured after a long moment, his fingers still moving gently along her back.

"Hmm?" She was already drifting, warm and sated in his arms.

"I like it." The quiet laughter in his chest vibrated against her, a phantom smile felt rather than seen. "It suits you."

"No one's called me that in nine years." She pressed closer, her leg sliding between his.

"Then I'll call you both." He yawned, exhaustion finally winning. "Nell in public. Eleanor in private. When we're like this."

"Like what?" She tipped her head back to look at him.

"Naked." His hand slid down her back, coming to rest possessively on her hip. "In my bed. Where you belong."

"Bold assumption." She raised an eyebrow, fighting a smile.

"Am I wrong?" He squeezed her hip, his eyes soft with certainty—and love.

She didn't answer. Because he wasn't wrong, though she did belong here. With him. In his arms.

"Sleep," she whispered, pressing a kiss to his shoulder. "You need rest."

"Stay." His arm tightened, holding her close.

"I'm not going anywhere." She settled against him, her head fitting perfectly into the hollow of his shoulder.

"Promise?" His words blurred as sleep claimed him.

"Promise." She kissed his collarbone.

His breathing slowed, deepened, evening out as he slipped fully into sleep. She watched him in the dark—this man who knew her secrets, who loved her anyway, who wanted her children as his own.

For the first time in nine years, she wasn't afraid.

Not running. Not hiding.

Just here. In his arms. Where she belonged.

"I love you," she whispered into the darkness, her lips brushing his skin.

Even asleep, his arm tightened around her.

She closed her eyes. And finally, peacefully, slept.

Chapter Twenty-Three

One week had passed since she'd told him everything. Seven days since she'd whispered her real name into the dark of his bedroom and waited for him to turn away. Seven days since he'd pulled her close instead and kissed her like she was something precious, something worth keeping.

Nell opened the shop that Tuesday morning and caught herself humming a low, lilting tune. She stopped at once. Then looked around the empty bakery like someone might have heard. The ovens crackled. The bread rose in its pans.

She was humming.

When had she started doing that? She couldn't remember the last time she'd hummed anything. Not since before Gabriel, yet not since before the fire. Not since she'd become the kind of woman who kept her head down and her mouth shut, never drawing attention to herself.

But this past week, something had shifted. The world felt lighter, brighter. It was like someone had scraped the grime off a window she hadn't realized was dirty. She woke up smiling, and she went to bed smiling. She smiled at customers who used to irritate her, at the weather that used to feel like a personal offense, and at the empty street that used to make her nervous.

It was terrifying.

Happiness never lasted. That was what life had taught her. Happiness was a trap, a lure, a pretty lie that made the fall hurt worse when it inevitably came. Gabriel had been charming once, too, but Gabriel had made her smile once, too.

But Dominic was not Gabriel.

She knew that now, knew it in the marrow of her bones, in the place where truth lived. Dominic was reckless and impulsive and maddening, but he was not cruel—and he didn't weaponize kindness. He didn't make her feel small so he could feel big. He looked at her as if she were the sun, and when she told him her darkest secrets, he'd held her closer instead of pulling away.

Still, the happiness scared her.

She went back to kneading dough, letting the familiar rhythm settle her nerves.

Press, fold, turn. Press, fold, turn.

The dough felt warm and alive under her palms, the yeast doing its quiet work. This, at least, she understood—yet this, at least, she could control.

The door to the back room creaked open.

Lily's head appeared, dark curls escaping her braid, her eyes bright with the particular gleam she wore when she was about to say something she thought was clever. Oliver followed a moment later, his whittling knife tucked into his belt and his expression carefully neutral in that way that meant he was paying very close attention to something.

"Mama is humming." Lily leaned toward her brother, her stage-whisper carrying easily across the room. She pressed one hand to her chest in mock horror, her eyes wide and mischievous. "Again."

"She has been doing that all week." Oliver rolled his eyes, but the corner of his mouth twitched upward as he leaned against the doorframe. "It's getting embarrassing."

"I can hear you both." Nell didn't look up from her dough, but she couldn't quite keep the smile off her face. "You are not as subtle as you think."

Lily bounced over to the counter, propping her chin in her hands and watching Nell work with that intense, curious focus she'd possessed since she was a baby. The girl had never learned to look at anything halfway. She gave everything the full force of her attention, whether it was a book, a butterfly, or her mother's suspicious good mood.

"Is it because of Lord Westmore?" Lily asked the question innocently enough, but her eyes were too sharp for nine years old. "Do you like him?"

Nell's hands stuttered on the dough. She recovered quickly, but not quickly enough.

"Lord Westmore and I are friends." Nell smoothed the top of the dough, but the word felt inadequate, almost laughably so.

What else could she say? She couldn't tell her nine-year-old children that she'd spent the past week sneaking to Bramwell Park after they fell asleep. She couldn't admit she'd slept in his bed more nights than her own, or that she'd told him she loved him and neither of them had taken it back since.

Oliver made a sound that might have been a cough or a snort.

"Friends." Lily drew the word out like taffy, her grin spreading. "Is that why you were humming?"

"I hum sometimes." Nell looked at the flour on her hands, avoiding their gaze.

"No, you don't." Oliver crossed his arms, leaning against the wood with an air of patient skepticism that made him look far too much like a tiny adult. "You never hum. You barely even smile. And now you are doing both. All the time."

"Since Lord Westmore." Lily added helpfully, tapping her fingers on the countertop.

Nell set down her dough. She wiped her hands on her apron and turned to face her children with what she hoped was a reasonable expression and not the flustered guilt she felt written across her face.

"Lord Westmore is..." She paused, trying again. "He has been… We've become..."

"You *do* like him." Lily's smile was so wide it threatened to split her face. "You *really*, *really* like him."

"I..." Nell began, but she was interrupted.

The shop bell jangled.

Nell's head snapped toward the sound with embarrassing speed. And there he was. Dominic filled the doorway as he always did, his broad shoulders blocking the morning light and his dark hair still slightly damp from a morning bath. The bruise at his temple had faded to a sickly yellow-green, and he moved a little stiffly still, but his eyes were clear and alert as they fixed on her.

A week. They had enjoyed a week together, and she still was not used to the way he looked at her. It was like she were something rare, something he couldn't quite believe was real.

“Lord Westmore.” Nell steadied herself against the counter, her heart hammering. “You are supposed to be resting.”

“I have rested enough.” He stepped inside, not bothering with the pretense of browsing the tarts. His eyes swept past the display cases and the bread cooling on the racks, seeing nothing but her. “I have business to attend to.”

“Business.” She raised an eyebrow, trying to find her composure. “In my bakery.”

“Important business.” He nodded toward the doorway where her children still stood, watching this exchange with fascination. “Can I meet the children?”

“Yes!” Lily waved from her spot, bouncing on her toes.

Oliver said nothing. He simply watched Dominic with that careful, measuring look he’d maintained since the first time they had met. The boy trusted slowly, and Nell loved him for it. She’d trusted herself slowly.

“Good.” Dominic moved past Nell without touching her, though she felt the heat of him as he passed. He was close enough that she could smell soap and something woodsy. “I need to speak with them.”

“Speak with them about what?” Nell stepped forward, reaching instinctively for his arm.

He turned to meet her eyes. Something in his expression made her breath catch, a mixture of nervous determination and barely contained joy.

"Trust me." He covered her hand with his and squeezed once, then let go. "Stay here."

"Dominic." She whispered his name, her hand falling back to her side.

But he was already walking toward the kitchen. Her children fell into step beside him as if it were the most natural thing in the world. Lily practically skipped. Even Oliver seemed curious, his earlier wariness softened into cautious interest.

The door swung shut behind them.

Nell stood alone in her shop, flour on her hands and confusion churning in her chest. What was he doing? What business could he possibly have with her children that required privacy? What required leaving her out here to wonder?

She moved toward the kitchen door but stopped herself. He'd asked her to trust him; he'd asked her to stay. She stayed, but she pressed her ear against the door anyway, just for a moment. The wood was thick. She could hear the low rumble of Dominic's voice and the higher pitch of Lily's, but no words reached her. It was just sound without meaning, tantalizing and frustrating.

Fine. She would wait.

She went back to her dough and kneaded it with more force than necessary, trying very hard not to think about what was happening in her kitchen.

In the kitchen, Dominic pulled the door shut and turned to face the two most important judges he would ever encounter.

Lily dropped into the chair by the fire and pulled her book into her lap, though her attention clearly had no interest in the story. She was all bright eyes and eager curiosity, bouncing slightly where she sat. Oliver settled at the table, picked up his whittling knife, and fixed Dominic with a look of serious appraisal.

These were Nell's children. Her fierce, protective, too-grown-up children who had watched their mother struggle to build something from nothing. They had learned that adults couldn't always be trusted — and now they were deciding whether to trust him.

Dominic had faced down cavalry charges at Waterloo. He'd held the line when men were dying around him. He'd stood before the entire ton in London after Vivienne broke off the engagement, let them stare at his scar, and dared a single one of them to speak. None of that had prepared him for this.

"Lord Westmore." Lily scrambled to her feet, her book tumbling to the floor. "Mama said you were hurt. Are you better now? Does it still ache? Mama says head wounds can be tricky."

"I was hurt." Dominic pulled out a chair and settled himself across from Oliver with deliberate calm. "I am better now. May I speak with you both?"

Oliver went still. His hand drifted back to his whittling knife, though he did not pick it up. He did not make a threat. He made it clear he was paying attention, and that he would protect what was his.

"Good." Dominic nodded, respecting the boy's vigilance.

"About what?" Oliver's voice was carefully flat as he picked up a scrap of wood.

"About your mother." Dominic kept his gaze steady.

The kitchen went quiet. Even the fire seemed to crackle more softly, as if it, too, were waiting to see what would happen next. Lily had gone still, her usual boundless energy temporarily suspended. Oliver's lips pressed into a thin line, his fingers curling tightly around the edge of the table.

Dominic took a breath and let it out slow.

"I love her." He offered no preamble, no pretty words, and no careful hedging. It was the truth, plain and simple. "I want to marry her."

Lily's mouth fell open, a small squeak of surprise escaping her. Her eyes went enormous, filling her whole face. Oliver didn't move. He didn't blink. He simply stared at Dominic with an expression that was impossible to read.

"Marry her?" Lily's voice came out breathless as she clutched her skirts. "You want to marry our Mama?"

"If she will have me." Dominic nodded, keeping his attention on both children. He watched their reactions, trying to read the thoughts hidden behind their youthful features. "But I wanted to ask you first."

"Ask us?" Oliver's frown deepened as he set the wood back down. "Why?"

"Because you are her family." Dominic leaned forward, resting his forearms on the table to meet the boy's suspicious gaze without flinching. "Because if I marry her, I am not just becoming her husband. I am becoming part of your lives too. That's not something I should decide without you."

Oliver said nothing, his mind clearly processing the mass of the statement. Lily, meanwhile, looked as if she might explode from the effort of staying quiet. Her hands were pressed over her mouth, and her whole body practically vibrated with what could only be described as violent joy.

“I know I am not your father.” Dominic remained perfectly still, his posture open and unthreatening. “But I would like to be… something. If you will let me.”

“Something like what?” Lily dropped her hands to her lap, her curiosity finally winning out over her attempt at restraint.

Dominic searched for the words to describe the life he was offering them.

“Like someone who is there.” He shrugged one shoulder, a small, genuine smile tugging at the corner of his mouth.

"Someone who takes you fishing. Someone who lets you read first editions until your eyes go crossed. Someone who makes your mother smile."

"She has been smiling more." Lily beamed, her wide, infectious grin returning. "She has been humming. Humming! She never hums."

"Has she?" Dominic couldn't quite suppress his own grin. The image of Nell happy enough to hum sent a strange, complicated thrum through his chest.

"You really love her?" Oliver's question landed hard.

Dominic met the boy's eyes and held them. "More than anything."

"She has been hurt before." Oliver's chin lifted with defiant pride, his small hands curling into fists on the tabletop. "Our father… I think he was not kind to her."

Dominic went stone-still. He'd known, of course — Nell had shared her truth in the quiet of his bedroom — but hearing it from Oliver was something else entirely. The boy had never met his father, yet he'd gathered enough to piece the story together on his own. He knew far more than Nell realized.

"I know." Dominic's response was a rough friction in his throat. He cleared it, forcing himself to settle. "She told me."

A crack formed in Oliver's expression—surprise, perhaps, that his mother had shared that particular secret with an outsider.

"And you still want to marry her?" Oliver's gaze searched Dominic's face for any hint of a lie.

"I want to spend the rest of my life making sure no one ever hurts her again." Dominic didn't blink, letting the boy see the iron-clad promise in his eyes. "Including me."

The room went still. Lily looked from one to the other like

a spectator at a match, her excitement suspended as she waited for her brother.

"What if you change your mind?" The question broke, betraying the fear beneath Oliver's bravado. "What if you decide you don't want us?"

"I won't." Dominic reached out, though he didn't touch the boy, keeping his hand palm-up on the table—an open invitation.

"How do you know?" Oliver pressed, his stare tracking.

Dominic leaned forward, ensuring their gazes were locked. "Because I have already decided. I am not asking your mother to marry me despite her having children, and I am asking her because of who she is. You are part of who she is. The best part, maybe."

Oliver's jaw worked. His eyes shone with unshed tears, though he fought to keep them back.

"If you hurt her..." The boy's words hitched, but he forced them out. "If you ever hurt her..."

"Then you've my permission to gut me." Dominic nodded toward the whittling blade on the table. "I mean it. You have my word. If I ever make her cry from cruelty, you can hold me to account."

Oliver's expression loosened by a degree. The suspicion didn't vanish—trust would take more than a single afternoon—but a crack appeared in his armor.

"Lily?" Dominic turned to the girl, who looked ready to burst. "What do you think?"

She bit her lip, clearly savoring the drama of the interrogation, before her face split into the widest grin he'd ever seen.

"I think you should have asked ages ago." She laughed, her heels drumming a happy rhythm against the chair legs.

Dominic's own laughter followed—a real, loose sound that felt entirely unrehearsed. Lily giggled in response, clapping her hands with delight.

"So?" He looked between them, his heart hammering harder than it had any right to. "Do I have your blessing?"

Lily's head bobbed so vigorously her curls bounced. "Yes. Absolutely yes. A thousand times yes."

They both looked at Oliver. The boy was silent, wrestling with the conflict playing out behind his too-old eyes.

"If you make her cry." Oliver spoke with a slow cadence, his eyes moving from the knife back to Dominic. "I will never forgive you."

"I will make her cry." Dominic met the threat with quiet honesty. "Sometimes. We will fight. We will disagree. But I will never make her cry from cruelty. Only from joy. Or from being stubborn."

"She is stubborn." The corner of Oliver's mouth twitched, just barely, as he looked down at his wood carving.

"Impossibly stubborn." Dominic agreed, leaning back with a small huff of a laugh. "I love that about her."

Another silence followed. It lasted longer this time, filled only by the rhythmic scraping of the boy's knife. Then Oliver nodded once, a sharp, decisive motion.

"Fine." He picked up his knife and went back to his whittling like the most important conversation of his young life were already behind him. "You can ask her."

"Thank you." Dominic rose from his chair, his expression solemn as he treated the moment with the gravity it deserved. "Both of you."

"When are you going to do it?" Lily bounced on her heels, unable to contain herself any longer. She clutched the back of a kitchen chair. “Can we watch? Please? Please, please, please?”

“Tonight.” Dominic headed for the door, his steps lighter than they had been when he entered. “At the carnival.”

“The carnival?” Lily gasped, pressing both hands to her cheeks. “In front of everyone?”

“In front of everyone.” He paused at the threshold and looked back at them. “She deserves to know I am not ashamed of her. I want the whole world to see.”

“That’s so romantic.” Lily sighed, the word coming out dreamy and drawn out as she stared at the ceiling. “Like something from a novel.”

Oliver rolled his eyes, but he was smiling now. He didn’t try to hide it anymore as he worked his blade.

“Not a word to your mother.” Dominic pointed a finger at them both, his eyes twinkling. “It’s a surprise.”

“We won’t tell.” Lily mimed locking her lips, then throwing away the key with a dramatic flourish. “Promise. Cross my heart.”

Dominic left the room. Behind him, he heard Lily squeal into her hands and something that might have been a rare laugh from Oliver.

Two down. One to go.

Nell was waiting when he emerged from the kitchen. She stood in the middle of her shop with her arms crossed and a smudge of flour on her cheek. She wore an expression that told him she’d spent the entire time he was gone trying to figure out what he was up to.

“What was that about?” She stepped toward him, her eyes bright and curious, a faint tilt to her head as she tried to read him.

"Nothing." He tried for an innocent smile, though his racing pulse betrayed him.

"Nothing." She echoed the word, her gaze narrowing as she crossed her arms. "You walked into my kitchen, shut the door, and had a private conversation with my children about nothing."

"That's right." He shrugged, letting a teasing smirk tug at his lips.

"You are a terrible liar." She shifted a step closer, eyes probing his face, searching for a crack in his composure.

"I am an excellent liar." He stepped forward, closing the space between them with measured ease, letting the heat from his body brush against hers. "You just know me too well."

She didn't flinch. Nell never did. Her chin lifted, her stance steady, her look sharp and unyielding, even as he pressed her gently back against the counter.

"Dominic..." She tilted her head slightly, a faint exhale escaping her as she studied him, the tension between them humming like a wire ready to snap.

"Are you going to the carnival tonight?" He changed the subject before she could interrogate him further, reaching out to steady himself on the wood beside her.

She blinked in confusion. "I… What?"

"The winter carnival." He reached up and tucked a strand of dark hair behind her ear, letting his fingers linger on the soft skin of her cheek. "In the village square. Are you going?"

"I usually take the children." She was distracted now. His nearness always scrambled her thoughts in a way that pleased him immensely. "Why?"

"I will meet you there." He leaned down and brushed his lips against her forehead. "Wear something pretty."

"What are you planning?" She reached for his lapels, her brow furrowing.

"Nothing." He pulled back just enough to meet her eyes. "I just want to see you."

"You are seeing me now." She pointed out, her breath hitching.

"I want to see you more." He kissed the corner of her mouth, a light and teasing touch. "I want to see you under the lanterns. Dancing."

Her composure fractured. He felt it, the tiny vibration in her chest.

"What did you say to my children?" She asked, though her resolve was clearly melting.

"Things." He grinned, stepping back toward the door.

"Dominic!" She called after him.

He kissed her properly this time. It was quick but thorough, enough to make her forget what she'd been asking, for when he pulled back, her eyes were slightly glazed.

"Tonight." He stepped away before she could recover. "The carnival. Do come please."

Then he was gone, out the door and into the morning sun. He left her standing in her bakery with flour on her hands and confusion on her face. From the kitchen, he heard the sound of muffled giggling.

Nell closed her eyes and drew a long breath. He was definitely up to something.

Chapter Twenty-Four

The first frost had come early this year, and the village had dressed itself accordingly. Braziers glowed at every corner, their coals spitting orange sparks into the black November sky. Evergreen boughs had been strung between the shopfronts, tied with red ribbon that snapped in the bitter wind. A bonfire crackled at the centre of the square, tall enough that the heat reached the far stalls, where vendors sold roasted chestnuts from iron drums and ladled mulled wine into tin cups that steamed in the cold. Children chased each other between the legs of adults, their cheeks raw and bright, their laughter sharp as glass in the frozen air. A fiddler played somewhere near the bakery, the notes thin and sweet against the crack and hiss of burning wood.

Nell arrived with the children as the sun was setting, painting the sky in shades of orange and pink. She'd worn her green silk dress, the one she'd worn at the harvest festival. The same one she'd kept hidden in the back of her wardrobe. It was perhaps a bit too fine for a village carnival, but Dominic had asked her to wear something pretty, and she'd found herself wanting to please him.

That alone should have told her something.

"Mama, you look so pretty." Lily had said it three times already, each time with the same breathless awe. She tugged on Nell's hand as they walked through the crowds. "Like a real princess. I adore this dress."

"It's just a dress." Nell adjusted her shawl, suddenly feeling quite self-conscious under the glow of the lanterns.

"It's the most beautiful dress ever!" Lily grinned, her expression far too knowing. "Can I have it when I am older?"

"Of course, my love." Nell smiled at her daughter, lovingly.

Oliver walked on her other side with his hands shoved in his pockets. He wore an expression of studied casualness that didn't fool her for a second, while he kept glancing at his sister, and Lily kept glancing back. They were both terrible at hiding things.

"All right." Nell stopped walking and turned to face them both. "What is going on?"

"Going on?" Lily's eyes went wide and innocent as she looked at a nearby stall. "Nothing is going on. Why would anything be going on?"

"You've been acting strange all day." Nell crossed her arms.

"We have not." Oliver muttered, looking at his boots.

"You helped me pick out this dress." Nell reminded them.

"Because you looked pretty in it." Lily bounced on her toes, gesturing to the silk. "Is it a crime to want your Mama to look pretty?"

Oliver coughed into his hand. Nell narrowed her eyes at him.

"Can we get sweets?" Lily grabbed her brother's arm, already tugging him toward the nearest vendor. "Please? I saw honey cakes. I love honey cakes."

"Go on." Nell sighed, recognizing a losing battle. "Stay together. Don't wander off."

"We won't." Lily was already pulling Oliver into the crowd. "Promise!"

They disappeared, their giggling trailing behind them. Nell stood alone in the middle of the carnival, surrounded by villagers and lantern light.

It was all so normal. So why did she feel as though the very air hummed before a storm?

"Nell." Daphne appeared at her elbow, materializing out of the crowd. Her grin was even wider than Lily's had been. "You look lovely."

"You too." Nell frowned at her friend, suspicious of everyone now. "You are smiling."

"I smile sometimes." Daphne smoothed her own bodice, her eyes darting toward the center of the square.

"Not like that." Nell's eyes narrowed further. "You know something."

"I know many things." Daphne linked their arms together, steering Nell through the crowd with determined cheerfulness. "Come. Let us walk."

"Daphne..." Nell tried to slow her pace.

"Look, there's Mrs. Potts. Wave to Mrs. Potts." Daphne urged, lifting her own hand.

Nell waved automatically, still trying to figure out the

mystery. Everyone she passed seemed to be smiling at her, like they were all participants in a secret she'd yet to be told.

There was Lady Philippa, standing near the cider vendor with her silver hair gleaming in the lantern light. She caught Nell's eye and offered a warm, encouraging smile that appeared slightly tearful. Nearby stood Lady Catherine, and beside her a tall man Nell did not recognise — lean and fair-haired, with an easy grin fixed on the stage like a boy at a puppet show. Both of them watched Nell with expressions of pure anticipation. Even Edmund hovered at the edge of the crowd, his kind face neutral but his eyes gentle as they met hers.

"Daphne." Nell stopped walking and gripped her friend's sleeve. "What is going on?"

"Look." Daphne simply nodded toward the small stage where the musicians had been playing.

The music had stopped. Dominic was climbing onto the platform.

Nell's heart seized in her chest. It forgot how to beat. She forgot everything except the sight of him. He looked tall and broad in his dark coat, the fading bruise at his temple barely visible in the golden light. He stood at the center of the stage and scanned the crowd until he found her.

Their eyes met, and he smiled. It was the smile that transformed his face, making him look young and hopeful, nothing like the brooding viscount he often pretended to be.

"What is he doing?" Nell's voice came out strangled as she pressed a hand to her throat.

"Just watch." Daphne squeezed her arm firmly. "Trust me."

"If you will indulge me." Dominic's voice carried across the square, cutting through the murmur of the crowd.

He waited as the village fell silent, faces turning toward their viscount with looks of curiosity and concern.

"I have an announcement." He cast the words to the furthest reaches of the square, his posture commanding and tall.

Whispers rippled through the gathered neighbors. Mrs. Pemberton, stationed near the front, began to fan herself with theatrical vigor.

"Some of you know that I recently had an accident." Dominic touched his temple where the mark was fading. "A stupid thing. A spooked horse. It was my own fault for riding in a storm."

Murmurs of sympathy rose from the villagers. Nell's hands were shaking, but she pressed them flat against her silk skirt, trying to anchor herself.

"What you may not know..." Dominic paused, his eyes locking onto hers across the sea of faces with a sudden, searing intensity. "…is that during my recovery, I had a visitor. Someone who sat by my bedside all night. Someone who held my hand and told me she loved me when she thought I couldn't hear."

Oh God.

Nell's face went hot, then cold. Every head in the crowd turned toward her, drawn by the direction of Dominic's stare like iron filings to a magnet.

"I could hear." He said it directly to her, ignoring the gasps and scandals erupting around them. "I heard every word."

Mrs. Pemberton let out a sound like a scandalized teakettle—and someone near the back whistled, low and impressed.

"Nell Ashford." He named her with a reverence that felt like a prayer. "Would you come up here?"

Her legs wouldn't move. She remained rooted to the spot, her heart hammering so hard she could feel the pulse in her throat. Daphne gave her a firm push.

"Go." Her friend's eyes were wet as she nudged her forward. "Go on."

The crowd parted like the Red Sea. Faces blurred past as she stumbled toward the stage, her own ragged breathing the only thing she could hear over the crunch of her shoes on the packed earth. She climbed the steps on legs that felt like they belonged to someone else. Dominic took her hand the moment she reached the top, his fingers wrapping around hers to steady her.

"Breathe." His lips brushed her ear, the word intended for her alone. "I have got you."

"What are you doing?" She breathed back, her fingers trembling against his palm.

"I know what you are going to say." He smiled against her temple, his grip tightening. "Just let me finish."

He turned to face the crowd, still holding her hand, and threw his words out to the square.

"This woman..." He lifted their joined hands for the assembled villagers to see. "…is the most stubborn, infuriating, magnificent person I have ever met."

Laughter rippled through the crowd. Nell felt her face burn.

"She threw a sovereign back at me the first time we met." Dominic grinned at the neighbors, his eyes dancing with the memory. More laughter followed. Somewhere in the crowd, Nell heard Lily's distinct giggle.

"I fell in love with her then." The performative edge drained from his expression, replaced by a quiet, raw sincerity. "I have been falling ever since."

He released her hand and stepped back. To the shock of every soul present, he went to one knee, sinking into the mud without a second thought. The crowd gasped as one. Mrs. Pemberton actually clutched her chest as if she might faint.

Nell couldn't breathe. The world had narrowed to this man and this impossible gesture.

"I have asked everyone who matters." He held up a small velvet box, his hand shaking with a visible tremor. "Daphne gave her blessing this afternoon. Your children gave theirs this morning. Now I am asking you."

"We said yes already!" Lily's shout rang out from the crowd, high and joyful.

Laughter rippled through the square. Even Nell laughed — a choked, wet sound. Dominic opened the box. Inside, a simple gold ring caught the lantern light like a drop of fire.

"Marry me, Nell." Her name broke in the back of his throat. This man who had faced cavalry charges at Waterloo was now openly trembling on a stage before the entire village. "Marry me because I love you. Because I have loved you since you slid my coin back across that counter and told me sixpence would do."

She was crying properly now, tears streaming down her cheeks.

"Marry me." He looked up at her with raw hope on his scarred face. "Please. Say yes. Put me out of my misery."

The whole square held its breath. Nell looked at him — this man who had asked her children's permission, who was kneeling before everyone he knew, risking everything because he loved her.

"Yes." The word came out broken and in a whisper.

"What?" He cupped his hand to his ear, a grin breaking across his face. "I couldn't hear you."

"Yes." She said it louder this time, laughing through her tears. "Yes, you impossible man. Yes."

He slid the ring onto her finger. His hands were still shaking, and hers were no better. Then he was on his feet, pulling her into his arms and lifting her clear off the ground as the crowd erupted.

"She said yes!" He announced it to the sky, his face radiant. "She said yes!"

Cheers exploded. Daphne was sobbing loudly into a handkerchief.

"I love you." Nell whispered against his chest, her face pressed to the wool of his coat. "I love you, you mad, reckless, wonderful man."

"I know." He tilted her chin up to look at him. His eyes were bright and suspiciously wet. "I love you, too."

He kissed her then, in front of everyone. Deep, sure, and unhurried — a kiss that left no doubt about his absolute commitment to the woman in his arms.

Chapter Twenty-Five

"Hold still." The modiste circled Nell like a hawk assessing prey, her pins bristling between her lips as she tugged the measuring tape taut across Nell's shoulder. "You keep fidgeting, and I cannot work."

"I am not fidgeting." Nell shifted her weight on the small platform, making the cream silk whisper against her legs as she tried to find a comfortable stance. "I am breathing. There's a difference."

"You are fidgeting." Philippa didn't look up from her embroidery in the corner, her needle flashing silver in the afternoon light as it pierced the fabric. "You've been doing it since Madame Dupont arrived. Stand still and let the woman work."

The modiste, a sharp-eyed Frenchwoman who had arrived from London with three trunks of fabric and opinions about everything, made a sound of agreement. She jabbed another pin into the bodice. Nell flinched, sucking air through her teeth as the point grazed her skin.

"The dress is too fine." Nell touched the silk draped across her body, half-pinned and half-flowing. She ran a cautious finger over the seed pearls scattered across the fabric like stars fallen from heaven. "I will ruin it before I reach the altar. I shall spill something, trip on the hem, or set it on fire somehow."

"You won't." Dominic's voice came from the doorway, low and certain.

Nell's head turned on its own, the movement nearly dislodging a pin. He leaned against the frame with that particular lazy grace he possessed, arms crossed over his broad chest. He watched her with an expression that made heat bloom beneath her skin. His glacial eyes traveled slowly down her body, over the silk and the pearls and the curves the modiste kept muttering about accentuating rather than hiding.

"You shouldn't be here." Nell pressed one hand to her flushed cheek, her words coming out breathless as she caught his eye. "It's bad luck. Seeing the dress before the wedding."

"I am not looking at the dress." His gaze lifted to meet hers, dark and hungry and utterly unapologetic as he straightened his posture. "I am looking at you."

"Lord Westmore." Madame Dupont straightened to her full height, the pins clicking between her teeth like the bones of small animals. "This is most irregular. The bride's gown is not meant for the groom's eyes until the ceremony."

"I own the house." He didn't move from the doorway, nor did he shift his attention from Nell even for a second. "I will be irregular if I please."

Philippa sighed, her embroidery hoop dropping to her lap with a soft thump that echoed in the quiet room. "Dominic, really. Some traditions exist for a reason. You will jinx the whole affair."

"I don't believe in jinxes." He pushed off the doorframe and crossed the room in three long strides that ate up the distance between them. He stopped at the edge of the platform. For once, they were nearly the same height, with her standing on the raised surface and him on the floor below. "I believe in her."

"You are impossible." Nell shook her head, but she was smiling. She felt her heart doing complicated things behind her ribs.

"You love it." He reached up and tucked a stray strand of dark hair behind her ear, his fingers lingering at her temple with a tender touch. "You are beautiful. You know that?"

"The dress is beautiful." She caught his wrist, intending to push him away, but her fingers simply rested there against the steady beat of his pulse.

"The dress is fabric and thread." His thumb brushed across her cheekbone, feather-light, tracing the line of her jaw. "You are the one who makes it worth looking at."

Madame Dupont threw up her hands with a torrent of French that Nell suspected was not complimentary, the movement causing a few pins to scatter from her lips to the floor. Philippa laughed, soft and fond. She looked like a woman who had long since given up trying to control her nephew's whims.

"One week." Dominic cupped her face in both hands, his piercing eyes boring into hers with an intensity that made the rest of the room fade. "One week and you will be mine."

"I am already yours." The words slipped out before she could catch them, tumbling free like birds escaping a cage. She felt her cheeks flush at her own boldness.

His eyes darkened, the grey turning nearly black, and his

grip on her face tightened just slightly. "Say that again when we are alone."

"Dominic..." She barely got his name out before his mouth covered hers.

He kissed her, quick and fierce and entirely inappropriate given their audience. Nell heard Madame Dupont's scandalized gasp and Philippa's knowing chuckle—his mouth was warm and demanding, tasting of tea and wanting. When he pulled back, his grin was wicked as sin.

"One week." He stepped away and straightened his coat, nodding to the modiste with perfect aristocratic courtesy as though he hadn't just kissed his betrothed senseless. "Make her something magnificent, Madame. Spare no expense. I want the ton to weep when they see her."

Then he was gone, his footsteps fading down the corridor. He left Nell flushed and breathless on her little platform with pins poking her ribs and her lips still tingling from his touch.

"That man." Philippa shook her head, setting aside her embroidery with a rueful smile. "He has no sense of propriety whatsoever. Never has. Even as a boy, he simply took what he wanted and damn the consequences."

"No." Nell touched her mouth, feeling the ghost of his kiss. Her fingers trembled slightly as she looked toward the empty doorway. "He doesn't."

She was smiling and found she couldn't seem to stop.

The kitchen of the shop smelled of cinnamon and yeast, with late afternoon light slanting golden through the windows. Nell stood at the worktable, her hands buried in dough, and she watched her son from the corner of her eye.

Oliver sat at the smaller table by the hearth, whittling something she couldn't quite make out. His knife moved in careful strokes, shaving curls of wood that drifted to the floor like pale snow. He'd been quiet all afternoon. He was quieter than usual, which was saying something for a boy who measured his words like a miser counting coins.

Lily had already bounced off to practice her flower girl walk for what must have been the hundredth time. This left mother and son alone with the bread and the silence.

"The wedding is in a week." Nell maintained a steady, rhythmic motion as she worked the dough, her eyes pinned to the worktable. She pressed, folded, and turned the heavy mass with practiced ease. "Philippa says everything is arranged. The church, the breakfast afterward, the flowers..."

"I know." Oliver didn't look up from his whittling, his knife biting deeper into the wood.

"Lord Westmore's friend Alistair will stand up with him as his witness." She hesitated, watching the tension gather in her son's shoulders like storm clouds. "We haven't discussed who might… That's, I wanted to ask if you..."

"I will do it." The words scraped out, catching in his throat with that unpredictable, jagged quality that had begun to plague him as he hovered between boy and man. His knife stilled against the wood, and he finally looked up at her.

Nell's hands stopped deep in the dough. "Do what?" She searched his face, her pulse quickening at his sudden, heavy gravity.

"Walk you down the aisle." He didn't look at her, his jaw

set in a hard, pale line as his eyes fixed on the half-carved shape in his hands. "Give you away. Someone should do it. Since there's no one else." He shaved a long sliver of wood from the block, the movement jerky and uncoordinated.

The words landed in her chest like stones dropped in still water, rippling outward through places she kept carefully guarded.

"Oliver." She moved around the table to stand beside him. "Look at me."

He obeyed with a slow, reluctant turn of his head. His eyes were bright, shimmering with a vulnerability he was fighting with everything he had.

"You don't have to." She crouched until they were eye-to-eye, one hand resting on his knee.

"I want to." His expression hardened into a stubborn mask she recognized from her own mirror. He gripped the whittling knife until his knuckles turned a bloodless white. "Someone should do it. Walk you down the aisle. Give you to someone who..." The words fractured, and he jerked his head away, blinking back the moisture. "Someone should."

"Oh, love." She reached out, her hand finding the tension coiled beneath his threadbare shirt.

He stiffened at her touch, a reflexive flinch before he allowed himself to lean, just an inch, into her warmth. Then his shoulders finally dropped.

"You don't have to be the man of the house anymore." She kept her words low, rubbing small circles against the ridge of his spine. "You don't have to take care of me. That's not your job. It never should have been."

"Someone had to." The defence was fierce, snapping

through the quiet of the kitchen. He jabbed his knife into the tabletop, the blade sticking upright and quivering. "There was no one else. It was just us, and you were — you were always tired, Mama. Always working. And sometimes you would get this look, like something far away was hurting you, and I didn't know what it was but I knew I had to make sure nothing hurt you here."

Her heart cracked clean down the middle.

This boy. Her boy. He had never known Gabriel, never lived through the worst of it, but he had grown up in the long shadow of it. He had read the bruises that were already gone by the time he was born — not on her skin, but in the way she startled at a slammed door, in the way she checked the locks twice every night, in the hollow behind her smile when she thought no one was watching. He had appointed himself her protector without ever understanding what he was guarding her from.

"I know." She pulled him into her arms. He resisted for a heartbeat — a final holdout of pride — before his forehead thudded against her shoulder and his hands fisted in the fabric of her dress. "I know you did. And I am so proud of you, Oliver, so proud of the man you are becoming. But you can be a boy now. You can let someone else carry the weight."

"Lord Westmore." The name was a muffled vibration against her shoulder, thick and heavy with the tears he was finally letting fall.

"Yes." She pressed a kiss to the top of his head, breathing in the familiar scent of wood shavings and youth.

A long pause followed. She could feel him gathering himself, the rise and fall of his breath as courage built for the question he needed to ask.

"Will he —" Oliver pulled back just enough to look at her face, his eyes red-rimmed but fierce. His throat worked around the words. "He won't hurt you? He won't — change?"

The question broke something loose inside her chest. He did not know the details. He did not know Gabriel's name or what that man had done. But he knew, the way children always know, that something had happened to his mother before he existed. Something that left marks he could feel but never see.

"He won't." She cupped his face in her hands, holding his gaze. "I promise you. I would never marry a man who would hurt us. Never."

"I know." Oliver drew a shaky breath, his Adam's apple bobbing in his thin throat. "I just — I wanted to make sure."

"I know, love. I know." She brushed a stray tear from his cheek with her thumb, pretending not to notice it.

He straightened his shoulders, pulling himself together with visible effort — bracing himself, deciding to be brave.

"I still want to do it." His chin lifted, stubborn and proud, and he wiped his face roughly with the back of his hand. "Walk you down the aisle. Give you away. Properly. The way it should be done."

Nell's eyes burned. She blinked, but the tears escaped anyway, sliding hot down her cheeks. "Then you will." A knot of emotion tightened in her throat, making the words struggle to surface. "I would be honoured. Truly."

"Good." He nodded once, sharp and decisive, like they were discussing something as simple as what to have for supper. Then he yanked his knife free from the table, grabbed an apple from the bowl, and disappeared out the back door.

He left her alone with her tears and her half-kneaded bread

and the fierce, aching love that threatened to split her chest wide open.

One week.

One week until she would walk down that aisle on her son's arm and marry a man who looked at her like she was something precious.

She couldn't quite believe it was real.

It was a Tuesday morning, one week before the wedding.

The air was bright and bitter, winter settled deep into the bones of Hampshire. Frost had crept across the windows overnight, forming lacy patterns that caught the first light. Nell's breath fogged in the early hours before she got the ovens going, before warmth filled the shop and chased away the chill.

She opened the shop alone. Daphne was running errands, seeking fabric for her maid-of-honor dress and salt from the merchant three streets over. A dozen small tasks had accumulated in the chaos of preparations. The children were at their lessons with the vicar's wife, conjugating Latin verbs and practicing their penmanship. The shop was quiet and peaceful, while the smell of fresh bread filled the room.

Nell was humming again.

It was indeed strange to be happy.

The ring caught the morning light as she shaped the loaves, the small ruby winking like it held secrets. One week until she would be Lady Westmore. One week until she would stand before God and the village and promise herself to a man who had knelt in the mud and asked for her hand.

The thought still didn't feel real.

She thought about Dominic as she worked, her hands moving through the familiar rhythm of shaping dough. She remembered last night, when he'd come to the shop after closing, letting himself in with the key she'd given him weeks ago. He'd pressed her against the wall in the back room and kissed her until her knees buckled, until her fingers tangled in his hair and her body arched into his.

"I want our wedding night to mean something." He'd murmured the words against her throat, his breath hot on her skin while his hands gripped her hips. "I want to do this properly. Court you. Marry you. Make love to you as my wife."

"You are killing me." She'd gasped the reply, half-laughing and half-desperate, her head falling back against the wall.

"Good." He'd pulled back with a wicked grin, straightening his coat as if he hadn't just reduced her to a trembling mess. "Suffer a little. I have been suffering for months."

He was a stubborn, impossible, and maddening man.

She loved him. She loved him so much it terrified her.

The bell above the door jangled.

Nell looked up with a smile, ready to greet whichever neighbor had braved the cold for fresh bread.

The smile died on her face.

A man stood in the doorway. He was tall and broad, dressed in travel-worn clothes that had seen better days. Dust coated his boots, mud splattered his coat, and his hat was pulled low over his eyes, casting his face in shadow.

She didn't recognize him at first. He seemed like just another stranger passing through, perhaps looking for a warm meal and directions to the next town.

Then he stepped into the light.

The right side of his face was the same. It was the face she remembered from seventeen, from foolish promises and secret vows. His dark hair was threaded with grey now, and he possessed a sharp jaw and that mouth that had whispered love and screamed curses in equal measure.

The left side of his face was a ruin.

She saw it in pieces because her mind refused to take it whole. The jaw first—that sharp jaw she remembered—warped now beneath a knot of scar tissue that twisted from chin to temple, the skin pulled taut and shining like melted tallow. The colour was wrong. Mottled white and livid pink where the flesh had fused back together, and beneath it, ridges she could not look at and could not look away from. His left eye had been dragged downward at the corner, the lid sealed nearly shut by the same rippled scarring, and what remained of his ear was a gnarled stub—the fire had taken it almost to the skull. His hairline on that side was eaten away in ragged patches, the scalp beneath it smooth and tight and wrong.

He was half a man and half a monster. The fire had split him down the middle, leaving enough of the handsome face she remembered to mock her while the other half bore witness to what she had left him to.

It screamed of what she'd left him to.

Gabriel Hyde was very much alive.

The room tilted. The bread paddle slipped from her nerveless fingers, clattering against the counter loud as a gunshot. She grabbed the edge of the wood to stay upright, her knuckles going white and her vision narrowing to a single, impossible point.

That face. That ruined, impossible face.

"Hello, Eleanor." Gabriel removed his hat, letting her see

the full horror of the damage. His good eye glittered with sharp, calculated malice. "You look well."

She couldn't speak. Her lungs seemed to have forgotten their basic function as she stared at the specter standing in her shop.

He smiled—a gesture that pulled at his scars and stretched the ruined flesh until the right side of his mouth curved upward and the left remained frozen by the old damage. "Nothing to say?" He stepped further inside, his boots thudding heavy on the floor. The door swung shut behind him, the bell jangling with a cheerful, obscene ring. "You used to have so much to say, Eleanor. Before you learned better."

"You are dead." The words scraped out of her, raw and broken. She gripped the counter so hard her knuckles turned the colour of bone. "You died in the fire. They found a body —"

"That wasn't mine." He shrugged one shoulder, the movement pulling at the scarred skin of his neck. "Some vagrant who had frozen in the alley. Wrong place, wrong time. I just —" He spread his hands, palms up, casual as the morning weather. "Made use of him. You know how the authorities were looking for me."

Made use of him. He'd dragged a dead man's body into a burning house and let everyone believe—let *her* believe for nine long years—that he was ash.

"You let me think you were dead." Nell hated the way her frame shuddered, betrayal and fear bleeding through her defences despite every effort to hold them back.

"You seemed happier that way." A sneer twisted the unscarred half of his face as he moved closer, his presence swelling until the small shop felt like a cage. "Running off.

Changing your name. Building your little bakery. Being a widow." He curled his lip as though the very word were a foul taste. "Did you mourn me, Eleanor? Did you wear black and weep?"

"I survived." Anger surged hot and fierce through the shock, and she straightened her spine, forcing herself to meet his gaze. "I survived you."

"Survived." A harsh laugh scraped out of him. He jabbed a twisted finger toward his melted cheek. "Look at what you left me with. Nine years I have worn this face because my own wife left me to die in flames."

"You were beating me." Her voice rose, vibrating with fury and terror. Her hands curled into fists at her sides. "You were going to kill me. You found my bag, my money, and you —"

"I was teaching you." He cut her off, his expression going bone-dry and empty—the same hollow stillness she remembered from the worst nights. "Teaching you your place. And you ran."

He was close now, far too close. She could smell road dust and sweat and something sour underneath.

"The law says I died in that fire." He tilted his head, studying her the way a cat studies a cornered bird. "But now you know the truth. I am alive, which means you are still my wife."

The word buried itself between her ribs. *Wife.* The marriage had never been dissolved—how could it have been? One couldn't divorce a corpse, and one couldn't annul a union with ashes.

"What do you want?" She forced the question through numb lips.

He reached out with his left hand—scarred as well, the

fingers twisted and stiff—and touched her cheek. She flinched away, revulsion crawling across her skin. His eyes darkened, rage flickering in their depths before his hand dropped and curled into a fist.

"Ten thousand pounds." He said it slowly, savouring each syllable. "From your viscount. Call it compensation—for the years, for this face, for everything you took when you ran."

"He will never —"

"He will." Gabriel slammed his palm down on the counter hard enough to make the bread paddles jump. "Or I destroy you."

He reached into his coat and pulled out a folded paper, yellowed with age and creased from frequent handling. "Marriage certificate. St. Michael's Church, 1800. Gabriel Hyde and Eleanor Whitmore. Witnessed and signed." He held it up between two twisted fingers, letting her see the familiar ink. "One piece of paper, Eleanor, and your whole pretty life comes apart. The widow everyone pities was never a widow at all."

She'd forgotten about that certificate. She'd tried to forget everything about those years.

He tucked it away, patting his coat pocket. "How do you think the ton will react when they learn Lord Westmore's engagement is a farce? That his bride is a bigamist and a liar?"

Nell's hands were shaking. "Why now? Why wait nine years?"

"Because now you've got something worth taking." He looked around the shop with greedy eyes. "When you were just a baker with two brats, you were not worth the trouble. But a viscountess? That's worth a great deal." His lips curved into that terrible half-smile. "Ten thousand pounds, and I disappear. You will never see this face again."

"And if I refuse?" She lifted her chin, and something cold and hard crystallised in her chest. "If I tell everyone you are alive? Tell the magistrates in Leeds too—I am sure they would love to know where to find the man who killed someone over a card game."

Gabriel's smirk faltered. Fear flickered behind his eyes before rage swallowed it whole.

"Then I take everything." His hand shot out and grabbed her wrist, squeezing until she gasped and her knees buckled. She could feel the stiffness of his scarred fingers and the unnatural strength in that damaged grip. "Your reputation. Your children. Your viscount. I will burn it all down, Eleanor—just like you burned me."

"I didn't start that fire —" Tears pricked her eyes as pain shot up her arm.

"You left me in it." His grip tightened, grinding the bones of her wrist together as he leaned in, his words dropping to a predatory whisper against her ear. "One week. Bring me ten thousand pounds, or I destroy everything you love."

The bell jangled.

Gabriel released her instantly and stepped back, his features smoothing into hollow pleasantry. The transformation was horrifying—the monster tucked away behind whatever remained of the man in the blink of an eye.

Mrs. Potts stood in the doorway, a market basket over one arm and her grey hair tucked beneath a sensible bonnet. She looked between Nell and Gabriel with mild curiosity, her brow furrowing at the heavy, stagnant air of the room.

"Mrs. Ashford!" The neighbor swept further into the shop, the bell above the door offering a final, oblivious jingle. She bustled toward the counter, shaking out her umbrella with a bright smile that didn't acknowledge the rot in the room. "I came for my Tuesday order. Am I interrupting something?"

Nell's throat was so tight it felt fused shut. She pressed her lips together, forcing the breath through the lump of fear lodged in her chest.

"Not at all." The words held, though they felt as brittle as glass. She pressed her throbbing wrist against her apron, hiding the darkening skin from view. "This gentleman was just leaving."

Gabriel tipped his hat, carefully keeping the scarred side of his face angled into the shadows. Even in his rage, he remained calculating.

"Think about what I said, Eleanor." He kept the reminder low, intended only for her, his good eye glittering with a final promise of violence. "One week."

He brushed past Mrs. Potts with a polite nod, playing the role of a gentleman traveler. "Ma'am."

The bell jangled again. He was gone.

Nell's knees buckled. She caught herself on the counter, her arms shaking with the effort of staying upright.

"Mrs. Ashford?" Mrs. Potts hurried forward, her basket swinging as concern creased her weathered face. "You've gone white as flour. Are you ill? Should I fetch the doctor?"

"I am fine." The lie tasted like poison on her tongue and she forced a lingering smile. "I just felt faint. The heat from the ovens, I suspect."

Mrs. Potts fussed about the shop. She fetched water from the pitcher on the back counter and insisted Nell sit on the stool behind the display case. She clucked and worried, offering remedies her mother had used for fainting spells.

Nell barely heard a word. Gabriel was alive. He was alive

and he wanted money, and if she didn't pay, the truth would be her undoing.

She was still his wife. She couldn't marry Dominic; everything she'd built and everything she'd finally allowed herself to want was gone.

Mrs. Potts left eventually, her bread tucked into her basket and worried backward glances thrown over her shoulder. Nell sat alone in the empty shop—yet the ring glinted on her finger. It was a simple gold band with a small ruby, a promise she could no longer keep.

One week until her wedding. One week until she was supposed to stand before God and the village and pledge herself to the man she loved. Except she couldn't. The law said she belonged to a monster with a ruined face and the power to destroy her.

She could pay him. She could beg Dominic for ten thousand pounds. It was a sum that would barely scratch a viscount's fortune. But what would she tell him? That her dead husband had crawled out of the grave? That their engagement was built on a foundation of lies?

He would hate her.

She could run. She could take the children in the night and disappear as she'd done once before. A new name, a new town, a new life, but she was so tired of running.

She could tell Dominic everything. She could trust that he loved her enough to help her find a way through. But what if there was no way through the law?

The bell jangled.

Nell's head snapped up, her heart slamming against her ribs as her whole body tensed for flight.

Daphne stood in the doorway with her arms full of parcels,

her cheeks pink from the cold. Her grin faded the instant she saw Nell's face.

"What happened?" She dumped the parcels on the nearest table and crossed to the counter in three quick strides. "You are shaking. You are white as death. What has happened?"

"Gabriel." The name scraped out. Nell pressed both hands flat on the counter to stop their trembling. "Gabriel is alive."

Daphne went very still, the colour draining from her face. "What?"

"He was here." The words tumbled over each other. "Just now. He is alive, Daphne. He didn't die in the fire. He faked it, put someone else's body in the house, and he has been alive this whole time. His face… half of it's ruined. He blames me. He knows about Dominic, and he wants money or he will destroy everything."

"Breathe." Daphne grabbed her hands, gripping them tight enough to hurt. "Slow down. Tell me everything."

So Nell did. She recounted every horrible word, the threats, the blackmail, and the marriage certificate.

When she finished, Daphne's face had gone hard as iron. Her jaw set tight enough to crack her teeth. "That bastard." The words came out quiet and deadly. Her fingers tightened on Nell's until the bones creaked. "That festering, worthless piece of filth."

"What am I going to do?" Nell's voice cracked, and she felt the hot pressure of tears building behind her eyes. "I cannot marry Dominic. Not legally. Not while Gabriel is alive. And if I don't pay, he will ruin me." She pressed her fists against her eyes, trying to hold back the flood.

"We need to think. We need a plan." Daphne said.

"There is no plan." Nell dropped her hands, her fingers

numb and clumsy as she gripped the edge of the counter. "He has the marriage certificate. He has nine years of silence on his side. The law will call me a bigamist and him a wronged husband, and there is nothing—"

"You have Dominic." Daphne set both palms flat on the counter and leaned forward, her dark eyes fierce. "He has solicitors. He has magistrates who owe him favours. He has a title and money and the kind of influence that makes problems disappear. But he cannot help you if he does not know."

The words sat between them, heavy and undeniable.

Nell stared at the ring on her finger. The ruby caught the last of the afternoon light, winking like a secret. One week. She had one week before she was supposed to stand in a church and promise herself to a man she had been lying to since the day they met.

Not lying. Surviving. But it would feel the same to him.

"I have to tell him." The decision settled into her chest like a stone finding the riverbed. Not because Daphne had pushed her there. Because it was the only road left that did not lead back into the dark.

"Yes." Daphne straightened, her jaw still tight. "You do."

"Stay here." Nell pulled the shawl around her shoulders and knotted it at her chest, her fingers fumbling with the wool. "The children will be back from their lessons within the hour."

"Are you going alone?" Daphne caught her arm near the elbow, her grip hard with worry.

"I have to." Nell covered Daphne's hand with her own, then gently removed it. "This is mine to tell. He deserves to hear it from me, and I need to be the one brave enough to say it."

Daphne looked into her eyes for a long moment, something

shifting behind her eyes—respect, maybe, or grief for the girl Nell had been before Gabriel Hyde had taught her that love could be a weapon.

She walked out of the bakery. The bell jangled behind her, and the cold hit her like a wall.

Chapter Twenty-Six

The walk to Bramwell Park took twenty minutes. Every one of them was a war.

Nell's boots crunched on the frost-hardened path, her breath rising in thin white ribbons that dissolved the instant they left her mouth. The cold gnawed through her shawl and into her bones, but she barely felt it. Her mind was loud with the words she would have to say, and none of them sounded right.

I lied to you. Not on purpose. I thought he was dead—everyone thought he was dead. But he is alive, and his face is burned, and he hates me, and I am still his wife, and I cannot marry you.

The hedgerows along the lane were bare and skeletal, their branches scratching at the grey sky like fingers clawing for purchase. A crow lifted from a fencepost as she passed, its wings beating the silence apart. Somewhere behind her, the village carried on with its Tuesday afternoon—bread bought, fires stoked, children called in from the cold. None of them knew that the baker on Mill Street had just watched a ghost walk into her shop and demand ten thousand pounds.

The gates of Bramwell Park rose before her, wrought iron twisted into elegant patterns of leaves and scrollwork. Beyond them the great house loomed, stone and glass and centuries of history. She had stood inside that house a week ago while a modiste jabbed pins into silk and Dominic kissed her in front of everyone. She had been happy. The memory felt like something that had happened to a different woman in a different life.

Nell's steps faltered at the gate. Her hand found the iron latch. The metal bit cold through her glove. She pushed.

The gravel drive crunched beneath her feet, each step louder than the last. Past the dormant gardens, brown and sleeping beneath the winter sky. Up the wide stone steps to the front door. She knocked before her courage could bleed away.

The butler admitted her. His eyebrows lifted a fraction at her pallor, though his expression smoothed back to professional blankness before she could read anything in it. He led her to the drawing room and went to fetch Lord Westmore.

Nell stopped in the centre of the room. She could not sit. The fire crackled in the hearth, casting restless shadows along the papered walls, and pale winter sunlight slanted through the tall windows to lay golden rectangles across the carpet. The clock on the mantel ticked with the steady, merciless patience of a thing that did not care what happened next.

One week ago she had stood in this room while Dominic cupped her face and told her she was beautiful. One week ago the hardest thing in her world had been holding still for pins.

Footsteps sounded in the corridor. Fast. Heavy. Coming closer.

The door swung open hard enough to knock against the wall.

Dominic filled the doorway, his cravat crooked, his dark hair shoved back from his forehead as though he had dragged both hands through it more than once. His gaze found her instantly—swept her face, the tear tracks, the pallor, the way she stood in the middle of his drawing room like a woman bracing for a blow.

Every trace of colour left his skin.

"What happened?" He crossed the room in three long strides and caught her hands in both of his, his grip warm and fierce and desperate. "Nell. Are the children—"

"The children are fine." The words cracked down the middle, a jagged breath stealing the rest. She clung to his fingers, her knuckles bone-white. "I am not hurt. No one is hurt. I just—"

She could not finish. The confession sat lodged in her throat like a piece of broken glass, too sharp to swallow and too sharp to speak.

He waited. That was the thing about Dominic—when it mattered, he did not rush her. He did not fill the silence with questions or demands. He simply held her hands and watched her face with those grey eyes that missed nothing, and he waited for her to find the words.

She drew a breath. Then another. She looked at the floor, at the fire, at the buttons on his waistcoat—anywhere but his eyes. Then she forced herself to meet them, because he deserved that much. He deserved to watch her face when the lie came apart.

"Gabriel is alive." Three words. They left her mouth and the room changed—the air thickened, the fire seemed to dim, and the clock's ticking grew obscenely loud in the silence that followed.

Dominic did not move. His fingers remained locked around hers, but she felt the stillness spread through him the way ice spreads across a pond—surface first, then deeper, then all the way down.

"My husband." She forced herself to continue, though each word cost her something she would not get back. "The man who was supposed to have died in the fire nine years ago. He came to the shop this morning. He is alive. His face is—" Her throat closed. "He is burned. Badly. And he blames me, and he knows about you, and he has our marriage certificate, and he wants ten thousand pounds or he will destroy everything."

The words poured out at the end, rushing like water through a crack in a dam. She watched Dominic's face the way a sailor watches the horizon for storms.

For a long, terrible moment he did not speak. He did not seem to breathe. His face was utterly still, carved from something harder than marble—and only the faintest tremor in his fingers, the barest tightening of his grip, told her he had heard her at all.

Then his jaw clenched. A tendon stood out along his neck, and something cold and dangerous moved behind his eyes.

He released her hands. Stepped back. Turned toward the desk and braced both palms flat against the mahogany, his arms locked straight and his head bowed between his shoulders.

The silence stretched so long she thought it might kill her.

"Tell me everything." He did not look up. His back was a rigid line beneath his coat, his knuckles white against the dark wood. "From the beginning. Every word he said. Every threat he made. Do not leave anything out."

So she told him.

The winter light was fading by the time Nell finished.

She had told him everything.

They stood in the Bramwell Park drawing room, the fire crackling low in the hearth. Shadows gathered in the corners as the pale sun sank toward the horizon. She had spoken without stopping for what felt like hours, pouring out the whole miserable story while Dominic listened with a focused, ferocious stillness that made her feel as though she were the only person in the world who mattered.

"He has our marriage certificate." Her throat had gone raw, and she cleared it to continue. "St. Michael's Church, 1800. It is proof that I am still his wife in the eyes of God and the law."

Dominic's expression had not changed throughout her telling, but she could feel the tension coiling through him the way heat coils inside an oven before the door opens. His thumbs moved in slow circles over her knuckles — a gesture of comfort that sat at odds with the storm gathering behind his grey eyes.

She pushed back her sleeve and held out her arm. The marks were dark against her skin, each one a perfect imprint of Gabriel's grip. "He grabbed me when I refused. Squeezed until I thought the bones would snap."

For a long moment Dominic simply stared at the bruises. Then something shifted in his face. It was a look she had never seen before — cold, measured, and utterly without mercy — and it reminded her that this was a man who had survived

Waterloo. Who had killed with his bare hands and walked through fire to come out the other side.

"He touched you." The words came out flat, his jaw locked tight.

"Yes." She met his gaze without flinching.

He released her hands. Turned on his heel and crossed to his desk in three long strides. She watched him pull out paper and ink, his pen moving across the page in quick, decisive strokes that spoke of a mind already working three moves ahead.

"What are you doing?" She followed him, her skirts brushing the carpet.

"Writing to Magistrate Harding." He did not look up, the nib scratching against the parchment. "Reporting an assault on my betrothed and a threat of blackmail against a peer's household. I am also sending men to search every inn and boarding house within twenty miles."

He sealed the letter with a firm press of his signet ring, the Westmore crest biting into crimson wax. He rang for Graves, handed over the letter with clipped instructions, and turned back to her with a look that brooked no argument.

"We need to think about the children." He placed his hands on her shoulders, grounding her. "Somewhere safe. Somewhere Gabriel does not know about."

And then it hit her.

The children. The lessons with the vicar's wife would have ended an hour ago. They would have walked back to the bakery the way they always did — down the lane, past the churchyard, through the front door with its jingling bell. They would have found Daphne behind the counter and Martha upstairs.

Suddenly, Nell had a presentiment that something was wrong. Something dreadful.

"Dominic." She gripped his wrist, her nails biting through his shirtsleeve. "The children are due back at the shop. Daphne and Martha are alone."

The colour left his face. He did not waste a single breath on words. He crossed to the desk, pulled open the bottom drawer, and took out a pistol — checked the flint, the powder, the ball — and shoved it into his belt. A second pistol followed from the cabinet near the door.

"Graves!" The shout carried down the corridor like a cannon report. "My horse. Now. Both horses."

They were mounted and riding before the last of the daylight bled from the sky. Dominic pushed his horse hard, leaning low over the animal's neck, and Nell kept pace beside him with her skirts bunched in one fist and the reins in the other. The frost-hardened lane rang beneath the hooves. Neither of them spoke. There was nothing left to say that the horses were not already saying with every stride.

Chapter Twenty-Seven

The village came into view as the first lamps were being lit in cottage windows — small, warm squares of gold against the gathering dark. Ordinary people living ordinary evenings. None of them knew what was coming.

Nell saw it before they reached the door. The dread in her bones had not been misplaced.

The bakery sign hung crooked above the entrance, knocked sideways by some violence she did not want to name. The front door stood ajar, and a wedge of lamplight spilled across the cobblestones. A bread knife lay on the ground near the step, its blade catching the last of the dusk.

She was off her horse before the animal had fully stopped, her boots hitting the cobblestones at a run. Dominic caught her arm.

"Behind me." Dominic ordered. He drew two pistols and went through the door first.

The shop was wrecked. Flour covered the floor in a fine white drift, disturbed by boot prints — large ones, a man's —

that tracked from the front room into the kitchen and out through the back. A stool lay on its side near the counter. The display case was cracked, a spider's web of broken glass glittering in the lamplight. One of the bread racks had been shoved sideways, its contents scattered across the floor like fallen soldiers.

"Daphne!" Nell pushed past Dominic the moment she saw there was no one standing in the room. "Martha!"

A sound came from behind the counter. Low, ragged, thick with pain.

Nell rounded the corner and found them. Daphne was propped against the wall with her legs stretched out in front of her, one hand pressed to her ribs and the other cradling her wrist at an angle that made Nell's stomach lurch. Blood matted the hair above her left ear, and her face was the colour of tallow. Martha knelt beside her, pressing a cloth to the wound. The girl's lip was split and swelling, her dress torn at the shoulder, and her hands shook so badly the cloth kept slipping.

"The children." Nell dropped to her knees, her fingers framing Daphne's bruised face. "Where are the children?"

"He took them." Daphne's voice came out scraped thin. She blinked, her eyes struggling to focus. "He came through the back, maybe ten minutes after you left. The children had just come in from the vicar's. Oliver was still hanging his coat."

"Tell me what happened." Dominic crouched beside them, one pistol resting across his thigh. His face was stone, but a vein beat hard at his temple.

"He had a pistol." Daphne swallowed, wincing at the effort. "Martha heard the kitchen door and went to check. He backhanded her into the wall before she could scream." She glanced at the girl, something fierce and protective cutting through the pain. "I grabbed the bread knife from under the counter. Went at him. But he was fast — caught my wrist, twisted it." She held up her damaged arm, her fingers dangling at a wrong angle. "Snapped it like kindling. Then threw me into the shelves."

"Oliver." Nell could barely form the word.

"Brave, stupid boy." Daphne's tears cut tracks through the flour dust on her face. "He grabbed the poker from the kitchen hearth and swung at Gabriel's knees. Caught him, too — Gabriel stumbled, cursing. But then he wrenched the poker away and shoved Oliver down. Put a boot on his chest. Lily was screaming. He bound Oliver's wrists with a curtain cord and dragged them both out through the back."

"Where?" Dominic's hand tightened on the pistol.

"He told me to deliver a message." Daphne's jaw clenched, and something dark and furious burned behind the glaze of pain. "He said — 'Tell Eleanor the old Hargrove cottage. Past the churchyard, through the east field. She comes alone, or they die.'"

Dominic went very still. "I know the cottage. It has been abandoned for years."

"It is on the edge of your estate." Daphne looked between them, her broken wrist held carefully against her chest. "He has been squatting there. He told me — bragged about it, the sick bastard. Said he has been living in that cottage for months, watching the village from the hill. Watching the bakery. Watching Nell."

Nell's stomach turned to ice. Months. He had been sleeping a mile from her children, eating in the dark while he planned this, watching the smoke rise from her ovens every morning.

Dominic stood. The motion was fluid and controlled, and the soldier in him had taken over completely — every trace of warmth, of tenderness, of the man who had kissed her in the drawing room a week ago, had been locked away behind something hard.

"Martha." He looked at the girl, his tone steady and commanding. "Can you ride?"

Martha nodded, wiping blood from her split lip with the back of her hand. "Yes, my lord."

"Take my horse. Ride to Bramwell Park. Tell Philippa to send the magistrate's men to the Hargrove cottage — east side, past the churchyard wall. Do you know it?"

"Yes, my lord." Martha was already on her feet, swaying slightly. "The one with the collapsed roof."

"That is the one. Tell them armed men are needed. Tell them children are inside. Go."

Martha fled out the front door. The sound of hooves followed moments later, fading fast into the dark.

"Stay with Daphne," Dominic said to Nell, reaching for the door.

"No." The word came out quiet and absolute. Nell stood, her hands steady for the first time since Gabriel had walked into her shop that morning. She looked at Dominic and did not blink. "He has my children. I am coming."

"He said alone. If he sees me —"

"Then we do not let him see you." She stepped closer, her chin lifting. "I walk in the front. You find another way in. The cottage has a back window — I remember it from when the Hargrove widow kept chickens. It has been boarded up for years, but the wood will be rotten."

Dominic stared at her. Something shifted behind his eyes

— the soldier reassessing, recalculating, factoring in a variable he had not expected. Then his jaw set.

"If he has a pistol aimed at one of the children, you do not rush him. You talk. You stall. You give me time to get inside." He gripped her arm above the elbow, his fingers fierce. "Promise me."

"I promise." She held his gaze. "Promise me you will not miss."

A muscle worked in his jaw. "I never miss."

They left Daphne with Mrs. Potts, who had already set water to boil and was pressing a clean cloth to the worst of the cuts, clucking softly as she worked. Daphne would be safe there.

The walk to the Hargrove cottage took fifteen minutes through the dark — past the churchyard with its leaning stones, through the east field where the frost crunched like broken teeth beneath their boots, and up the gentle rise to where the cottage crouched against the tree line like something that had been trying to hide for a very long time.

The building was a ruin. Half the thatch had collapsed inward, and the walls were black with damp. A single window faced the lane, its glass long since shattered, and a faint glow leaked around the edges of a board that had been nailed across the frame from inside. Firelight. Someone had lit a fire in the old hearth.

Dominic pressed his mouth to her ear. "Two minutes. Give me two minutes to reach the back, then go in." His lips brushed her temple — not a kiss, not quite, but a touch that said everything a kiss would have said if there had been time.

Then he melted into the darkness around the side of the cottage, moving with the trained silence of a man who had stalked French sentries across Spanish hillsides.

Nell counted her heartbeats. One. Two. Three. She made it to sixty before she could not bear it anymore, and she had promised him a hundred and twenty but her children were inside that cottage with a monster who had nothing left to lose.

She pushed the door open.

The cottage was a single room, low-ceilinged and filthy. A fire burned in the old hearth, throwing jumping shadows across crumbling plaster walls. The floor was packed earth, and the air stank of smoke and damp wool and something sour underneath — the smell of a man who had been living like an animal for too long.

Gabriel stood in the centre of the room.

He looked worse than he had that morning. Wilder. More desperate. The ruined half of his face twitched with a rhythmic tic she did not remember, and his eyes burned with a feverish, unhinged light that told her Daphne had been right — there was nothing human left in him. His clothes were splattered with blood that was not his own.

He was gripping Lily by one arm. Oliver sat against the far wall, his wrists bound with curtain cord, a bruise darkening along his jaw where he had hit the floor at Daphne's. His dark eyes were wide and bright with fury, not fear. He was watching Gabriel the way a cornered dog watches a bigger animal — looking for the moment to bite.

"Mama!" Lily's scream pierced the close air, and she reached toward Nell with her free hand. "Mama, he is hurting us!"

"Let them go." Nell held her hands out, palms open, her

posture rigid as she fought to keep her composure from cracking apart. "This is between us, Gabriel. They have nothing to do with what happened between you and me."

"They have everything to do with it." Gabriel shoved Oliver hard against the wall, making the boy grunt as his shoulder cracked against the plaster. He yanked Lily against his chest and pulled out a rusted pistol, pressing the barrel against the girl's temple. "You ran from me carrying a bellyful of child, Eleanor. You let me burn and then you brought my blood into this world and raised them without me. Gave them a life so sweet they do not even know my name."

"You were supposed to be dead." She took a cautious step forward, her eyes locked on the weapon. She knew she had him talking to give Dominic time. "Everyone believed you were dead. I buried an empty grave and I mourned you, Gabriel, even after everything you did to me."

"Mourned me." He laughed — a thin, cracked sound. "Mourned me so hard you opened a bakery and got yourself engaged to a viscount."

Behind Gabriel, barely visible in the shadows beyond the boarded window, something shifted. A board easing outward. An inch of dark air where there had been none.

"What do you want?" She took another slow, measured step. Her heart was a fist pounding against her ribs, but her hands were steady. She needed her hands steady. "You said ten thousand this morning. I will get you twenty. Forty. Name it and let them go."

"You think this is still about money?" Something shifted in his face. The greed drained away and the thing beneath it surfaced — raw and festering and older than the burns. "I sat in this cottage all day after you left, staring at this face, and I thought about you standing in that shop with flour on your hands and a ring on your finger and that look — that look like the world owed you something good. And I realised no amount of money was ever going to make that feeling stop."

His grip on Lily tightened until the girl whimpered. His voice dropped, and the words came out slow and poisonous.

"You were supposed to suffer, Eleanor. You were supposed to be as wretched as I am. Instead you built a life and fell in love and now your children will be calling another man Papa! All the while I rotted in this hole with half a face and nothing to my name. The money was never going to fix it. Nothing fixes it. Nothing except making sure you lose everything the way I did."

Another inch of dark air behind the board. Dominic moved like smoke.

"You hurt my mother." The voice came from the wall. Small and shaking and white-hot with fury.

Oliver had pulled himself upright against the plaster, his bound wrists held tight against his chest, blood drying on his jaw. He was looking at Gabriel with an expression no nine-year-old should know how to wear — not fear, not confusion, but a hatred so pure and clean it could have cut glass.

"I know who you are. You are my father." The words came out one at a time, bitten off like thread, as though he had been rehearsing them since the moment this man dragged him from the bakery. "I may never have met you before, but I know you hurt my mother. And I hate you for that." His chin lifted, trembling but refusing to drop. "I hate you."

Gabriel stared at the boy. For one flickering instant something almost human passed behind his eyes — not guilt, not shame, but the brief, startled recognition of being seen for exactly what he was by a child who had never met him and understood him completely.

Then it was gone. His face hardened.

"Your son has your mouth, Eleanor." He turned back to Nell, dismissing the boy like he had always dismissed anything that did not serve him.

He raised the pistol, the heavy iron steady as he took deliberate aim at Lily's temple. Nell's world narrowed to a single point — the dark circle of that barrel and the wide, liquid terror in her daughter's eyes.

"GABRIEL, NO!" The scream tore from her lungs as she lunged forward.

Behind Gabriel, Oliver moved.

He had freed his hands. The cord lay in a loose coil at his feet, and the boy launched himself at Gabriel from behind with all the strength his small body could muster. His thin arms wrapped around the man's gun hand, yanking it away from his sister's head with a strength born of pure, animal desperation.

"Leave her alone!" Oliver's cry was a jagged, frantic thing, fracturing as he strained against the man's weight.

Gabriel stumbled, thrown off balance. The pistol swung wide. Lily tore herself from his grip with a shriek, scrambling toward Nell on her hands and knees.

"Run, Lily!" Oliver clung to Gabriel's arm, kicking at the man's shins, biting at his twisted wrist. "Run!"

Nell caught her daughter and shoved her toward the open door. "Get out! Run toward the churchyard — do not stop!"

Lily fled into the dark, her sobs swallowed by the night.

Gabriel roared — a raw, inhuman sound — and his free hand cracked across Oliver's face in a vicious backhand that snapped the boy's head sideways. Oliver hit the ground hard, his cheek splitting open against the hearthstone. He lay gasping on the packed earth, his limbs tangled beneath him, too stunned to rise.

"Oliver!" The scream tore from Nell's throat.

She never reached him.

Gabriel's hand closed around her throat and slammed her back against the wall. The crumbling plaster gave way behind her head. He pinned her there, his fingers crushing her windpipe, cutting off her air, and the firelight painted his ruined face in shades of copper and shadow.

"You were mine." His breath was hot and sour against her skin. "Mine to keep and mine to break. You do not get to be happy when I am this."

Black spots danced at the edges of her vision. Her lungs burned.

The boarded window exploded inward.

Dominic came through the rotten frame in a shower of splintered wood and rusted nails, both pistols drawn, his face a mask of cold, controlled fury. His eyes swept the room in a single tactical glance — Gabriel's hand on Nell's throat, Oliver on the floor, the firelight, the shadows, the angles.

The man Nell loved disappeared. In his place stood the soldier who had survived Waterloo — hard and utterly without mercy.

"Get your hands off her." The command rang off the walls before anyone could breathe. He did not blink. His aim did not waver.

Gabriel spun, dragging Nell with him, her body a shield between them. The pistol jammed against her temple, the barrel a cold iron circle against her skin.

"One more step and I kill her." The words came out high and thin, the first fraying edge of panic breaking through.

"Let her go." Dominic's pistols stayed level.

"Shoot me and she dies first." Gabriel's grip on her throat tightened, and she gasped for a sliver of air. "The bullet will go right through her skull."

The standoff hung in the firelit room like a held breath. Smoke drifted from the hearth. Oliver lay still on the ground, his eyes open now, watching, his bloodied cheek pressed to the earth. "You are not walking out of here." Dominic adjusted his stance, his boots grinding against the packed floor. "The only question is whether you die fast or slow."

"Big words from a man whose woman has a gun to her head." Gabriel laughed, the sound high and cracked and wrong. He pulled Nell closer, his fingers digging into the bruised skin of her throat. "Here is what is going to happen, my lord. You are going to put down those pretty pistols and let me walk out of here with my wife. Then you are going to forget you ever saw my face, and perhaps I will let her live."

"She is not your wife." Dominic's finger tightened on the trigger. "She stopped being your wife the moment you raised your hand to her."

"The law says different." Gabriel sneered, pressing the pistol harder against Nell's temple.

"The law can hang itself." Dominic took another step. "And so can you."

Gabriel's pistol swung toward him — away from Nell's temple — for just a second.

It was long enough.

Nell threw herself sideways with every ounce of strength

she had left, her elbow catching Gabriel hard in the ribs. He stumbled. His grip loosened.

Dominic fired.

The shot was deafening in the small cottage, the sound slamming off the stone walls. Gabriel screamed, blood blooming from his shoulder as he clutched at the wound. Nell tore free, hit the ground, and crawled toward Oliver.

Gabriel raised his pistol toward Dominic, his ruined face twisted with rage.

Dominic fired again.

The second bullet took Gabriel in the chest. He staggered backward, his eyes going wide with shock, and collapsed against the far wall. Blood spread across his shirt, dark and wet. The pistol slipped from his fingers and clattered to the earth.

He looked down at the wound. Then he looked up at Nell, who was gathering Oliver into her arms on the floor.

"You —" Blood bubbled at his lips. His ruined face twisted with pure, final hatred. "You were supposed to… suffer..."

He slid down the wall and did not move again.

Silence. The fire crackled. Smoke hung in the low ceiling like a shroud.

Oliver stirred in Nell's lap, pushing himself upright on shaking arms. Blood ran from the split on his cheekbone where the hearthstone had caught him, and his eyes were glassy, but they were open and fierce and fixed on his mother's face.

"Is it over?" The words came out scraped raw.

"It is over." Nell pulled him against her chest, her tears hot against his hair. She pressed her lips to the top of his head and held him so tight she could feel his heart beating against her ribs. "It is over, love. He cannot hurt us anymore."

Small footsteps crossed the floor behind them. Lily pressed herself into Nell's side without a word, her fingers clutching a fistful of her mother's dress. Dominic knelt beside them, his arms gathering all three of them in, his chin resting against Nell's temple. Nobody spoke. Nobody needed to.

Outside, distant shouts carried across the frozen field — the magistrate's men, coming fast from the direction of the village. Torchlight bobbed through the dark like fallen stars. Inside the cottage, surrounded by the ruins of a dead man's hatred, a family held each other close and refused to let go.

Chapter Twenty-Eight

Christmas morning dawned soft and white. Snow fell past the windows in fat, lazy flakes that blanketed the world in silence.

Nell woke before the sun had fully risen, her eyes opening to the grey half-light of a winter dawn and the unfamiliar canopy of the guest chamber at Bramwell Park. The bed beside her was empty, the sheets cool where Dominic should have been. Tradition, Philippa had insisted, required the bride and groom to spend their last unmarried night apart.

Three weeks had passed since Gabriel died in a derelict cottage at the edge of the estate, with a curse on his lips and hatred in his eyes. Those weeks had been a blur of magistrate inquiries, formal statements, and waiting. She had watched men in wigs decide whether Dominic would face charges for killing a man in defence of his family. The ruling had come five days ago — self-defence, justified, no charges to be filed. Nell's past was finally in the past. She was free.

The scandal had threatened to swallow them whole in those first terrible days. Whispers spread through the ton like wildfire — the viscount's fiancée had been married all along. Her first husband had faked his death. Lord Westmore had shot the man dead. Bigamy, some whispered. Murder, others hissed.

But Philippa had managed the gossip with an iron will that Nell could only admire. Dominic's name carried weight that money alone could not buy. The narrative had been carefully shaped — a brave woman who had escaped an abusive monster, and a heroic viscount who had protected his family from a blackmailer and a murderer. Some still whispered behind their fans. Let them. Nell had survived worse than whispers.

The hardest part had not been the magistrate or the ton.

It had been the children.

They had asked, of course. In the days after the cottage, when the bruises were still dark and the nightmares still came every night, Oliver had sat at the kitchen table with his jaw set in that hard, pale line and asked the question Nell had been dreading.

"How long did he hurt you?" Oliver had not looked up from the wood grain he was tracing with his thumbnail. "Before us. How long?"

Lily had gone very still beside him, her spoon frozen halfway to her mouth.

Nell had set down the bread she was shaping. She pulled out a chair, sat between them, took a breath, then another, and gave them what they were owed — not all of it, not the worst of it, but enough.

"Almost the whole marriage." She kept her tone steady, though her hands wanted to shake. "I was very young when I married him. I did not know what kind of man he was until it was too late."

"But you got out." Oliver's thumbnail stopped moving. His jaw worked, the muscle jumping beneath the fading bruise on his cheekbone.

"I got out." She nodded. "I changed our name. I built a life where you would be safe. Where no one could find us."

"You never told us any of it." He looked up then, and the expression on his face was older than any nine-year-old boy's face had a right to be. "All those years. You carried it alone."

"I had you." She reached across the table and covered his hand with hers. "Both of you. That was enough."

"I already knew." Oliver's fingers turned beneath hers, gripping back. "Not everything. But enough. The way you flinched at loud sounds. The way you checked the locks three times every night. I knew something had happened to you. I just didn't know his name until he told me."

Nell's throat closed. She had spent years trying to hide it, and her boy had been quietly reading her scars the whole time.

Lily had crawled into her lap — too big for it, really, but neither of them cared — and pressed her face against Nell's neck. "I am glad he is dead," she whispered, and there was no child left in her voice when she said it. "I am glad Lord Westmore killed him."

Nell had held them both for a long time after that, the bread going cold on the counter. She did not cry. She had spent all her tears on Gabriel Hyde years ago, and she refused to give him another drop.

That conversation lived in her chest now, a tender bruise she carried alongside the healing ones. But the weight of it was different from the weight of the secret. Lighter. Shared.

. . .

She reached across the cold sheets and pressed her hand to Dominic's pillow. She breathed in the lingering scent of him — sandalwood, and beneath it something that was simply him. Today she would become Lady Westmore. The thought still did not feel real.

A knock at the door made her sit up, pulling the covers to her chest.

"Mama?" Lily's voice came through the wood, high and eager. "Are you awake? It is Christmas and your wedding day!"

"Come in, loves." Nell smiled as the door burst open and her children tumbled through, still in their nightclothes, their faces bright despite the early hour.

Lily launched herself onto the bed with the abandon of a girl who had never learned to contain her enthusiasm. Oliver followed more slowly, his movements careful, his eyes sweeping the room before he allowed himself to relax. Even now, even safe, he checked for threats. Some habits, Nell knew, would take years to fade.

The mark on his cheekbone had faded to a dull yellow stain, barely visible unless you knew where to look. Edmund had pronounced him fully recovered ten days ago — no lasting damage beyond a headache that lingered for the first week and a tender spot he still flinched from when Lily hugged him too roughly. That was why they had waited these three weeks, despite Dominic's protests that he wanted to marry her the day after Gabriel died. Nell had insisted — not until her son was well, not until she could walk down the aisle knowing both her children were whole.

"It is snowing!" Lily bounced on the mattress, making the whole bed shake as she jabbed a finger toward the frosted glass. "Real snow, Mama! On Christmas! On your wedding day!"

"I can see that, sweetheart." Nell pulled both children close, tucking Lily under one arm and reaching for Oliver with the other. He allowed the embrace, leaning into her side with a sigh that spoke of exhaustion finally releasing its grip.

They stayed like that for a long moment — the three of them tangled together in the warmth of the bed while snow fell silent outside the window. Safe. Whole. Together.

"Are you nervous?" Lily tilted her head back to look up at Nell's face.

"A little." Nell smoothed a hand over her daughter's wild curls, tucking a stray strand behind her ear. "Are you?"

"Why would I be nervous?" Lily's brow furrowed, and she gave a small, dramatic shrug. "I am not the one getting married. I am just throwing flowers."

"Very important flowers." Nell leaned down to kiss her forehead.

"Do not be nervous, Mama." Oliver reached out and patted his mother's hand with a gravity that was too old for a nine-year-old, yet lighter than it had been in months. "He loves you. Anyone can see it."

Nell's throat tightened. "When did you get so wise?"

"I have always been wise." The corner of his mouth twitched — not quite a smile, but close.

Another knock sounded, and the door swung open to admit Daphne, Martha, and Philippa in a flurry of silk and chatter. Daphne's temple still showed faint bruising where Gabriel had thrown her against the bakery shelves, the yellow-green of a healing wound, and her left wrist was splinted and bound in clean linen. She had refused to miss this day.

"Up, up!" Philippa clapped her hands, her eyes already bright with tears she was fighting to contain as she swept toward the curtains. "We have a bride to prepare! Children, off to Martha for breakfast. You will see your mother at the church."

"But—" Lily started, her lower lip jutting forward.

"No arguments." Martha scooped the girl off the bed with practised ease, settling her on one hip despite the fading bruise on her own jaw. "Come along. There is chocolate and toast waiting in the nursery."

The promise of chocolate worked its magic, and Lily allowed herself to be carried off with only a few backward glances. Oliver followed more slowly. He paused at the door, his hand resting on the brass handle, and looked back at his mother.

"You look happy." He said it quietly, almost to himself, a small nod of approval accompanying the words. "I am glad."

Then he was gone, and Nell was left with her three attendants and a heart so full it threatened to overflow.

The next hours slipped by in warm water and rose petals, in careful hands and low instructions. Martha pinned Nell's dark hair in an elaborate arrangement threaded with small white flowers, leaving a few loose curls to frame her face. The white streak at her temple gleamed silver against the darker strands. For once, Nell did not try to hide it. Let them see. Let them know what she had survived.

"Mama." Lily stopped in the doorway when she returned, her flower-girl gown of white silk and pink ribbons forgotten entirely. "You look like someone out of a painting."

"She looks like a viscountess." Daphne corrected, her good hand working the last of the tiny silk buttons up the back of

Nell's dress while she braced the splinted wrist against her hip. "Which is what she is about to become."

The dress was cream silk scattered with seed pearls. It fit like it had been made for her, every seam crafted to flatter her curves rather than hide them. Nell stared at her reflection in the full-length mirror and barely recognised the woman looking back. She was not the baker with flour on her hands and exhaustion in her eyes. She was not the widow running from her past. She was not the woman with bruises on her throat and terror in her heart.

She was someone new. Someone whole. Someone free.

"Oh, my dear." Philippa pressed a lace handkerchief to her eyes, giving up any pretence of composure as she stepped closer to adjust the veil. "My nephew is the luckiest man in England. In the world. He does not deserve you."

"He saved my life." Nell turned from the mirror and took Philippa's hands in hers, squeezing gently. "He saved my children. I think that earns him a little luck."

"He would say you saved him right back." Philippa squeezed her fingers in return. "And he would be right."

Oliver appeared in the doorway, dressed in his first proper suit — dark blue wool with a cream waistcoat, his dark hair combed back from his face. He looked uncomfortable and proud, his shoulders squared as he attempted to appear impossibly grown up. Nell's eyes burned at the sight of him.

"The carriage is ready." A sudden, jagged catch in his throat betrayed him as he adjusted the fit of his new waistcoat, the sound hovering between boy and man. "Are you — are you ready?"

Nell crossed to him and cupped his face in her hands. "Ready to walk me down the aisle?"

"Ready." He covered her hands with his own — his palms startlingly large and warm against her skin — and gave a single, solemn nod. "Let us go get you married."

The carriage ride through the village felt like a dream. Snow had blanketed everything in white, turning the familiar streets into something magical and strange. Villagers had come out despite the cold to watch the procession pass, calling out blessings and throwing dried flowers and winter berries that scattered across the snow like crimson confetti.

The church rose before them, its ancient stone walls draped in holly and winter roses, candles glowing warm in every window. Half the ton had come, it seemed — carriages lined the lane while footmen stamped their feet against the cold and fine ladies in furs hurried inside.

Some had come to celebrate. Others had come to gawk and whisper behind their fans about the baker who had caught a viscount. Let them all see. Let them witness what love looked like when it refused to be defeated.

Nell waited in the vestibule while the guests settled, Oliver standing solid and steady at her side. Through the closed doors she could hear the murmur of the crowd, the rustle of silk, the first strains of music.

The doors swung open.

Lily went first, scattering rose petals with the serious concentration of a child performing a holy task, her brow furrowed as she ensured the path was perfect.

Then Nell and Oliver stepped through the doorway, and the world fell away.

She saw Dominic at the altar, and nothing else existed. He stood tall and straight in a dark blue coat and cream waistcoat, his dark hair brushed back from his face. The candlelight caught the silver of the scar on his jaw, and his grey eyes fixed on her with an intensity that stole the breath from her lungs.

His friend, Alistair, stood beside him, grinning broadly as he nudged Dominic's arm. Catherine dabbed at her eyes in the front pew. Philippa was already openly weeping. Near the back, Edmund stood with his arms crossed, watching with a quiet, resigned peace. None of it registered beyond a faint awareness. There was only Dominic.

The walk down the aisle felt endless. The walk down the aisle was over too soon.

Oliver placed her hand in Dominic's, his small fingers steady as they transferred her from son to husband. "Take care of her." The request fractured, catching on a wave of emotion he was fighting to contain.

"Always." Dominic's hand closed around hers, warm and strong. He met Oliver's eyes with the solemnity of a soldier's vow and gave a short, firm nod. "I swear it."

Oliver stepped back to stand beside his sister. His hand found Lily's, and they watched together — the children Nell had borne and raised and protected, witnessing their mother pledge herself to a man who had earned their trust with blood and bullet and promise.

The vicar began to speak, the familiar words of the marriage service washing over Nell like music.

The vicar turned to Dominic, prayer book open in his weathered hands. "Do you, Dominic James Westmore, Viscount Westmore, take this woman to be your lawfully wedded wife?"

"I do." Dominic spoke without a trace of doubt, the words ringing through the rafters as he squeezed her fingers.

The vicar shifted his attention to her, his expression softening. "And do you, Eleanor Whitmore, take this man to be your lawfully wedded husband?"

"I do." She lifted her chin and held his gaze without hesitation. The gold band slid onto her finger beside the ruby, a perfect circle that completed the promise.

The vicar raised his hands in a small gesture of blessing. "You may kiss the bride."

Dominic leaned in, one hand cradling her face, the other settling at the small of her back. "Finally." He pressed the word against her lips so softly that only she could feel it.

Their kiss deepened, full of promise and relief. She pressed into him, her hands fisting in the lapels of his coat, and when they parted the church erupted in cheers and applause. Lily's delighted squeal of "They are married!" bounced off the rafters.

Nell laughed through tears, and Dominic laughed too, pulling her against him and holding her the way a man holds something he never intends to let go.

He pressed a warm kiss into her hair, murmuring her name against the strands.

She tipped her head back to look at him. "Take me home."

Bramwell Park had transformed into a vision of light and colour. Flowers and candles filled every corner, casting warm glows that chased away the grey of winter. Musicians played in the gallery, the strains of violin and pianoforte drifting through the halls. Nell moved through the crowd in a happy daze, shaking hands and accepting congratulations, but her hand never left Dominic's. He stayed close, fingers threaded tightly through hers, shadowing her with a steady, protective presence.

When the crowd thinned for a moment, he leaned toward her, his thumb tracing lazy circles over the back of her hand.

She pressed her cheek to his shoulder, inhaling the scent of sandalwood.

He pressed a teasing hand lower on her back, leaning close until she felt the warmth of his chest against her. Her cheeks flamed, and he laughed quietly — a low, delighted sound that made her heart ache.

Daphne rose from the head table, a glass of champagne held high in her good hand. The splinted wrist rested in her lap, but her eyes were clear and fierce and bright. Silence fell over the room.

"A toast." She gestured toward the couple with the glass. "To the woman who survived everything life threw at her and found love anyway. To Nell — Lady Westmore now — the bravest person I know. And to Lord Westmore, who had the good sense to recognise a treasure when he found one." She winked, mischief sparkling. "May you have the happiness you deserve. Both of you. Always."

Alistair Thorne, the Marquess of Waverly, was watching Daphne with an expression that made Nell's breath catch. There was something sharp and hungry in his gaze, a look that felt entirely too familiar. He was the only son of the Duke of Patterson and the sole heir to one of England's oldest titles, yet he watched Daphne Wells the way a starving man watches a locked kitchen.

"Your friend is staring at Daphne." Nell murmured the words to Dominic, nodding subtly in Alistair's direction.

"Is he?" Dominic glanced over, and a smirk curved his lips as he adjusted his cuff. "They have been sniping at each other all day. She called him an arrogant peacock with more hair than sense. He called her a sharp-tongued menace who would not know a compliment if it bit her."

"That sounds like trouble." Nell leaned her shoulder into his.

"That sounds like the beginning of something." His smirk widened into a grin as he took a long draught from his glass. "I recognise the signs."

Indeed, Alistair was approaching Daphne now, cutting through the crowd with the easy confidence of a man who had never been told no in his life. Daphne saw him coming and stiffened, her chin lifting in that stubborn way Nell knew so well. Alistair said something — Nell could not hear what — but Daphne's cheeks flushed red with anger. She snapped something back, sharp enough to make nearby guests wince, and Alistair threw his head back and laughed.

Daphne turned on her heel and stalked away, her silk skirts swishing with every furious step. Alistair watched her go with an expression Nell recognised all too well. It was the same look Dominic had worn in those early days, when he had been fighting his attraction with every stubborn bone in his body. Poor Daphne had no idea what was coming.

The children had been swept up by a group of well-wishers. Lily basked in the attention like a flower turning toward the sun, chattering happily about her flower-girl duties and displaying her pink ribbons to anyone who would listen. Oliver stood nearby, watchful as always, but there was a lightness to his shoulders that had not been there before. He looked like a boy at last — not a protector, but a nine-year-old in a new suit eating cake and trying not to get cream on his waistcoat.

Philippa was weeping into her handkerchief again, declaring to anyone within earshot that this was the happiest day of her life and that she had always known Dominic would find someone worthy.

Edmund found them near the windows, a glass of champagne in hand and a genuine smile softening his features. "Congratulations." He clasped Dominic's hand firmly, then turned to Nell with warmth in his brown eyes. "Both of you. I have never seen two people more deserving of happiness."

"Thank you, Edmund." Nell squeezed his arm. "For everything. You were there when we needed you most."

"That is what friends do." He raised his glass. "To the future. May it be kinder than the past."

They drank together, and for a moment the three of them stood in comfortable silence, watching the snow fall soft against the windows. The candlelight caught Edmund's face, and Nell thought he looked lighter than she had ever seen him — like some old weight had finally begun to lift.

"Now." Edmund set down his glass and gestured toward the dance floor. "I believe the music is starting, and I would very much like to see Lord Westmore attempt a waltz without stepping on his bride's feet."

Dominic laughed. "I will have you know my footwork is impeccable."

"We shall see." Edmund's eyes crinkled. "We shall see."

The evening deepened and the candles burned low. The children were drooping with exhaustion, and Martha appeared to shepherd them off to the nursery wing.

"Be good for Martha." Nell crouched to kiss them both, smoothing Lily's wild curls and straightening Oliver's already crooked cravat.

"Have fun!" Lily giggled, poking her brother in the ribs.

Oliver rolled his eyes with all the world-weary exasperation of a boy twice his age.

But then Oliver hugged her. Tight and fierce, his thin arms wrapped around her neck. He pressed his face into her shoulder for just a moment before pulling back.

"I am glad you are happy, Mama." He said it quietly, just for her. "You deserve it."

Then they were gone, Martha herding them up the stairs with promises of bedtime story. Nell stood in the emptying ballroom with tears on her lashes, and arms wrapped around her from behind. Dominic pulled her back against his chest, his chin resting on top of her head.

"Ready to go upstairs, Lady Westmore?" He pressed the question against the curve of her ear, the words a low vibration in his chest.

She turned in his arms and looped her hands around his neck. "I thought you would never ask."

Chapter Twenty-Nine

Dominic closed the door behind them with a quiet click. The bedchamber was warm, the fire already built high, candles lit along the mantelpiece so the room glowed amber and gold. Someone — his aunt, probably — had scattered white rose petals across the turned-down sheets. He would thank her tomorrow. Or never mention it. One of the two.

Nell stood in the centre of the room with her back to him, her fingers already working at the pins in her hair. She pulled them free one by one, dropping them onto the dressing table with small metallic clicks, and her dark hair tumbled down her back in loose waves threaded with white. She hadn't asked for help. She never did.

"I have been waiting for this." He crossed to her slowly, each step deliberate, and stopped close enough to feel the warmth of her through the silk. His fingers found the first button at the back of her gown. "All day. All week. All my life, I think."

"The wedding night?" She tilted her head, giving him the long, pale line of her throat.

"You." He pressed his mouth to the curve of her neck, just below her ear, and felt the familiar shiver run through her. "As my wife. In my bed. Where you belong."

He knew her body. He'd learned it in stolen, breathless fragments — his fingers working inside her in the storage room, him between her thighs in the maze, her on top of him when he was hurt after the accident. He knew the sounds she made when she was close. He knew the way her fingers dug into whatever she could reach — his hair, his shoulders, the bedsheets — when she lost control. But those encounters had been frantic, desperate, shadowed by guilt or fear or the knowledge that it shouldn't be happening.

Tonight there was no guilt. No rushing. No voice in the back of his skull whispering that she would regret this in the morning.

He unfastened the buttons one by one. Two dozen of them at least, each small and silk-covered, and he took his time with every last one. His knuckles grazed her spine as the fabric loosened and parted. The scent of her rose through the widening gap — rosewater and warm skin and something deeper, something that was simply Nell — and it made his head swim the same way it had the first time she'd stood close enough for him to breathe her in, back in her shop when he'd reached past her for a tart he didn't want.

The gown slipped from her shoulders. He eased it past her hips until it pooled at her feet. She reached for the laces of her stays, but he covered her hands with his.

"Let me." He turned her to face him. Her eyes were dark, her lips parted, the rise and fall of her breathing quickening beneath the boned fabric. He worked the laces free with steady hands — steadier than he felt — and loosened the stays until they gaped and he could lift them over her head. The chemise beneath was thin, near sheer, and the candlelight turned it golden against the swell of her breasts and the soft curve of her belly.

She didn't cross her arms. She used to — every time, that instinctive folding inward, the shielding, the making herself smaller. In the maze she'd tried to keep her bodice pulled up even as his mouth worked between her legs. When she'd ridden him she'd kept her chemise on, gathered at her waist, as though she couldn't bear to be fully bare in front of him even while she took him apart.

Not tonight. She stood still and let him look.

He lifted the chemise over her head. The linen caught on her hips and he eased it free, and then she was standing before him in nothing but candlelight and the gold ring he'd placed on her finger that morning.

He'd seen her body before, in pieces — the maze had been dark, the night in his bedchamber lit by a single guttering candle while his injuries kept him pinned to the mattress. He had never seen her like this. Fully bare, fully lit, fully his.

Full breasts that rose and fell with each unsteady breath, the nipples drawn tight in the warm air. A waist that gave way to generous hips, wide and strong. The soft belly marked with silver where her skin had stretched to carry the children who were now sleeping down the hall in their new bedrooms in his house. Thighs that were thick and warm, the same thighs that had gripped his hips hard enough to bruise when she'd ridden him, and he'd loved every second of it.

"You are staring." Her lips curved, but her chin lifted — that stubborn tilt he knew so well.

"I am." He pulled his shirt over his head and let it drop. "I intend to stare a great deal more before the night is done."

She watched him strip with open appreciation, her gaze travelling down his chest.

He crossed to her and ran his hands down her sides — over the swell of her breasts, the dip of her waist, the generous flare of her hips. She leaned into his touch, her breath catching, her palms flat against his bare chest.

"Every time before," he said against her temple, his fingers pressing into the soft flesh of her hips, "there was something in the way. The dark. Your chemise. My injury. Not tonight."

"Not tonight." She tipped her face up to his.

He kissed her. Not the careful kisses he'd given her at the altar, but a deep, thorough taking that tasted of champagne and the sugared almonds Lily had been sneaking to everyone at the reception. Nell's hands slid up his chest and into his hair, gripping hard, and the sound she made against his mouth — low, wanting, impatient — sent his blood south so fast his head spun.

He walked her backward until her thighs hit the bed. She sat, and he followed her down onto the sheets, bracing himself above her. For a moment he simply looked. The candlelight played across her skin, catching the flush that spread from her cheeks down her throat to the tops of her breasts. Rose petals clung to her hair, her shoulders, the curve of her hip.

"I want to taste you." He kissed the hollow of her throat, then lower, his mouth dragging between her breasts. "Properly this time. Not in a bloody maze with one ear listening for footsteps."

She laughed — a real, startled laugh — and her fingers tightened in his hair. "That was your idea, if I recall."

"Best idea I ever had." He kissed her nipple, then drew it into his mouth, and the laugh dissolved into a sharp, hitching gasp. He took his time with her breasts, cupping their weight in his hands, running his thumbs across the peaked flesh until she was arching into him, her nails raking down his shoulders.

He kissed lower. Down the soft swell of her belly, his lips tracing the silver marks there, each one a testament to the life her body had carried. Lower still, along the crease of her hip, to the sensitive skin of her inner thigh. She spread for him without hesitation — not the nervous, uncertain parting of the maze, but a confident opening, her thighs falling wide as her fingers threaded through his hair and guided him where she wanted him.

"You are not shy tonight." He pressed a kiss to her inner thigh, close enough that his breath ghosted across the heat of her.

"I am your wife." She tugged his hair, pulling him closer. "I am done being shy."

Something primal and possessive roared through his chest. He lowered his mouth to her and gave her everything he'd been too rushed, too reckless, too desperate to give her properly in that maze. He was slow. He was thorough. He catalogued every response — the gasp when he used the flat of his tongue in long, dragging strokes; the bitten-off cry when he circled the place where she was most sensitive; the way her thighs clamped against his ears when he pressed two fingers inside her and curled them forward.

"Dominic—" Her hips lifted off the mattress, and he pinned them down with his forearm across her belly, holding her there, keeping her still while he worked her with his mouth. She cursed — something filthy and entirely un-ladylike that made him groan against her — and gripped his hair so hard his scalp burned.

He didn't stop. He pressed closer, firmer, finding the rhythm that made her breathing fracture, and held it there until her whole body went rigid. She came with a sound that was half his name and half a sob, her spine bowing off the bed, her thighs shaking against his shoulders, and he worked her through it, gentling his mouth, easing her down with slow, unhurried strokes until she went boneless against the sheets.

He kissed the inside of her thigh, then her hip, then the soft slope of her belly. When he looked up, her eyes were glassy, her chest heaving, her lips bitten red.

"Come here." She reached for him, her hands fumbling, her coordination wrecked. "I need you. Now."

He shed his trousers and settled between her legs. She wrapped her thighs around his hips — those strong, generous thighs — and pulled him against her. The contact drew a groan from deep in his chest.

"I love you." He braced himself on one arm and cupped her face with his free hand, his thumb stroking her flushed cheek. "I love you, Lady Westmore."

"Then show me." She rolled her hips against him, and his vision went dark at the edges.

He pushed into her slowly. Not because she needed the care — she was slick and ready and her body took him with an ease that nearly ended him on the spot — but because he wanted to feel every inch of it. He wanted to remember this. The first time he entered *his wife*. The first time there was nothing forbidden about it.

She gasped when he filled her completely, her nails biting into his back, her head tipping into the pillow. He held still, buried deep, and pressed his forehead to hers.

"All right?" His arms shook with the effort of not moving.

"If you don't move I will kill you." She dug her heels into the small of his back.

He moved. Slow at first, long deep strokes that drew ragged sounds from both of them. He angled his hips the way he'd learned she liked — tilted upward, pressing against the spot inside her that made her go quiet before she went loud. Her nails dragged down his back, leaving welts he would wear like medals in the morning.

"Harder." She gripped his shoulders, pulling him deeper. "Dominic. Harder."

He obeyed. The pace shifted, his hips driving into her with a force that made the bed frame protest beneath them. The sound of skin against skin filled the room, punctuated by her gasps and his low, guttural groans. Her breasts moved with each thrust and he dipped his head to take one into his mouth, sucking hard enough to make her cry out and clench around him so tight his rhythm faltered.

"I'm going to—" She couldn't finish the sentence. Her thighs locked around him, her body drawing taut as a bowstring, and he reached between them, his fingers finding the swollen bud of her and pressing firm circles against it.

She shattered. Her whole body seized beneath him, her back arching, her walls gripping him in rhythmic, pulsing waves that dragged him to the edge. He held on — barely, his jaw clenched, his arms trembling — because he wanted to watch her face. He wanted to see the moment when everything else fell away and there was nothing left but pleasure and him and the knowledge that she was his wife and this was their bed and nobody could take this from them.

When the tremors eased, he let himself go. Two more thrusts, deep and desperate, and he followed her over, burying himself to the hilt as the release tore through him. Her name left his mouth, broken and raw and reverent and she held him through it, her arms wrapped around his back, her fingers stroking his damp hair while his body shuddered against hers.

He collapsed beside her, pulling her against his chest, their legs tangled in sheets and scattered rose petals. Their breathing came in ragged, uneven gasps that gradually slowed. The fire crackled. A candle guttered and went out, dimming the room to a warm, honeyed glow.

She pressed her lips to his chest, just above his heart. "I love you."

"I love you too." His arms tightened around her. "Lady Westmore."

"That is going to take some getting used to." She traced the line of his scar with one finger, from his temple down to the corner of his mouth, and he turned his head to press a kiss to her palm.

"You have the rest of your life." He drew the coverlet over them both and tucked her closer against him, her back to his chest, his chin resting on the top of her head.

She was quiet for a moment. Then, softly: "Dominic?"

"Hmm?"

"This bed is absurdly comfortable."

He laughed against her hair — a real laugh, warm and unguarded, the kind of laugh he'd forgotten he was capable of before she walked into his life with flour on her sleeve and fire in her eyes.

She settled deeper into his arms, her breathing slowing, her body heavy with satisfaction and sleep. He held her in the quiet, listening to the fire and the soft fall of snow against the windows and the steady, trusting rhythm of her breathing.

She was staying. She was his. And tomorrow, when the sun came through those windows and found them still tangled together, there would be no guilt, no rushing, no pulling away.

Just this. Just them. Just the rest of their lives.

Epilogue — One Year Later

It was Christmas morning again.

Nell woke slowly, dragged from sleep by the familiar weight of Dominic's arm across her waist and the pressure of her swollen belly against the mattress. Eight months along now, the baby was a constant presence — making sleep difficult and breathing a challenge. Edmund monitored her weekly, his careful hands and careful eyes watching for every sign of trouble. The risk had not gone away. She had simply decided it would not decide for her.

She shifted carefully, and Dominic's arm tightened. "Stop squirming." The words came out rough with sleep, muffled against her hair. "Too early."

"Your child is using my bladder as a cushion." She pushed at his arm with a weary laugh, though she did not truly struggle. "I need to get up."

"Five more minutes." His hand slid around to rest on her belly, warm and possessive, fingers splayed wide.

The baby kicked — a solid thump against his palm — and he laughed, low and delighted. "Good morning to you too." He pressed a kiss to her neck, stubble grazing her skin. "Tell your mother to stay."

The door burst open.

"MERRY CHRISTMAS!" Lily launched herself onto the bed, bouncing across the mattress without any regard for her very pregnant mother, waving a discarded ribbon in the air like a flag of surrender.

Oliver followed more slowly, a real smile on his face — the kind that reached his eyes. At ten years old he was all long limbs and sharp angles, more serious than any boy his age had a right to be. But the seriousness sat lighter on him now. He wore it like a coat he could take off, not armour he could never remove.

"Lily, careful." He caught his sister's shoulder before she could bounce onto Nell's stomach, his expression turning stern. "The baby, remember?"

"I was being careful." Lily pouted, but allowed herself to be redirected, wedging between Nell and Dominic with the boneless flexibility of childhood.

"Come here." Dominic reached past Nell to pull Oliver closer, his hand settling on the boy's shoulder. "Christmas morning tradition. All of us together."

They lay tangled in the warmth of the bed while snow fell silent outside. The four of them, soon to be five, wrapped in each other's arms.

"Does the baby kick a lot?" Lily pressed her small hand to Nell's belly, her dark eyes wide.

"All the time." Nell covered her daughter's hand with her own, guiding it to where the movement was strongest. "Especially at night."

The baby obliged with a solid kick, and Lily's eyes went round. "I felt it!" She giggled, looking up at Dominic.

"Strong." Oliver had let himself be pulled closer, his hand joining the rest atop the quilt. "Like a fighter."

"Like their brother." Dominic reached out to ruffle Oliver's hair, his gaze full of pride. "The baby is going to need someone to show them how to be brave."

Oliver ducked his head, but not before Nell caught the flush of pleasure on his cheeks. He had started calling Dominic "Papa" six months ago — quietly at first, then more often. It still made Dominic's eyes go soft every single time.

"Can we stay here forever?" Lily snuggled deeper into the blankets, letting out a long, contented sigh. "Just like this?"

"We have presents downstairs." Nell reminded her, though she made no move to get up.

"Presents can wait." Lily yawned, resting her head on Nell's shoulder. "This is better."

Nell met Dominic's eyes over their children's heads. Grey eyes, warm with love and soft with wonder at the family they had built from the wreckage of so much pain.

One year since the wedding. One year since Gabriel died and the nightmare ended. One year of peace, of healing, of happiness she had never dared to hope for.

"Happy?" Dominic mouthed the word, his eyebrows lifting.

"Terrified." She mouthed back, her lips curving.

His answering smile said everything. I know. Me too. The good kind.

Outside, snow fell soft and silent, blanketing the world in white. Inside, a family lay tangled together in the warmth of a bed that had become home.

Book Two Prologue

The Gentleman Loves Like Ruin

Two years after the wedding. Hampshire. Late autumn.

The surgery on Mill Street had the best light in the village.

Edmund had chosen the building for precisely that reason —tall windows facing east, glass-fronted cabinets filled with brown bottles, an examination table worn smooth from use. The smell of dried lavender mingled with vinegar and beeswax, his coal stove crackled against the autumn chill.

He had arrived in this village nearly three years ago with nothing but a medical bag and the raw wound of a broken engagement he refused to speak of. He had needed to disappear—from London, from society, from the pitying glances of everyone who knew that the baron's daughter had made a fool of him.

Now his name was known in every cottage for miles. Dr. Hartley, who came when you called. Dr. Hartley, who didn't charge the families who couldn't pay.

He had just turned forty-one years old. His hair had gone more silver than brown; his hands were steady, and his life was quiet, and he had made peace with that.

Mostly.

The clock chimed six. He extinguished the lamps, locked the laudanum cabinet, reached for his coat—

The door burst open.

Mrs. Briggs stood gasping, her round face flushed from running, one hand pressed to her heaving chest. "Dr. Hartley." She gulped air between words. "Express rider from London. He said it was urgent."

She thrust the letter toward him. Cream paper. The Pembroke seal pressed into red wax—a stag's head crowned with roses.

He broke the seal.

My dear Edmund,

She's back.

She arrived in London three days ago. Edward turned her away from the door—my own son turned his sister away, and I couldn't do a thing.

I cannot find her. She looked like death itself. I am desperate.

You loved her once. If any part of you remembers the girl she was, I beg you: help me find her.

— Helena

Edmund read the letter twice.

Three years of silence. Three years of pretending he had forgotten her face. And now this. *Looked like death itself.* Edward had slammed the door in her face.

"Mrs. Briggs." He folded the letter and slipped it into his breast pocket, his movements precise despite the tremor threatening his fingers. "I've been summoned to London. Send for Dr. Fenton in Thornbury if there are emergencies."

"Sir?" She stepped closer, her brow creasing as she searched his face. "Is everything all right?"

He paused at the door, one hand on the frame. Looked back at the surgery he had built, the life he had made, the peace he had fought so hard to find.

"I don't know." He pulled on his hat and stepped into the cold. "I honestly don't know."

Then he was gone, boots striking cobblestones as the first flakes of snow began to fall.

London was a few hours away.

She was back.

And God help him, he was going to find her.

A Note from Arabella

You just finished my first book.

I need a moment with that. Because for a very long time, this story lived only in my head — in the shower, on long drives, in the middle of the night when I should have been sleeping. Nell existed before she had a name. Dominic existed before he deserved one.

I wrote this book because I wanted to read it. I wanted a heroine who looked like the women I know — soft, fierce, taking up space without apology — and a hero who didn't need convincing that she was the most magnificent thing in the room. He just needed her to let him close enough to prove it.

If you picked up this book not knowing my name, thank you. That kind of trust from a stranger is no small thing, and I don't take it lightly.

If Nell and Dominic made you feel something — if you laughed, or held your breath, or stayed up past your bedtime — then I did what I came here to do.

There are more stories coming. More heroes brought to

their knees. More heroines who refuse to shrink. I hope you'll stick around for all of it.

With love and gratitude,

Arabella

Acknowledgments

To my readers — you took a chance on a debut author whose name you'd never seen before. You opened this book on faith. Every download, every page turn, every review means more to me than I have the words to say, and I'm a woman who writes for a living. Thank you for being the reason this dream became real.

To my husband — who never once asked me if this was a good idea. Who brought me tea during late-night edits and pretended not to notice when I cried over fictional people. You are the reason I know how to write a hero worth keeping. I love you more than any book could hold.

To my children — who remind me every single day that the bravest thing a woman can do is build something and put it into the world. Everything I make, I make for you. Even the parts you're not allowed to read yet.

Did You Enjoy This Book?

If Nell and Dominic's story made you feel something, I'd be so grateful if you left a review.

It doesn't need to be long. A sentence or two is more than enough. For a debut author, every single review matters — it helps other readers find this book, and it tells me that the late nights and rewrites and moments of doubt were worth it.

You can leave a review on Amazon, Goodreads, or BookBub.

Thank you. From the bottom of my heart.

Coming Soon

THE GENTLEMAN LOVES LIKE RUIN

Thorns & Temptations — Book 2

She left him for another man. He married her when that man was done with her. This is not a love story. Not yet.

Jasmine Pembroke broke Edmund Hartley in ways he'll never admit out loud. He loved her for four years. She called him boring, let his flowers die, and ran off to Paris with a French count without so much as a goodbye.

Now she's back. Broke. Ruined. Pregnant with another man's child.

He should hate her. He does hate her. He marries her anyway.

Four years. His rules. His roof. His terms. One year for every year she wasted.

What follows is not forgiveness. It's war. A slow, devastating, unbearable war fought in silences and slammed doors and the space between two people who cannot stop wanting each other no matter how hard they try.

She broke him once. He won't survive it twice. But God help him, he's already burning.

Coming July 31, 2026

About the Author

Arabella Kent discovered historical romance at fourteen when she stole her mother's copy of The Bride by Julie Garwood. She read it in three days under the covers with a flashlight and never recovered.

Two decades of Julia Quinn, Lisa Kleypas, and Tessa Dare later, she started wondering where the heroines who looked like her were hiding. The ones with soft bellies and thick thighs who still got the brooding hero on his knees.

She couldn't find enough of them. So she started writing her own.

Arabella writes steamy, mature historical romance featuring plus-size heroines who don't shrink themselves and heroes completely wrecked by them.

Connect with Arabella

Email: authorarabellakent@gmail.com

www.ingramcontent.com/pod-product-compliance
Lightning Source LLC
LaVergne TN
LVHW100505110826
845146LV00002B/522

* 9 7 9 8 9 9 3 0 5 2 6 4 9 *